For Marilyn

The Road to Grantchester

James Runcie

LARGE
PRINT

First published in Great Britain 2019
by
Bloomsbury Publishing

First Isis Edition
published 2019
by arrangement with
Bloomsbury Publishing

A catalogue record for this book is available from the British Library.

ISBN 978–1–78541–742–9 (hb)
ISBN 978–1–78541–748–1 (pb)

Published by
F. A. Thorpe (Publishing)
Anstey, Leicestershire

Set by Words & Graphics Ltd.
Anstey, Leicestershire
Printed and bound in Great Britain by
T. J. International Ltd., Padstow, Cornwall

This book is printed on acid-free paper

PART ONE

WAR

CHAPTER ONE

London, 28 February 1938

They are in the Caledonian Club, dancing the quickstep. Sidney is eighteen. Amanda, his best friend's little sister, is three years younger. The band is playing "*Bei Mir Bist Du Schoen*": "To Me, You're Beautiful". He has asked her to dance out of politeness. He has good manners, everyone thinks so, but he enjoys the dance more than he had expected.

She is gracious, poised and moves more elegantly than he does, making sure they keep time and look good together. All around them there is gaiety. The guests are well prepared. They have practised their steps and their behaviour. Slow, slow, quick, quick, slow. The conversation is easy, the laughter assured.

When the music comes to an end, Sidney acknowledges his partner with a bow. Amanda returns with a mock curtsey and a complicit smile that he can't quite read. He escorts her back to her seat as etiquette demands but, straight away, she leaves to find her brother, Robert. She wants to be by his side for their father's speech and the midnight birthday toast.

"This is the moment," Sir Cecil Kendall announces, after the twelfth stroke of the clock and a general hurrah, "when my son comes of age and we let him loose into the world. All I can say is" — here he stops to make sure that he has command of the silence, ready for the laugh that will surely follow — "*God help the world*. A new star has arrived in the firmament, ready to set our lives *ablaze*."

The room is filled with youth and age across the generations. There is wealth, ease and confidence, despite the political anxiety. No one believes there will be another war and, even if there is one, how can it possibly ruin the memory of this golden evening, with everyone in their finery, dancing on a polished wooden floor under the chandeliers with the orchestra playing and the candles ablaze?

Five years later, Sidney Chambers is on a transport ship with the 2nd Battalion, Scots Guards, preparing for landing south of Salerno. Officers tell the troops they have trained so well that victory is assured. They only have to stay alert, watch out for their comrades (a fighting force is only as good as its weakest link) and show no vulnerability.

The night is bright with barely a kiss of wind. Water hisses along the hull. A bosun's whistle rings out. The ship swings on its moorings. Below decks, a group of men are gambling their rum rations on a game of cards.

Sidney checks his uniform and his kitbag. He pats his breast pocket to confirm that he has his notebook and recent letters from home. He doesn't know if the queasiness he feels is hunger, seasickness or the fear of impending battle. He closes his eyes and tries not to think of anything at all.

During his peacetime education, the history of warfare had been academic. He read Homer, the classics, Shakespeare's history plays. There had been debates at school. A gas-blind brigadier from the Great War, a man who had survived Passchendaele and yet never expected to grow old, spoke about the limits of diplomacy, the problem of conscientious objection and the necessary evil of a just war.

It was during Prize Day in the summer term of 1937, and the old-boy hero was wearing a double-breasted navy blazer with medals and grey flannel trousers. He appeared to have wet himself. He couldn't keep his left hand still and clamped it over a walking stick with his right.

The brigadier went back to the Headmaster's Lodge and said, after three large whiskies — Glenlivet, water, no ice — that "the young have no knowledge of terror. They can't imagine the future. All they have is the present. That is the advantage of having a ready supply. It is their glory and their tragedy."

Sidney never imagined he would become a soldier. In fact, he has thought very little about a career or how he might "turn out". So far, his life has been one of study, friendship, peace and parties. He's never even been abroad. His idea of Italy, before all this, had been of ancient Rome and the Renaissance; classical sculpture, architecture, rhetoric and philosophy, beautiful paintings in grand palazzi. He'd always imagined that his first visit to the country might be on a modern, updated version of the Grand Tour, with friends, family, or even someone he loved: a honeymoon, perhaps.

As they approach land, he's given a government-issue guide to the Italian language. It includes not only the words for "lobster", "oyster" and "butter", but five pages of medical instruction: *Come Fermare un' Emorragia*. Sidney thinks that if his father, a medical officer in the Great War, were with them then at least he would know how to "stop the bleeding" rather than command someone else to do it.

Some of the troops read bits out loud. "*What is your name? Where do you live?*" Others make up phrases. "*Ciao, bella. When are you going to take off your clothes?*"

None of them can quite understand how they have come to be sitting in this boat, dressed in uniform, with guns over their shoulders and fear in their hearts.

Robert Kendall starts telling jokes. "What's got six reverse gears and one forward gear? An Italian tank. The forward gear is in case they get attacked from behind."

Freddie Hawthorne is pretending the invasion is just another show. "In peacetime, people would pay hundreds of pounds for this. Never mind 'see Naples and die'. See Naples and live. That's what I say."

They sit on wooden benches, each soldier pressed against his neighbour, cramped by kitbags and equipment. The air is stale with the smell of men; sweat through thick battledress, tobacco breath, boot polish and excrement. Sidney thinks of Dante: the dead lining up for purgatory.

Aitchison, Armstrong, Brennan, Campbell, Carnegie, Clarke, Cummins. There are so many. *Donaldson, Duff, Ford, Hart, Howe*. Sidney has to remember the names — *Gatchell, Gilchrist, Hawthorne, Kendall, Lawlor, Logan*. If, and when, one of them dies — *Macrae, McDermott, McDonald* — their loved ones will ask how it happened. *MacGregor, Mackay, McKenzie*. Parents will want to know if their son felt fear — *Naylor, Paterson, Quigley* — if he realised he was dying — *Redmond, Reekie, Robertson, Ronson* — and how much pain he suffered at the end — *Sweenie, Swint, Thomson, Thorburn*. Can they be proud? *Wallace, Ward, Wichary, Wilson*.

The boat slows, the engine grinds down. After another anti-Italian joke (the national flag is a white cross on a white background) there's an unexpected silence, an angel passing overhead, and Kendall says he doesn't want to talk any more. Hawthorne is writing a "just-in-case" letter to his parents.

If you get this, then you'll know the worst.

There is a loosing of chains, the lowering of the gangplanks on each side of the bow, the rush of water and the start of light; a pale grey dawn, brightening to a duck-egg blue without its usual wash of pink, the day undecided.

Sidney jumps into a shock of cold water. The men wade towards the land in single file, holding their equipment above their heads. It is heavier going than anyone has anticipated. Even though the tide is coming in, the currents spill around their legs, pulling them under as their uniforms weigh heavy with the wet.

Lawlor, a young ginger-haired boy from Falkirk who has lied about his age in order to join up, calls out: "So, this is sunny Italy?"

As soon as he gets to the shore he treads on a landmine and is killed. Half a mile from the beaches, the Germans send shells over that throw up geysers all around them. Tracer fire bounces off the ramp. Machine-gun fire starts up.

Once ashore, the men are fighting in the open crescent of a plain without cover of vegetation or terrain. The plan is to get footholds in the hills so they can fight on equal terms, but the enemy knows every point on the bridgehead.

"Bloody hell," says Hawthorne, "it's like a theatre. We're on stage. They can watch our every move and we can't see a single one of the bastards."

Luftwaffe planes attack with flares, bombs and torpedoes. Sidney's battalion is ordered to take out a series of warehouses situated in a prominent defensive position between Bellizzi and Battipaglia. It is known as "the tobacco factory" even though there is no sign of a cigarette. The two-floor buildings have been commandeered by the Germans as a munitions store, filled with grenades and sub-machine guns.

The men follow the battle drill they have been taught, moving forward behind an artillery barrage, covered by smoke from a burning farm silo, but they are exposed too soon and repulsed by a German counter-attack that cuts them apart with its power, speed and brutality. Bodies are thrown back, uniform and flesh ripped open. Violent anatomy; death faster than pain.

They are fired on from behind. They keep their heads down as bullets from the first two rounds soar over them, but the next volley is lower, too low for some of the men. Watson cries out, "I'm hit. Help me . . . help me . . . I'm hit . . ." and dies.

Those who risk a recce are shot so quickly they have no time to understand what has happened. The only way for a soldier to survive is to learn from the death of his friends.

"I thought they were supposed to be on the point of surrendering," says Hawthorne.

"We have to get round," Kendall replies. "There're never as many of them as you think."

"It only takes one of them to kill us."

"Don't think like that. Get at them."

Kendall treats any fire directed towards him as a personal affront. At school, everyone loved him. What has he ever done to deserve being shot at? He repeats orders, shouts out instructions, rallying the troops as he did when he was captain of the rugby first fifteen. He isn't interested in taking prisoners. He tells everyone that he will murder the entire German army on his own if he has to. "Have at you, scum," he shouts.

"Get back," Sidney warns. "Keep low."

"Don't let up, Chambers. We have to let the bastards know who they're dealing with."

They shift position while hiding out of sight, creating new angles of attack, getting the Bren guns going with sustained rounds before encouraging another assault with grenades and close fire. Sidney remembers an old commander saying that "you must never allow men to lie down in a battle". His instructor believed that the more courageous you were, dashing straight into enemy lines, the swifter your chance of success. You just had to have the guts to do it.

They start another charge, ten yards apart and no two abreast. The Bren gunners fire first and then the riflemen advance, each man carrying four hand grenades. Sidney runs in a darting motion, throwing the first grenade on command and the other three as soon as he can. Each one weighs heavy in his hands. He worries about them slipping in his sweat, his own manual dexterity, getting the pins out in time. He doesn't want to blow his own legs off. He's seen Gascoigne do that already. The only thing he has to do is to keep on running, firing his rifle when he has finished off the grenades, moving left when he is out of ammunition. The man next to him has his jaw blown off. There is no time to reload. He can't stop. If he stays on the move, he tells himself, if he keeps breathing, if he changes direction, he will be safe.

Between the bursts of explosion and commands he can just make out Germans shouting, "Grenade! Grenade!", firing from their machine-gun positions before throwing their own and scrambling for cover.

Sidney concentrates on the immediacy of attack, defence and survival. He knows he has to feel more alive than he has ever felt before just to keep on living. He sees an object thrown in his direction: a grenade silhouetted against a blaze of gunfire. It lands three feet away, but he is gone by the time it explodes. He runs back low into cover, vaulting sandbags and barbed wire, throwing himself down on to the ground, bruising his right side, exhausted, breathless, relieved and yet exhilarated.

"I've never seen you move like that," says Kendall. "You know you run like a girl?"

"And you can bugger off too," Sidney replies.

"So easy to get a rise out of you."

"How are we ever going to get out of this?"

"You just have to keep on until there's nothing left to do. Get up and be brave."

The next day, the American forces open an airstrip near Paestum. They plan to set up a series of airborne attacks in support, but it is five days of fighting before it is operational. By that time, the battalion has lost a third of its men. Their training had assumed a full fighting force. No one has taught them how to cope when exhausted and under-strength. It doesn't take long to work out the mathematics. At this rate, they'll all be dead in a fortnight.

Sidney makes his way back to the bivouac area, passing the already decaying dead, listening to bursts of fire from far away. He can smell the tang of what he takes to be salt and blood in the wind; pine, earth and explosives. He looks out at the sea, struck by the unyielding rhythm of its tides.

He sees a bell tower in the distance, standing proud and unharmed, its brickwork the colour of warm sand at dusk. He wonders where the priest might be, if there are any faithful left to worship, when anyone last said Mass or prayed for peace.

He sits down on his helmet and reads from the prayer book his mother has given him. *Thou shalt not be afraid for the terror by night; nor for the arrow that flieth by day; nor for the pestilence that walketh in darkness; nor for the destruction that wasteth at noonday. A thousand shall fall at thy side, and ten thousand at thy right hand; but it shall not come nigh thee*. He hopes it is true, but he can't quite believe it.

After their sixth attempt to take the tobacco factory, and with no returning fire, the Scots Guards realise the Germans have withdrawn to form a stronger defensive line further north, spanning the peninsula to the east of Naples.

"It's rude of them, really," says Kendall. "They could have let us know they were leaving. Saved us the bother."

The battalion advances through destroyed villages, watching defeated Italians fleeing both sides of the war, following the railway line en route to their homes in the south. In the fields, a few remaining villagers are stripping the last of the corn, hiding from enemy fire, looking for chestnuts, fungi and plantains. They pick dandelions and put them in paper bags. Sidney is told that some of them have secret stores buried underground — ham, sausages, Parmesan cheese and last year's wine — but it's too dangerous to go back and recover them.

A couple of shepherd boys herd four sheep into the undergrowth to prevent them being requisitioned or stolen. There is only the odd roadside maize field standing, the brown stalks higher than a man. It would be a good place to hide, Sidney thinks, imagining being trapped there for weeks.

They find an empty palazzo near Avellino to use as a base; a brick-built villa with a bullet-pocked Palladian façade and a medieval oratory in the courtyard. The windows are broken, only one half of a swagged curtain remains, and the terrazzo floor in the hall is gouged down the middle. The washed-pink walls contain dark rectangles where the paintings have been. Even the nails and picture hooks have been taken. Nothing remains that cannot be sold or burned for warmth, apart from an old chandelier that was clearly too heavy to remove and a grand piano that is now badly out of tune. Kendall hauls over a munitions box, sits at the keyboard and starts vamping a piece of Gilbert and Sullivan. Freddie Hawthorne steps up to sing "A Wandering Minstrel, I" from *The Mikado* but stops short of performing "I Am the Very Model of a Modern Major-General", not out of tact but because he isn't sure if he can remember all the words.

He is a small, boyish, blond man who was once a child star in the West End. He closes his eyes when he eats his rations, remembering first nights and number-one dressing rooms, pretending that he is at the Mayfair Hotel with his theatrical friends enjoying smoked trout or quails' eggs and champagne. The bully beef is boeuf bourguignon, the hard tack is a cheese-and-rosemary sablé, the water is fine wine. "If you think you're somewhere else, you can be somewhere else," he says. "It's the only way to survive."

Each night Hawthorne inspects his nails before trying to sleep, filing them down, ensuring they are smooth and clean. "I like to keep them neat."

"You know they grow on after you die?" says Sweenie.

Kendall cuts in. "But he's not going to die. No actor likes to leave the stage early. They want the applause."

"I'm glad you're so confident."

"You have to keep cheerful."

Other soldiers are amused by Hawthorne's camp manner and tell him to watch out. There are going to be times when he is the nearest thing to a woman they can find. Every time he takes a shower or a tin bath, Kendall sings "The Strip Polka", amused by how annoying his friend finds it.

"My old man," says Sweenie, "never spoke about the last war, except to tell me about the time the mules got drunk or how his teeth were taken out by a Canadian doctor who had never taken out a tooth in his life. I spent my childhood thinking that war was about mules getting drunk and toothache."

They prepare for bed in the ground-floor rooms with mattresses of chestnut cones and with greatcoats as blankets. When McIntyre, who moans about everything, complains of a sleepless night Kendall tells him not to worry. "At least you're still alive. You can rest all you like when you're dead."

"Thanks very much."

"Why don't you ask Hawthorne to warm you up a bit? He's always game for a cuddle."

"Stop it."

"Only trying to help."

Despite the early success, the Germans have instituted a series of delaying tactics — blowing up harbour breakwaters, polluting the water supply, destroying bridges, roads, railway sidings and yards. They have killed most of the cattle, stripped most of the fields and burned out the beehives.

There is sporadic fire from pockets of retreating soldiers before they leave their positions — mortar and Spandau, a final salvo — and it comes from all over the place. The valleys contain so many echoes it is impossible to pinpoint the direction.

Sidney never sees more than two or three of the enemy alive, but many lie dead in the hedges and ditches along the roadside. The belts around their waists, fastened by gilt buckles, are engraved with the belief that God is on their side: *GOTT MIT UNS!*

There have been hasty burials. A bayonet is stuck to a dead man's rifle and stabbed into the head of his grave. Dog tags hang on the stock with a helmet on top of the butt. Around them are rotting cows, dead dogs, abandoned farm machinery. Who will plough the earth now? Back at home, Sidney realises, they will be celebrating Harvest Festival.

"They're so quick to get out," the Commanding Officer tells them. "We have to keep hammering away. Deny them the initiative."

Lieutenant Colonel Sandy Buchanan is an old Etonian, Balliol classicist, and Scottish cross-country running champion. "You're a Herodotus man, aren't you?" he says to Sidney. "Read Greats at Oxford?"

"Classics. At Cambridge."

"Pity. You know Oxford's the better place? And why the Scots Guards? You don't sound very Scottish."

"My father was with the regiment in the last war," Sidney replies. "We come from the Borders."

"Landed gentry?"

"Farming stock."

"Never mind, you can't have everything. Is your old man still alive?"

"Yes. He was a medical officer."

"We could do with him now. It's not going to be as straightforward as many of us had hoped. Still, we carry on."

The Lieutenant Colonel argues that the infantry is ultimately about hand-to-hand combat. It's all about the battle for "the next hundred yards". In junior athletics, Kendall had run that distance in thirteen seconds. Now, he says, it's going to take them a week to cover the same length of ground.

Buchanan is an old warhorse who knows where he is going to suffer casualties. "The enemy may have withdrawn for the time being, but they are fanatics," he says. "They've been told to fight with a holy hatred. If one of them surrenders it's only because he wants to distract your attention so that one of his mates can shoot you. Remember: you are always at your weakest when you think you've won."

He is speaking in the mess tent. Sidney, Hawthorne and Kendall eat their hard tack and bully beef and can't imagine what it will be like to think they have "won" at all. It is more a question of survival, of getting through each day.

The Germans switch their positions so often that the men never quite know when they are within sight and range. An advance patrol is ambushed by machine-gun fire. A sniper wounds McCallum in the shoulder. Dalrymple is hit by a grenade thrown by a German who is running away — a last act of defiance.

"It's slow going," says Hawthorne, once everyone has split into groups for a smoke and a rest. "All roads may lead to Rome but most of them are mined."

Buchanan overhears as he is passing back to his quarters. "That's why we've got the engineers. Although we do seem to have run into a spot of bother."

"What do you mean?" Sidney asks.

"It's tiresome. A group of sappers is trapped in one of the fields."

"You've sent out a search party?"

"They haven't come back. Clarke, Naylor and Cummins are missing; Gilmour and McDonald have not returned. I'm going to ask for a second group of men."

"We'll do it," says Kendall. "We've done the training. Let's sort this out."

"You don't mind?"

"Someone has to go and it might as well be us. Come on, chaps . . ."

It is just before ten at night. They set out down a dark lane lit by the faintest moonlight. They know the rules. No noise. No coughs. Tools and equipment padded. No lights. No smoking.

They arrive at a potato field surrounded by barbed wire and deep ditches. The engineers have marked out a winding single-line track with white tape, but something has gone wrong. They must have missed a section. A mine has exploded in an area that they thought had already been cleared. The first soldier Sidney comes across is lying face-down dead with a detector on his back.

Ahead is a man who thanks God they have got there at last. He is told to keep his voice down.

"How many of you are left?" Kendall asks.

"Clarkie won't answer but I think he's alive."

"So that's two of you."

The standard procedure is to throw out a rope and pull the men back through the cleared area, but the rescue party can't trust that method any more. "We'll have to check again," says Kendall, "and we'll do it by hand."

"It'll take ages."

"And you're a long time dead. Take any metal out of your pockets. Get down on the ground, crawl forward. Use the short bayonet. Prod ahead and at an angle. If you feel any resistance, dig down with your hands and uncover."

Sidney gets down on his knees. "I thought they'd cleared this."

"So did Gilchrist. Now look at him."

They move through the mud and cold. There is just enough give in the ground to feel down for the mines. "This is worse than a wet night in Paisley," says Hawthorne.

"Have you ever been to Paisley?"

"You'd be surprised where I've been."

One man ahead is moaning. Sidney isn't sure if it is a complaint or a prayer. The only other sounds are of frogs from the nearby riverbank, the first spots of rain.

He moves forward, spearing the bayonet into the earth as gently as he can, careful with the pressure, five times with his left hand, five times with his right, only an inch or two apart. After fifteen minutes, he feels a tap of resistance, metal on metal. "I think I've got one."

"Stay calm, Chambers," says Kendall. "You know what to do."

"It's been a while since the training."

"Take it slowly. Don't let your hands shake."

"How am I supposed to do that? It's bloody cold."

"You can't play with fire without risking your fingers."

Sidney uses his fingertips to feel for the three prongs of the spring. God, he could blow his hand off at any minute and that would only be the start. How many more of these bloody mines are there?

Hawthorne uses his body to shield and direct a beam of torchlight. "Christ, this is dangerous."

"Don't bring him into it," says Kendall.

"Shut up," says Sidney.

Something catches in his eye; he doesn't know if it is sweat, earth, an insect or a strand of his own hair. He finds the first prong of the mine. It almost catches underneath his fingernail. Then he discovers two more. He claws away the earth around the cover plate. "Have you got a pin?" he asks.

"Ready and waiting," Kendall replies. "Just make sure you don't drop it."

"How many of them have we got?"

"Enough."

"That means you don't know."

"Twenty."

"Then let's hope there aren't any more mines than that."

Using Hawthorne's light, Sidney places the pin through the hole below the prongs to create a safety catch. He then takes out the pressure springs, plugs and detonators. Once he has done so, he lies still for a moment, letting his breathing return to normal.

"Are you all right?" Hawthorne asks.

"Of course he's all right."

Sidney gets back on his knees, stands up, and takes the dismantled mine beyond the white tape before they resume their task.

A voice rises out of the darkness. "Are you still coming?"

"Give us a chance."

"No hurry," returns another voice. "Anyone would think we'd got all night."

"No sign of the enemy?"

"They're either having a kip or a laugh. Perhaps they're going to shoot as soon as we think we're safe."

"Don't joke about it."

"Get on with it then."

It takes another two hours to reach the stranded men. Ward and Cummins are dead. Brennan has shrapnel wounds in the chest. Thorburn isn't sure he can walk but it turns out to be the shock and the cold. He puts his arms around Sidney and thanks him for saving his life.

"I'll do the same for you one day."

"I very much hope you don't have to," says Sidney.

"Thank God that's over," Hawthorne replies.

"Nothing is over," says Thorburn, "and I don't think God has much to do with any of this."

Kendall puts an arm round Sidney's shoulder as they walk back to base. "Well done, old boy. I'm proud of you."

"We should be proud of each other."

Sidney looks back at the minefield in the early dawn. He realises that no matter how much they do now, or how swiftly they win the war, this Italian land will never be truly cleared; that whenever the peace finally comes, the mines will still be there in the fields, to wound and kill the farmers who till the soil and the children who play there.

CHAPTER TWO

"Who chose this place for a holiday?" Robert asks.

It is the beginning of October. The three friends are in Naples.

Before they left the city, the Germans destroyed the gas and electricity plants, cut off the water supply, and carried away the buses and trams. There is no oil for lamps or heat, just the wood from destroyed buildings and smashed furniture in makeshift street fires. Piles of stone and rubble have been left uncleared. Ruined houses have had their rafters blown off; dead dogs lie beneath half-sloughed plaster walls and broken windows.

"If all the towns in Germany get knocked about like this then they'll regret ever starting this war," says Robert.

The streets are filled with gaunt men too old or weak to fight, their wives wait for their luck to change, praying to the Virgin Mary, and children beg for biscuits, chocolates and cigarettes.

A seventy-year-old woman, wearing a bridal veil and football boots, stirs a cauldron of soup. A cripple, lying chest down on a wheeled platform only a few inches from the ground, propels himself forward at speed, reaching out to beg or steal with his one good arm. A thin and vague old lady, in a black-velvet dressing gown with three layers of pearls, wanders through the streets of Santa Lucia, carrying the family jewels, uncertain who will buy them and where to go next. She is telling anyone who will listen that her cousin has sold twelve silver spoons to pay for a ham and that she is La Principessa Lucrezia Bianca della Robbia.

Anything of use is for sale; cigarettes made from butt-ends collected in the street, hospital blankets, army socks, jeep tyres, chairs with missing legs, manhole covers, even gravestones.

Having nothing to cook, most of the restaurants are closed; a few offer macaroni or sea bass they claim to have caught recently but display heads that don't belong to the fish beneath them or veal that turns out to be horse.

A group of blind girls move in a line from table to table, clinging on to each other for direction, weeping and begging for food. They are ignored.

After Sidney has paid over the odds to a wild-eyed old man for a pair of American combat boots, they pass a row of women sitting with their backs to the wall, a yard apart, with an empty ration tin in front of them. This is the price of sex. A tin of rations. Some of them do it there and then without undressing at all; a hitch of the skirt, the man's fly unbuttoned, a short burst of rhythmic movement and it's over.

In this city, they say that you can catch venereal disease simply by shaking hands with a priest. Freddie tells his friends he wants nothing to do with flesh and the devil. He has heard that there are up to 40,000 women offering themselves in Naples alone — do they really want the clap?

A girl of twelve offers to strip for twenty lira. It is less than the price of an egg. Another offers Sidney a "trip to the cemetery" where no one will disturb them.

"For God's sake," says Robert. "They're younger than our sisters."

Men in Naples pimp their daughters from the age of ten, while doctors offer services to "restore" a woman's virginity if the right man comes along. Sidney remembers losing his own to a young Irish girl, Caitlín Delaney, at the age of nineteen and how she had asked him, just before the crucial moment: "This will be all right, won't it?"

He wonders where she is now. She went back to Ireland and married a local boy. Will he be fighting or has he managed to avoid the whole damned thing?

"Come on, Chambers," says Robert. "I should light a candle for my mother. It'll be something to tell her I've done. There must be a chapel round here somewhere."

They are on the edge of the Spanish Quarter. The church of Santa Chiara has been bombed so badly that they have to step over mounds of rubble to get into it. Parts of the roof are missing, windows are smashed and the door at the west end is about to come off its hinges. The decorated columns in the majolica cloister garden are still standing and depict scenes of rural peace and leisure (boar hunting, bowling and dancing) that are at odds with the destruction around them. The only vines, oranges, lemons and figs available are ceramic.

Inside, a priest is saying Mass and the people in attendance are women and children. One side chapel has candles that the sexton is selling for the same price as a prostitute. Sidney holds back as Robert hands over the money, tilts his candle towards one that is already lit, places it in position and lowers his head. He does not make the sign of the Cross or appear to pray, but takes his time as the Mass continues in the distance and the priest provides the final benediction.

"You've never struck me as being religious," says Sidney as they return to the streets.

"I'm never quite sure what I believe," Robert replies, "but it doesn't matter when I'm in there because Mother does. She always likes to know I've been thinking of her. This will be something to write home about."

There's a bar in the Piazza del Gesù Nuovo and they stop for a quick drink. It is standing room only and they are just inside the doorway when they hear the strains of "Giovinezza" on the radio from Munich.

Some Italian fascists have remained true to the cause, despite the surrender, and are swearing an oath: *I believe in God, Lord of Heaven and earth. I believe in justice and truth. I believe in the resurrection of Fascist Italy. I believe in Mussolini and the final Italian victory.*

"I'm not sure we'll be welcome here," Robert whispers, just before a man sitting at a table at the far end is shot for refusing to stand to attention.

"Bloody hell. Let's get out of here."

When they leave Naples and are moving through the surrounding fields, Sidney sees a woman with a little girl and a basket of washing walking along with a mule. The mother is leading, wearing a black dress. Her daughter is riding side-saddle. They are heading towards the river.

Ten minutes later Sidney hears an explosion. He turns around. There is bloodstained laundry in the trees.

The battalion moves on towards Rocchetta e Croce and Pignataro just north of Caserta, and bed in below "Monastery Hill". Sidney is given a Bren gun and asked to winkle out a sniper who has dispatched three of their men already. He is to wait for "as long as necessary" to get rid of the man.

He edges his way into a small terraced house that is just within range. There are a couple of long-dead geraniums in the remains of a wire-framed window box, torn curtains, a broken rocking chair, a bed without a mattress, a pitted alcove that might have been a shrine. He can't tell who has lived here before the war — it could have been a young family, an elderly couple, a widow, the local doctor or a policeman — it doesn't matter now. Their history has gone.

Sidney secures his position, watches sniper fire just miss a fellow Guardsman below and does not retaliate. He cannot give his location away. He estimates that he will have less than three seconds for the kill and that he might have to wait until dusk or darkness.

After what must have been over two hours of waiting, the German fires off a salvo at a house over to the right. The ensuing silence is broken only by the sound of a distant explosion and an armoured vehicle climbing up the hill behind them. Then there is movement, a glint of gun in the low sunlight, the turn of a head, a glimpse of back and shoulder.

Sidney shoots off a round in eight seconds. Then he lets the time pass. He still does not want to risk being seen. But there is no response. After five or six minutes, he approaches the enemy position, keeping down, looking out for movement, approaching round the back. He throws in a grenade. He waits for the explosion and then for signs of life. There is no further sound, no sense of a trap or counter-attack.

He sees the dead sniper in the dust and rubble. There are wounds to the head and neck. The man is lying on his side, his cork-blacked face turned to the left, burned flesh visible, blood still seeping from a body that seems too incongruously large to be lifeless.

Before this moment, any death Sidney has caused has been in the heat and hazard of battle. Whether people have lived or died has been a matter of luck as much as anything else. This more deliberate killing feels closer to murder.

He leans against a wall, making sure he is clear of the window and well out of sight, puts down his gun and is dizzyingly sick. His head hurts, his mouth is dry and his sight blurs. He wonders if he is going to pass out. He just stops himself from falling forward on to the ground.

He should get out, he knows. But something makes him stay longer. He wonders how his life has led to this moment and if he could have avoided it altogether.

What might it have been like had he been born in a different time or place or even refused to join up? Who is the man he has just killed? Had the German felt confident and impregnable as he took up his position, or scared and on edge? Was he able to discard his own feelings and remain calm, ignoring the morality of his actions as he picked off enemy troops? How aware was he that he might die that day?

Sidney kneels down and searches the breast pocket of the man's uniform. He finds a studio portrait of a girl. She looks too young to be a girlfriend. Could it be the man's little sister? He wonders what she might be called. The men are used to calling the enemy "Hans" and "Fritz" but he once met a young couple in Cambridge called Wolfgang and Ilse. He tries to imagine where they might be now — back in Lübeck perhaps — if they have become Nazis (they seemed so civilised, so studious, so well mannered), and whether they are still alive.

He looks at the sniper and wonders how soon the body will be recovered and buried. Will the Germans come back for him or will their own padre have to do it? He hasn't met the new man yet. They say he is recovering from the jaundice he's caught in Sicily.

Sidney thinks about praying for forgiveness, for mercy on the sniper's soul and on his own, but he doesn't have the words and it doesn't feel right. He tries to work out how soon the news of death will reach the sniper's home. He studies the photograph. The blonde woman's face. He imagines the end of her smile. A room in silence. The drawn curtains. A thickening light.

As the weather worsens they advance towards Monte Camino. The fertile valleys are knee-deep in black mud. The Germans have destroyed every bridge and culvert. The rivers rise. The rain only stops when they are asleep. Thousands of men stay in wet clothing for weeks.

One of the scouts conscripts a shepherd to herd his flock of sheep across a field that might be full of landmines. The man is old, he can't have that much more time to live, and he knows what will happen. It doesn't take long for a couple of lambs to stumble and set off a series of explosions that scatter the way ahead with legs, bones, shoulders, heads and stomachs.

Robert watches everything. "There must be a better way to prepare dinner," he says.

The battalion marches for seven miles, passing through a series of "liberated" villages that have been blown apart. Sidney remembers a line from Tacitus. *They make this place a wilderness and call it peace*. He cannot stop thinking about the sniper. The dead man's face haunts his dreams.

The men arrive at a "Long Stop" position on a low ridge. Sidney's Number 3 Company stay in place in the rain for a couple of days, waiting for the push on Camino. They live in foxholes in the ground — it is a case of dig or die. They set up the latrines: one yard for twenty men. "Let's just shit for victory," says Kendall.

As they sit on their helmets and eat their rations, the army padre pays them a visit. He has arrived at last and is enlisting support for the church service the following morning.

"You won't get many of us going to that," Hawthorne tells him.

"Even one of you sinners would be enough."

"Sin? Fat chance of any of that round here."

"Rev Nev" Finnie is an Episcopalian from Markinch in Fife. He is an asthmatic in his early forties, technically too old for service, but he is a family friend of the Colonel. He has been offered leave but he has a determination to continue with his ministry, wherever it takes him, and people can't be bothered to argue about his age or suitability. He is only a priest. There are plenty of soldiers to console and bury.

He is a tall man with a slight stoop and a shy smile who gives out cigarettes and tots of whisky whenever a case arrives from his father's distillery. Some people joke they would rather have the whisky than the communion wine, but he tells them that one is a precondition of the other.

"I know what you're all thinking when I heave into sight," he says. "Here come the bloody clergy."

Not many of the soldiers are eager participants in the singing of "Onward Christian Soldiers", "Soldiers of the Cross, Arise!" and "Fight the Good Fight". Sidney remembers how, at school, after they had been told to "Stand up, Stand up for Jesus", Kendall had said: "I think I'd prefer to sit down if it's all the same to you."

"What does a priest do in the middle of all this?" Sidney's friend asks.

"You know perfectly well, Kendall. I take services. I provide Holy Communion. I hear confessions. I help people write letters home. I negotiate with the Red Cross. I anoint the wounded. I bury the dead."

"I suppose someone has to do it . . ."

Rev Nev's kitbag is packed with "just-in-case" letters home from the soldiers in his charge.

"Just as long as you don't bury me . . ."

"I hope and I pray that I won't have to do that. I think that what I'm really here to do is to provide some kind of stability; to remind people that there is an alternative to this hell. There is another world."

"But not one that we live in. Perhaps you offer a future state to keep us quiet about this one?"

"That is not the intention."

"But it is the reality. What does your wife think?"

"I'm not married."

"So, you're married to the Church?"

Nev speaks with an otherworldly but weary hopefulness born from a belief that the real enemy is not the German army ranged against them but death itself; and that when the strife is o'er, the battle done, there will be an eternal victory far greater than anything achieved on earth.

"I believe there is no higher calling than to be a priest in the service of God and God's people; to offer some kind of stability in a bewildered world."

"Blimey," says Kendall. "You've certainly come to the right place."

"But I can tell," the padre continues, "that I am depressing you all. Too many memories of school chapel, I can see. Would you like some whisky?"

"That's more like it."

"My father's a director at John Haig and Company. We don't have to talk about religion. There's always football, although my knowledge is mainly confined to Raith Rovers and West Ham."

"You don't need to entertain us," says Hawthorne.

Kendall laughs. "Hawthorne is perfectly good at doing that on his own. You should see his strip routine . . ."

"Don't start all that again . . ."

"He's quite the showman."

Rev Nev waits for the conversation to die down. He has advice to impart. "I've been in the wars for a fair bit longer than you all, if you don't mind my saying so," he continues, "and so I can also advise on practical matters."

"Oh really?"

"Your foxhole, Kendall."

"What about it?"

"It's not deep enough. It should go at least six feet down."

"I'll be all right. Besides, I'm not sure if I've time to do any more. The earth's frozen."

"Make time. You won't regret it."

"Really?"

"It could be a matter of life and death."

"I can't see a few inches of earth making much difference."

"I've seen it do so."

"All right then. If you say."

The men go back to dig the ditch deeper, straight at the ends, sloping at the sides, filling sandbags with the hard and claggy earth and laying them down at front and back to act as cover. Around them, people are singing: "Nobody knows how bored we are and nobody seems to care." Then they begin work on the roof, putting strong branches across the top of the hole and pitching it up with bits of wood so that any grenade that falls directly will roll off. That is the theory. Hawthorne digs a storage pit for weapons and ammunition.

"It reminds me of the early Christians living underground in their catacombs," says Rev Nev, "decorating the walls with scenes from the Bible, sharing meals with the living and the dead as if, perhaps, there is no distinction between them but time . . ."

"I think there is a distinction," says Kendall, "and I know which I prefer."

"The important thing is that no matter what their suffering entailed, they still believed. It's what we have to do now. We have to trust in everything we hold dear."

"I do. I'm just not sure I need to be walled up in a foxhole to do that."

"Imagine you're camping if it helps."

"I'm the only one doing the camping round here," says Hawthorne.

"And then, if we do get killed all you have to do is leave us," adds Kendall. "Who needs gravediggers?"

They wait for orders. This is how it is, the oscillation between boredom and terror; soldiers oiling their Tommy guns even when they are already oiled because there is little else to do.

Wait. Watch. Stalk. Patrol. Dig in.

Eat. Guard. Try to sleep.

Wait again. Contain the fear.

Some men's hands shake so much they can hardly light a cigarette.

Sidney tries to imagine the landscape without war; the last of the cicadas, a stretch of autumn pine and cedar, preparing the vines for the winter, the first taste of that year's wine. He wonders if, because the summer is so much hotter than in England and burns everything away, winter comes sooner here. The first frost is that night.

He tells Rev Nev about the sniper; the guilt and the horror; the fact that the man's death feels so personal and deliberate. It is Sidney's most frequent resting thought. He cannot shake off the memory of the dead man's face, the photograph of the young girl, the blood drying on a dusty floor.

"You have to remember that the enemy would have had no qualms about killing you, Chambers."

"I know that. But it doesn't seem to help."

"This is war. There are very few rules. But you have to harden your heart. You're of no use to your friends if you lose your stomach for the fight."

"I don't know how you keep your faith in the middle of all this."

Nev hands Sidney his hip flask. "In the creed, we say that we believe in the one God and we remind ourselves of the facts of Christ's life, death and resurrection. And in wartime there is one sentence that always stands out. *He descended into hell*. Christ knew suffering. And we know it too. We witness what human beings are capable of doing to each other. Having experienced the worst, we must live for the best. We have to turn away from the horror."

"And yet we confront it every day."

"I try to think of St Paul's letter to the Romans, Chambers: 'Do not be overcome by evil but overcome evil with good.' We must fight our way out of the darkness, even if we do not live to see the light ourselves."

"And how do we do that?"

"Despite battle, we love and work and believe in righteousness. And we pray."

"I have thought about doing that. But I can't find the words."

"I have some," says Rev Nev. "So, perhaps we should try?"

"I can't see what good it's going to do."

"But what harm can come of it, either? I'll say the words. You just come in with the 'Amens'."

His voice is steady and assured. Perhaps he thinks it is because, if he sounds confident, people will *become* confident in his presence.

"Have mercy upon me, O God, according to thy loving kindness: according unto the multitude of thy tender mercies blot out my transgressions. Wash me thoroughly from mine iniquity, and cleanse me from my sin. For I acknowledge my transgressions: and my sin is ever before me . . ."

Sidney wonders what sin he has committed, apart from the death of the sniper, to warrant this fawning submission to an unknown presence. He finds little reassurance in words said amidst the cold, the damp and the darkness; and even if these prayers can provide hope for the night ahead, how can it last into the light of the returning day, the daily repeat of dread and battle?

CHAPTER THREE

For sixteen days and nights the battalion dig in on the tops of the hills. They survive on limited rations with no hot food and little water to wash or shave. They go to breakfast in the dark, one group at a time, eat quickly and return to their foxholes so the next group can take their turn. Lunch is eaten in their holes. Dinner is the same as breakfast.

The advance party forms outside Battalion HQ. The first few hours are spent watching Brigade, Divisional and Corps Commanders spying out the land.

"They're taking too much time," says Kendall. "That's a bad sign. We'll just have to hope the others don't notice. We need to keep up morale. People are starting to go mad."

It takes different guises. Some men stop moving. They stare into space and refuse any order, abandoning themselves to whatever fate holds for them. Others shake until they are too exhausted to continue and fall over to one side, still trembling but anticipating constraint, trying to prevent anyone touching them. Others repeat words for no reason — *larkspur, hen, majesty* — or they say little phrases over and over — *very peculiar, it's all very peculiar* — or they start to sing: *Joshua, Joshua, nicer than lemon squash you are . . .*

Kendall tries to comfort them by organising word games and general-knowledge quizzes with bizarre rules that no one understands but everyone seems to enjoy. They are necessary distractions.

Company Commanders spend half an hour issuing orders and another quarter studying the mountain. The main objective is to take the high ridge that they have christened "Bare Arse".

Sidney is told to "advance to contact".

"You know what that means? Very little advance and far too much contact," says Kendall. "I heard you talking to Rev Nev last night. I didn't want to interrupt."

"That means you disapprove."

"You can do what you like, Chambers, anything that helps. But I was just thinking —"

"You don't want to do too much of that, Kendall. It's not your strong point."

"Shut up and listen. You've nothing else to do."

"Go on then."

"Well, Jesus got off quite lightly when you think about it. Nev can talk as much as he likes about the suffering but, let's face it, it was only in the last couple of weeks, after your man had gone to Jerusalem, that he had all the trouble. If he'd stayed in Galilee he'd have been all right. We're going to be in Italy a lot longer than Jesus was under arrest and we'll see a lot more of hell than he did. He was only down there for three days. You could think of it as a long weekend, if you like. We've got months, years even."

"I don't think you can compare the two situations."

"I've got a point, though, haven't I? I'm not as stupid as you think I am."

"I don't think you're stupid at all, Kendall. It's just that sometimes . . ."

"I talk too much?"

"Yes."

"Well, you could help out a bit more if you don't like it, Chambers. It can't be left just to me and Hawthorne to cheer everyone up. That's all I'm trying to do."

They don't get to the top of Bare Arse until near dawn, a nine-and-a-half-hour climb.

"Well, Hawthorne," says Kendall. "You're on your first bare arse."

"What makes you think it's the first?" his friend replies.

It is hard rock with crevices large enough to get a foot caught, all set off at a slope to the west. The climb would have been difficult enough by day, but on a pitch-black night it is, Hawthorne says, "damn near impossible".

As dawn appears, a captain from the London Irish comes over with news. He's survived earlier skirmishes but lost a couple of fingers. He tells them the battle is going badly and he doesn't think that more than a platoon's worth of men is in one piece.

Sidney's company form up in single file and march. They are told to imagine that it's a bit like going for a grouse drive through a wood in the Borders. As they come over the summit, German patrols let loose from all directions. Mills bombs are thrown, machine guns fired and the wounded are stranded. "Bones" McKay is caught in the chest by a burst of Spandau and dies within minutes. Two stretcher-bearers are killed. Even when retrenched there is no respite. Allan Proudie is dispatched in his foxhole by a mortar that lands right on top of him — his helmet looks like a kitchen colander. Brocklebank is sitting up in a shallow slit trench. Sidney doesn't realise the man is dead until he taps him on the shoulder to ask how he is.

Rev Nev proves that he is a man for more than communion, going out again and again with the stretcher-bearers under cover of smoke to bring back the wounded. He is one of few men oblivious to risk.

"The only truth that matters," he says, "is that without God we cannot live. We can only take a longer or a shorter time to die."

Sidney remembers his father talking to him about a colleague in the last war — Douglas Dougan — *Duggie, Duggie* — singing his way to the front, trying to pretend that it was all a lark; there was no point being afraid: *Everybody does that Charlie Chaplin walk*.

Duggie told Alec Chambers that the third time he went over the top would be his last and it was. He just knew. Just like the third light of a cigarette; the first to spot you, the second to aim, the third to fire. He wanted to leave the world with a smile. Sidney's father didn't think he had ever seen such bravery.

They are at the front for thirty-six hours. A wounded engineer asks one of the stretcher-bearers to shoot him rather than attempt to save his life. Another commits suicide to avoid having to go back to fight.

"Lucky bastard," says Kendall.

"Every man has a string so long," says Hawthorne, "yet none of us know how long our own is until we come to the end of it."

"Do you know, sometimes you surprise me, Hawthorne. You really do."

At last they are relieved of their positions. Sidney and his men hand over what little ammunition they have and start the journey down. Not one of them has expected to come back from the mountain alive.

They lodge in caves at Miele. Those who take their boots off cannot get them back on again. Their feet have swollen to twice the size with trench foot.

Sidney shares a tin bath with Robert. It is so cold they keep their vests on to wash their legs before drying themselves and switching over. It reminds them of school. All that manly jocularity in the washrooms; the cold showers, cross-country runs, rugby in winter and assault courses in the CCF.

"Do you remember waking up in the dorms and the windows were frozen on the inside?" Sidney asks.

"You always wanted to stay in bed or read a book. I couldn't wait to jump out and get on with the day. I'm not so keen now, though."

"Too bloody right; it's not history first thing but mortar fire. What do you fancy? Latin verbs or being bombed?"

Sidney laughs but Robert does not. He hands his friend the soap. "Which do you think is worse? To die of heat or of cold? Burn or freeze?"

"I can't imagine ever being warm again. Someone once told me that hypothermia's quite nice. It's a bit like falling asleep."

"Buried alive or suffocation?"

"Aren't they the same thing?"

"I suppose drowning is also an option."

"Hard to do in this bath, though. Not enough room."

"I'm sure we could find a way."

Robert starts to dry himself with a towel that's too damp to be effective. "This is about as useful as a eunuch in a brothel." He throws it across to his friend. "But at least it passes the time. Stops you thinking. You know that's bad for you."

It is the kind of thing Sidney's mother says. "You mustn't *dwell*. It makes you moody."

Iris Chambers believes that most of the bad events in a life can be alleviated by a hot bath and a stiff whisky — it's important to have an ordered routine, to keep your body clean and your clothes fresh and to do everything "nicely" — whether it be washing and drying, ironing linen, folding the sheets, starching shirts, baking scones, or even laying a table for dinner. It never takes that much effort to do things properly, she says. You just have to take the trouble. Then everything looks, and feels, better. Sidney wonders what she would think of him now. Can you wage a war "nicely"?

He opens his rations and imagines what his mother would do to improve matters. She would lay everything out with a napkin, he thinks, or with a handkerchief that she would conjure from nowhere. She would tell him to enjoy the moment.

Sidney lies down on the ground and closes his eyes. He lets himself remember saying goodbye to his family and what London had been like at the time. He had just broken up with Caitlín Delaney. He wonders what it might have been like if they had stayed together. Would she have persuaded him not to fight? He could have become a teacher, missed the war and lived with her in the south of Ireland instead.

Thinking of her stops him dwelling on the sniper. Caitlín was the first member of her family to go to university (they met while she was reading Classics at Girton) and she was serious and generous and had made up her mind that Sidney was the man for her. She invited him to her older sister's wedding in Listowel. It was a Catholic affair with a Mass, a dinner and a dance and all the relations assumed he was going to propose that very weekend but the longer it went on the more Sidney felt incapable of saying anything. The two of them walked along the cliffs at Ballybunnion — they were the last he saw before coming to Italy — and they stopped at Collins's Seaweed Baths and Sidney had laughed at the ridiculousness of that hot, oily luxury and being next to each other, divided by a partition yet still able to talk, unaware that he would never bathe so well again, or that he would be stuck in the future in a freezing tin bath in the middle of nowhere with Robert Kendall making grim jokes about the best way to die. Perhaps this was his punishment for telling Caitlín he didn't think he could love her as much as she expected, as much as she wanted, as much as she *deserved*.

"I think you're ashamed of being with me, aren't you, Sidney?" she had said.

"It's not that."

"You're embarrassed by my family."

"No, I'm not."

"They've guessed something's up. It's humiliating. How am I supposed to recover?"

"I'm sorry. I didn't think it would be like this."

"You shouldn't have come so."

"You invited me."

"And you came. You should have realised what would have been expected of you. You should have thought more about who we are. My family. You're a snob. I can see that now."

He thinks of all that was good and lovable about her and how he let her down and how his life would have been different if he had just got on with it and proposed.

"You can't behave as if you're a character in a book," she said to him. "People have feelings. Real feelings. You have to live your life by taking account of others."

Well, I'm certainly living it now, he thinks. And I wonder how much of it I've got left.

He is too tired to sleep. He listens to the sound of loose shutters banging in the windows of derelict houses and the rasping of the wind in the wires supporting the vines.

In the near distance, flickering lights move quickly but uncertainly in the night sky. It looks like silent gunfire but it is not. Two village boys have caught some bats, tied them to rags, soaked them in petrol stolen from Allied jeeps and set them alight to create living fireworks, burning to death.

CHAPTER FOUR

The roads are deep with glutinous mud. Sidney tries to imagine they are like milk chocolate because he cannot stop thinking that the ground beneath his feet is the colour of shit. It gets everywhere: on his boots, his clothes, his hands, face and hair. It is another layer of skin. There are times when he can smell nothing else and thinks he will never be clean again.

It freezes every day. At night, the water bottles are solid. One man is so desperate for cleanliness that he lays out his wet blankets to dry in the faint afternoon sun and returns to find they have frozen hard. They look like a giant water biscuit.

They pass ruined olive groves, wrecked orchards, bombed buildings and booby-trapped roads. There is nothing in the fields. Village children are so hungry they suck at the teats of goats.

Sidney marches through the wet, with a pack on his back, his Bren and his gear, as men die around him. At one point, he thinks he sees a large mushroom poking out of the ground before he recognises it is human bone; the bruised white weather-beaten dome is part of a soldier's skull.

The German machine-gun positions are wired in and the bands of fire interlock. They have developed a technique of low-grazing shooting that can hit a man in the legs no matter how close he keeps to the earth. Alternatively, the shelling comes straight down. A soldier can be in a slit trench and the mortar drops right in with him.

Jock Wilson is shot in the chest, his beating heart exposed, the flesh flapping around it. Sidney grips his shoulder. "It's all right, Jock. It's going to be fine."

He knows it's a lie.

One platoon advances through trees and is trapped in a minefield. Only eight out of the thirty emerge unscathed.

"What is it like?" he asks a survivor.

The question is repeated back twice — "What is it like?" — as if the person asking is beyond stupidity. "What is it like? It's like a butcher's shop."

It takes so long to fall asleep at night that Sidney is surprised when he wakes to find that he ever lost consciousness. He has missed the moment of dawn, sleeping through it in the blackness below ground, amidst the worms, the roots and the wildlife, preferring the comfort of darkness to the threat of another day, shifting position and stretching only because his back aches, his legs are stiff and his mouth is dry. It is always dry. He is able to survive on little food. It is fresh water he misses; fresh water in a summer garden with his friends, the anticipation of wine and a party, people dancing, smiling and laughing. It is so long since he has heard anyone laugh unrestrainedly. The laughter in war is ironic, half-hearted and resentful. He wants to enjoy the freedom of a joke amidst good company, warmth and a conversation that can be ended on its own terms rather than by the actions of the enemy. What would it be like to have no enemy? He cannot imagine.

"Here we are again," says Kendall cheerfully, as he walks beside Sidney, refusing to let his energy drain away. "It hasn't been a bad dream after all."

More soldiers go mad or pretend to do so. No one can believe they can make a proper attack in this weather, up a mountain, and at two in the morning. Others hope for "holiday wounds", pieces of shrapnel in their arms or legs, just enough to take them away from the front. More of them injure themselves deliberately.

One of their number, Swinton, a quiet man from Galashiels who has taken to sketching the fields and villages when they stop to rest, is missing. They don't hear if he has been wounded or taken prisoner and they never find his body. Either he has crawled into a foxhole, never to come out, or he has gone native and is being hidden by an Italian family.

Another, Gatchell, says he thinks he might run away before the next attack. He can't stand it any more.

Kendall's having none of it. "If you're going to desert us, you might as well leave now, at night, so we can find someone to take your place. If you run away in the middle of a fight I'll shoot you. You can't let us down."

"You would kill one of your own?"

"If it meant survival, and if it was for the greater good of all of us, then of course I would."

"I didn't expect you to be so heartless."

"It's not that at all. Fear is contagious. We can't show it. You should know that by now, Gatchell." He turns to Sidney. "Come on, Chambers. Walk with me."

Kendall marches amongst the troops exuding calm and resolve, but quietly assessing how much the men can endure and what can be expected of them. He has "a good stride on him", the men remark. "They can't hit me," he says to them, "they just can't hit me," and, for the moment, the enemy don't.

"You have to step in," he tells Sidney afterwards, "and distract them. It's not that different from captaining the rugby. You have to make them believe they're going to win, whatever the score. *Audentes fortuna juvat*."

"You remember that?"

"*Fortune favours the brave*. I may not be an intellectual like you, old bean, but I remember a lot more than you think I do."

Some of the men are talking about their sweethearts: how they'd met, whether they are "good girls" or "flighty bints", how long they might wait for them, if they can trust them. Sidney is asked about Caitlín Delaney. One of the men met her in Dublin a few years before and describes her as "frisky as a mare". He implies he's had her first.

Sidney feels he has to say something in defence or denial but can't decide whether to lie or tell the truth. All this masculine company. All this bravado in the face of death. Sometimes he wonders whether anything with Caitlín counted at all. The sex had been so bad that they were embarrassed to continue. It had been perfunctory, humiliating and unloving, and it haunted Sidney so much that he made enough of a confession to Robert for him to offer to organise a meeting with a game girl at Newnham whom he promised would put Sidney right and pass on a few tips to help him perform better next time. Sidney had said no thanks and then, later that weekend, he'd seen them in a punt together, laughing away, and wished he'd joined them.

They find an old two-man trench that saves them the bother of digging a new one. They don't discuss what might have happened to the previous occupants. It is only two or three feet deep and rested over with a framework of wood and bracken. The entrance is a mere slit, so they lie flat on the ground and wriggle in on their stomachs. Robert goes in first and Sidney passes him their two blankets before sliding in himself. They can hear guns in the distance. Earth falls into the trench with each tremor. The space is more cramped than they had anticipated and they are forced to lie facing the same way, close up against roots and damp earth, puddles forming underneath as the rain continues to fall. They draw up their knees; their bodies curled one inside the other. If one of them wants to change position the other has to follow suit.

"You know this is mad," says Robert. "To think that I got a cricket blue and you got a first. We're supposed to be the cream of England. You've got the brains and I've got the beauty. Now look at us. We should be tucked up in clean sheets with beautiful women who smell of roses and lily of the valley. Oh God, how I miss my own bed."

Sidney thinks of his family back in London and then of Robert's sister. She has sent her regards in a letter. The last time he saw Amanda the family all went to a Myra Hess concert at the National Gallery. She sat next to him and told him about her love of Dutch still life and said that one day she wanted to be a curator and have a career in art. She was never going to be content just to be "someone's little wife".

"Besides," she argued, "I know I'd be bored. Men are never entertaining enough for a woman to spend all her time with them. A girl has to find something else to do."

"I hope I'm not boring," Sidney replied.

"Oh, you're different," she said. "You don't count. You're my brother's best friend."

She calls him by his surname, "Chambers", as if she's at school with him. He imagines her on the lacrosse field, tearing into the opposition, her stick held high, flinging the ball into the goal and celebrating with her friends, running back to the centre circle with an enormous grin on her face, glad to be so triumphantly alive. He remembers her at a Christmas party in a black, low-scooped, long-sleeved, silk cocktail dress and pearls, the clothes accentuating her willowy grace; how he had been surprised by the incongruous depth of her voice; the way she held a cigarette as if she had forgotten all about it; the fact that sometimes she came too close to him; the smell of her perfume, Jean Patou's Joy; the chuckle at the beginning of her laugh that was like a car starting up; the way she turned for a last look before she left the room because she knew people were watching her.

"Come on," says Robert, waking him up. "You need to move first. Show Rev Nev that you can rise from the dead."

The battalion moves up the mule track between the two Camino ridges, through steep slopes, seamed with deep ravines, minor ridges, knolls and hollows confused together. It is an eight-hour hike through the hills to the forward positions. To avoid artillery and mortar attack it has to be done in the dark on mountain slopes guided only by a small white patch tied to the pack of the man in front.

They march on, shoulders dropping, legs unwilling, packs heavy on their backs. Each time a loose rock is dislodged and falls noisily to the valley below, they stop in their tracks. Enemy forces fire flares into the sky. No one speaks or coughs or breathes too loudly in case they give their position away.

There is hardly a time when it isn't raining. The gorges are choked with thorn; other approaches are blocked with boulders, barbed wire and abandoned machinery. Supplies of water, rifle ammunition, mortar bombs and food are brought to the rear areas by truck and then loaded on to smaller vehicles. As the mountains start to rise, the goods are transferred on to mules and then finally carried on the backs of the men themselves.

They take only the lightest and most essential provisions, abandoning the warmth of heavy greatcoats and blankets. "To think," says Kendall, "we've come all this way in order to learn that a string vest is no substitute for a greatcoat."

Fraser Dunbar, the son of a vet from Kelso, is put in charge of the animals. He knows his horses and it is presumed that mules can't be that different. When asked why, he says: "I know nature's way of things, that's all. People in cities have no idea."

"Then you should tell them," says Sidney.

"We don't talk much where I come from. It's not what a man says but what he does that counts."

Taking one mountain mass after another establishes no tactical advantage. There is always another mountain mass beyond. Every advantage lies with the defending forces.

The mules lose their footholds. Sidney tries to stop one of them, laden with heavy radios and batteries, slipping and plunging over the edge but can do nothing to prevent it without falling himself. On each journey, a third of the animals either collapse, or expire, or are shot.

The battalion suffers so many casualties that the men are forced to become their own stretcher-bearers. Where the track is wide enough there are four to a victim, but often it is two men stumbling over the rocks while the wounded man lies cursing in the dark.

Sidney has to search for the missing and help bury the dead. They work for three days, wrapping bodies in blankets and signal wire, collecting personal effects, noting names and numbers and building small cairns of stone to mark the sites.

He gets a nick across the throat with a bit of gravel that sprays up from a burst of gunfire. He lays up at the side of the hill and puts up sangars, shelter amidst the rocks and stones. From Aquapendola, they can look down on the River Garigliano below with the Liri winding its way north-west past Cassino towards Rome, and begin to feel some relief that the Camino massif is behind them. Then, over the next ridge, they see an enormous building in the far distance on top of a high steep hill: the Benedictine monastery of Cassino.

"So that's what we're supposed to capture?" says Hawthorne.

"Seems straightforward enough," Kendall replies. "A steady climb at night, in winter, while under constant fire from well-defended positions by people who know the territory. Piece of cake."

CHAPTER FIVE

On Armistice Day, Rev Nev holds a special service and insists that his friends join him; otherwise "no one else might come". The men are aware of the irony of commemorating the sacrifices made on the anniversary of the end of the Great War while serving in another. They stay away.

"They're dog tired," says Robert.

"Everyone needs a moment of reflection in the midst of all this."

"Some of them think too much already."

"There's no harm in that."

"On the contrary, there's plenty. What was it Virgil said? 'Fear is proof of a degenerate mind.' "

"Very impressive."

"I can read as well as write, you know. You'd be amazed."

"Nothing about you surprises me, Kendall."

Rev Nev is reading Thomas à Kempis. He has a copy of *The Imitation of Christ* with him at all times. Contemplating death makes him appreciate life, he says. *A man is blessed if he is able to keep the hour of his death continually before his eyes, and every day to hold himself in readiness for death*.

"So, there are advantages," he explains, as they began to dig their foxholes for another night of defending their position, the blades of their shovels blunted, the mud thick and wet, their lower backs aching.

"To this?" says Robert. "What do you mean?"

"We are made ready. In peacetime we would be distracted by worldly superficiality. Here we are unsurprised by the inevitable."

"Give me worldly superficiality any time you like."

"If you are always worrying about death then doesn't it ruin every day?" Freddie asks.

"What would you think about instead?" Nev replies.

"Women," says Robert as he stops digging to stretch. "Do you know, Nev, if you ever did change your mind and marry, you should find a girl called Beverley. Then you could be Bev and Nev Rev."

"Yes, yes and we could probably have twins called Kevin and Trevor. Then we'd be Bev, Nev, Kev and Trev."

"It'd be worth it just for the Christmas cards."

They resume their digging, first for safety and then, only if they have time, for comfort. Freddie talks about the theatre, imagining himself on stage, acting in *Cavalcade* or *French Without Tears*, getting the laughs, hearing the applause, going out to dinner with friends, feeling secure in the company of the like-minded.

The next night they get lost. The track they are on dwindles into a diverging maze of minor trails. They hold on to the same line, uphill and westward, moving forward, talking little, listening hard. The trail they are following leads them across two vertiginous gullies and towards a long spur. As they approach, the ground falls away steeply in front of them into a dark void. High above them, on the opposite side, the monastery rises in the moonlight.

They can go no further, realise that they might be seen by the enemy, and dig in by a battered white farmhouse on a terraced hill. Just below it, they spot a line of sleeping figures with room to spare at the end. They unroll their waterproof bags, use their kitbags as pillows and sleep for the few hours left until morning.

Sidney is kicked awake by a soldier from another battalion. "You're not fussy who you sleep with, then?"

He looks to his left. His sleeping companions have their faces covered in blankets. They are American corpses.

"It's the dead that keep us alive," says Robert.

The damp air smells of wood-rot and cordite. There is a thick clammy mist and little sense of day or night. It is a world that never gets properly light. Sometimes the firing is so close that men start to tremble without speaking.

Hawthorne says, "The next one's going to bury me, I know it." Sidney sees there are tears in his eyes. "It's just this bloody smoke," he says, and turns away.

Sidney and Robert find a foxhole someone has started the night before. It is only ten inches deep and there is a dead man sitting upright, as if he's just stopped for tea. He's been hit between the eyes and his helmet is lying to one side, cast down to give him a bit of air and take the weight of his head. He'd probably just stopped to wipe the sweat away. He has a trusting look that has been preserved in the moment of a death that he had not expected. Perhaps, Sidney wonders, he had been thinking of home, a sweetheart, a family Christmas. He has never seen such a neat death before, just a trace of blood on a pale face framed by a shock of dark hair, the kind of hair, Sidney thinks, the man's mother must have loved to brush.

"Stop dreaming," says Robert.

They move the body and deepen the hole as shells scream past and artillery and machine-gun fire bounce around them. The equipment lying outside is blown apart. The dirt that they have piled up is thrown back into the foxhole.

Every time he stands up to try and work out what is going on, Sidney sees other soldiers being lined up and taken prisoner.

The enemy have tanks dug right in up to the barrel. They are fortified as bunkers with steel and concrete two feet thick. Anyone caught above ground is gone. Sidney digs down six feet and water starts coming in. He stops. His nose is bleeding. The side of the hole is caving in from direct hits.

Most soldiers in the foxholes are too scared to move. They want to wait until it is over. But it will never be over.

Sidney remembers his father describing the trenches in the last war, three feet deep with corpses underfoot and corpses on the parapet, duckboard walks running behind them past graves, shell-holes and ditches. The breastworks, with their wooden fire-steps, their roofs of corrugated iron or old doors, had no protection against the back-blast of shells.

"The only thing they could keep out were tennis balls."

His father's best friend, a lance corporal, had been killed while boiling a billycan of water for tea. Alec Chambers had bid him a good night and, after he had moved on, a shell had dropped down straight on top of him.

The bombs had their own rhythm, he said.

Ri-tiddley-i-ti . . .
Pom POM.

On the Western Front, people used less-frightening names for them: plum puddings, footballs and woolly bears. The grim humour had been the only thing that had kept them going. *You've got to have a laugh*.

Here in Italy, on the shortest day, the sun goes by early afternoon. The light, rather than fading, falls in clear drops: darkness visible, inevitable night.

In London, Sidney imagines, people will be struggling with wind, rain, huddled into coats and sheltering umbrellas, safe, dry and still complaining.

He thinks he hears a blackbird sing. It pauses to let a burst of cannon fire go by. Then it resumes.

Sidney can still hear his mother's voice, reading Oliver Herford's poem from a silvered greetings card at Christmas, when he was five years old.

I heard a bird sing

In the dark of December.
A magical thing
And sweet to remember.

CHAPTER SIX

Christmas Eve is not a silent night. Hawthorne and Kendall decorate a tree with white tape, red cellophane from cigarette packets, the pull-tops of ration tins and ripped silver paper from a bar of chocolate. But there is no celebration.

"A bit ironic, isn't it?" says Kendall. "Most of our Christmas customs are German."

Sidney's parents met each other at the front in December 1917. His father was a doctor, his mother a nurse. They hosted a Christmas dinner on a train, enlisting the wounded to make paper decorations, sing songs and recite whatever poetry they could remember from their childhood. Alec Chambers had chosen "The Mistletoe Kiss".

> The dearest thoughts in the heart lie deep
> Through snows of winter and rose-time heat,
> But if your memory tries to sleep,
> Remember the mistletoe kiss, my sweet!

Iris Willoughby had kissed him for the first time once he'd finished and Sidney was born four years later. Now Sidney is in the same situation. Christmas at the front. At one point the enemy fire over sixty shells a minute. The dead bodies of soldiers from both sides ring a mountain pool just below the monastery. Thirst has got the better of common sense. Undercover snipers wait for the next man to risk a drink.

No one dares rescue the wounded or bury the dead. Survival is as much a matter of patience as bravery and luck.

Sidney remembers his father talking about field placing in cricket: being in the right place at the right time; lulling your opponent into making mistakes. The importance of patience and concentration, not letting the game get away from you. Taking your chances.

Mortar bombs continue to fall. The smoke shells mean there is no day. In one brief lull Robert calls out: "Is that it then? Have you quite finished?" Sidney can see that even he is losing heart. His eyes are red-rimmed, and raw chilblains cover his knuckles. His lips are dry. He has a little tin of peas. He takes them out one by one and crushes them against his lips to ease the chapping.

Someone starts to sing "We Wish You a Merry Christmas" and other soldiers join in, as if they are singing a rugby song. They don't worry how loud they are, who hears them or if they are out of tune. It is the sound of men who know they are going to die soon.

On the early afternoon of New Year's Day, during a lull in the fighting, Robert organises a duck shoot.

"It'll be a laugh," he says.

He has seen geese in the days before, coming inland at dusk to feed and spend the night on flight ponds, splashes and pools. He finds a flat wooden hunting boat that looks like an old gondola anchored at the entrance of a creek. It is full of painted cork decoys — wigeons and pintails — and it has been camouflaged on the sides with reed panels. He shows Sidney and Freddie how to set up a couple of hides, facing the open water and with the land at their back. He demonstrates the whistling calls needed to lure the ducks out and towards the decoy. He is a little boy again, Sidney thinks, twelve years old and having fun.

"There's a heron," says Freddie. "My grandmother thought they brought bad luck. She used to take to her bed as soon as she saw one."

"And when the hell did she get up again?" Robert asks.

"Someone had to tell her it had gone away. One time my grandfather asked me to hang on for just a bit longer after it had flown off. 'Life's so much more peaceful when she's out of the way.' "

"You don't believe in any of that nonsense, do you?"

"I'm not sure I believe in anything any more."

Sidney remembers the ponds near his grandparents' house in the Tweed Valley, ducks zipping about in the low light, the hunters sitting in their butts and waiting for the birds to start flighting in. There was always so much waiting. The shooting lasted less than an hour. The important thing, his grandfather told him, was not to fire too early.

They kill six in all that day (a pair of pintails, a grey goose, a mallard and two wigeon) and Robert takes them back to the cookhouse.

"Do we have any oranges?" Freddie asks.

"In January?"

"Perhaps they make marmalade round here?"

He tells them of a duck à l'orange he enjoyed with some of his theatrical friends after a first night in 1938. "We were so naughty that night. Everyone was there, all the stars: Noël, Gertie, Hermione and Celia. I don't suppose I'll ever see those times again."

Sidney remembers his mother plucking pheasants. The first time he saw her do it, he hadn't realised how strong she was, anchoring down the skin, using quick snaps of the wrists to yank out the feathers, one or two at a time, watching for where the wings met the body, saving the breast for last, then gutting and saving the liver, heart and gizzard for pâté, stock and gravy.

He strips the last of the meat from a leg. "What a weird day it's been," he says.

"What's weird about it?" Robert replies. "I thought it was perfectly normal. I always go duck shooting on New Year's Day. Better to shoot ducks than Germans. At least they don't fire back."

Hawthorne starts to whistle an old music-hall song. "I'm Not Such A Goose As I Look".

"That's the spirit," Robert continues. "Keep cheerful. It's our only hope."

He hugs Freddie to him and they sing the chorus in crazy harmony.

CHAPTER SEVEN

In order to advance they have to cross the Garigliano River. Although only twenty-five to thirty feet wide, it is up to twelve feet deep and has steep banks and freezing, fast-flowing water. On the near side are numerous mines; on the far, the Germans have constructed a layer of dugouts protected by barbed wire, machine-gun nests, booby traps and tripwire mines.

The Royal Engineers mark a single-line track across country with tapes to avoid the mines that lie in their path. This is good enough in daylight, but difficult for men carrying 400-pound wooden boats on their backs for two miles in the dark.

"I don't know how we can do this," says Hawthorne. "First, it's hard enough for us to get to the river. Second, if we do get there, we can't cross with our supplies. Third, even if by some miracle we get to the other side, there's nowhere to go without being blown to bits."

"Don't be a gloomy bastard," Kendall replies. "What's the worst that can happen?"

"We die."

"Might as well get it over with, then."

They see the river, its water running smooth and oily, catching unexpected reflections from the sky; a cloud that looks like the aftermath of an explosion; the branch of a tree that appears to be a machine gun. The advance company starts crossing in dinghies and thirteen-foot-long assault boats. There aren't enough paddles and few of the men know how to steer. A small man holds his pack over his head with one hand and clutches on to a rope with the other, walking underwater, only coming up every few paces to breathe. The first boat slides into the water and overturns.

"What's your plan to make it across, Rev?" Kendall asks Nev. "Are you going to walk on water?"

They are ten men per boat, each one weighed down with a fifty-pound haversack, their gun, ammunition, six grenades and one day's ration.

There is no response from the enemy — no gunfire, no shellfire; do they not have scouts and spies? Sidney cannot believe how eerily silent it is.

His boat wobbles as he sits down. Kendall pushes away, Hawthorne paddles, but they are caught in a current they had not anticipated and lose sight of the far shore.

Back on land, Gordon Docherty stands on a mine. His left foot is ripped away. Majors Watson and McKenzie, who were moving up to join him, are blinded as shrapnel rips into their faces. More mines go off. Bright-green flares soar into the sky. Defensive fire from machine guns and mortars hits the river's edge — a heavy stonk — shooting at pre-registered targets.

There are only so many places where they can cross. The Germans know them all.

On the shore and in the dark, the troops have not anticipated the currents of the river, the way in which a combination of battle cordite, smoke and mist hampers visibility, how easily they can be swept away.

On Sidney's boat, Gavin Allan stands up to try and assess the situation and falls back. They are mid-capsize. An overcorrection makes it turn completely and Sidney is pulled underwater, weighed down by his kit.

He struggles to get the weight off his back but one of the clips catches in his belt. The current and gravity force him down. He does not have the strength to free himself and hold his breath at the same time.

He is more aware of weight than water, heaviness than cold. The pain and pressure rise in his chest. As he reaches up for the surface, he senses himself falling, bumping against the bottom of the river. Why does he not float up? Perhaps if he lets himself go and surrenders to the moment, he will become weightless? But that is mad. He should fight. The pain in his chest tightens. He takes in gulps of water: three, four, five, six. He starts to choke. He does not know whether water is coming in or out of him.

There are lights, torches he thinks, or perhaps they are flares or gunshots. All sound is a roar about his ears, constant rather than in waves. He begins to give in to the heaviness, he's not sure if he has any strength left to fight (perhaps one more push?), and then he realises that this, surely, must be death. He is momentarily puzzled by the timeless freedom of this abandonment, and he is almost enjoying the hypothermic ease as he starts to lose consciousness.

Then he feels a series of tugs and pulls at his clothing. He thinks it might be some kind of animal. He doesn't know what. Can a fish do this? Perhaps it is the enemy. Have the Germans stationed troops underwater?

He cannot decide if he is breathing or choking or fighting for life. He feels a buffeting against earth, a landing, a weight across his arm, air forced into his mouth, a suffocation and a breathing. Air coming in, water coming out and up from his lungs, a sickness, a desire to vomit. This can't be death, surely?

There is pressure on his mouth, his lips; someone is either trying to kiss or suffocate him, he can't tell. He wants to cough, he does cough, water comes up, he vomits and then he hears a voice.

"Jesus. I didn't expect that."

There is the smell of blood. He doesn't know if it is from his mouth or a wound from somewhere or somebody else.

Blood. The need for air. Water. A drink. Even if he has taken in too much water already. He also wants light. To see things clearly. To understand what has happened. Where is he?

He feels cold. He tries to speak. He thinks he says the word "blanket" or perhaps it is someone else who says it. He can't imagine speaking. He does not feel that he is living in his own body. He is watching the scene: darkness, boats, flares, stretcher-bearers. A foreign face smiles at him. An Indian? A Gurkha? All he wants to do is shiver. He can't stop it. And then he returns to the dark. Another sleep.

He feels himself raised up — is this a stretcher? There is support now, but he is weightless, wet and cold. He tries to work out whether he is wetter than the canvas on which he lies. Nothing absorbs water, he thinks. It runs off us and into us all.

He is taken to a respite area. He develops a fever. He dreams of his parents, of his home in London, of Caitlín Delaney naked underneath him, fearfully asking if it is going to be all right — is he sure? And then he dreams of Amanda Kendall dancing, men marching, mines, stretchers, blood and bombs, darkness and bright flares, the thrust and roar of battle. He is underwater once more, drowning all over again, unable to breathe, swamped by the weight of water, the pressure on his face and chest, the heaviness in his legs, the sensation of sinking; yes, surely, this is dying, it isn't so bad after all, he will surrender to this until he hears Buchanan's voice (is it his?), *We will not surrender, we will never give in, we must keep the momentum*.

Now, there is a bright light. Someone is shining something in his eyes. There are voices, something muffled, someone is speaking, could it be Robert and is he talking to him? Should he answer? He doesn't know if he can. He still thinks he is underwater. He tries to push up and feels material rather than water, a warmer weight.

"Whoa there," he hears. "Steady."

What is he now? Has he become a horse?

"Sidney . . ."

It is Robert's voice. He is sure now. And he is alive. The room is floating away high above him. And then a face, interrupting the view of rough tenting, a pale sun behind it — day, light, cold.

He shivers. Why is he shivering? He is too hot to shiver.

"About bloody time."

"Where am I?"

"You're in Italy, and you're still with me."

"And me," says Freddie.

"You nearly drowned, Sidney."

"I don't remember. What about the others?"

"Too many dead."

"But not you," says Freddie. "Robert saved you."

"He did?"

"I pulled you out," his friend replies. "That's all. Someone had to do it. I thought about leaving you down there but then I decided I'd miss you too much."

"You saved my life?"

"Don't worry. It wasn't that hard. You would have done the same for me. And it saves me the bother of having to go and tell your mother you'd gone and bought it."

"I suppose so."

"I didn't want to have to go through the bother. So, you were doing me a favour when you think about it. You allowed yourself to be rescued. I should be thanking you. I might even get a medal. But don't think you're ever going to get another kiss from me."

"What do you mean?"

"The kiss of life," says Freddie. "I think if I'd been you I'd have lain there for a bit longer. If it had happened to me I really would have been in heaven."

All but one of the battalion's twelve craft are damaged. There have been direct hits on the crowded boats. Others overturned, throwing their occupants into the freezing water. One man says that he could feel hands grabbing his feet from below as he was swimming towards the bank.

The Germans have opened up the sluices of a dam and the river is six feet deeper. Boats begin to spin and those already on the water become confused as to which bank they are supposed to be heading towards. Are they advancing or retreating?

As Sidney recovers, the sappers construct Bailey bridges, manoeuvring ten-foot-long prefabricated panels into position, lining them up on rollers linked with girders strung between them. Every time three or four panels are built, they are brought to a point of balance. Six men work at once, easing the bridge over the water, adding more panels and girders on the bank before pushing them across so the structure begins to span the river. It is straightforward in dry daylight. It is not so easy at night whilst under fire and over an unknown, rapidly rising, river in the rain.

New defences are entrenched but the smoke, fog and river mist have cleared to reveal the challenge ahead: an exposed stretch of land some ten miles wide flanked by two superb artillery positions: Monte Maio to the south and Monte Cassino to the north.

This is what stands between the Allies and Rome: the Gustav Line.

The valley has been flooded to make it impassable and the higher, drier ground is studded with concrete dugouts, gun turrets, machine-gun posts, pillboxes and reinforced stone houses. From these positions, the enemy have fields of fire that range over the flats between the river and the hill. In order to increase their effectiveness, they have cut all the trees and brush. There is no cover.

“We’ve crossed the river,” says Hawthorne. “Now we’re sitting ducks.”

In order to protect the advancing soldiers from attack there is a constant laying-down of smoke shells around the base of the monastery and on the hillside. The shells come with an explosive charge and base plugs that are ejected at such force they become weapons in themselves. One man is hit by a plug and runs forty yards downhill, chasing after his own brains before collapsing on to the ground. It is impossible to know which has given up first, his head or his legs.

The land is filled with harassing fire: machine gun, automatic weapon, rifle, mortar and artillery. They cannot leave their foxholes at night. They are on half-rations. Fifteen men share three loaves of bread. There are no hot meals. There is no chance of a wash. They look for food in dead men’s kit. At one point Freddie is convinced that Germans are scurrying above and around them, but the sound is nothing more than rats in search of more corpses.

It is now a question of which side has more men to risk. Attrition and numbers matter as much as tactics and skill. "We're only going to survive if there's nothing left alive to shoot at us," he says.

On the morning of 22 January, Sidney's company had consisted of three officers and 140 enlisted men. Twenty-four hours later, all the officers have been wounded and only fifteen of the enlisted men make it back to safety.

Sidney helps Rev Nev bury the dead. His back aches from the shovelling of earth, the lowering of bodies, the nights spent lying on frozen soil, too cold to sleep, but too tired to do anything else but try.

For days on end no ground is taken.

The German regimental commander sends an English-speaking officer to ask for a truce in which they can pick up their dead. The break in fighting is arranged between eight and ten in the morning. A white flag appears on the lines. The Americans set off down the valley carrying the Stars and Stripes. At a plateau, they find two Germans with a Red Cross flag. A third watches from behind a bush in case anything goes wrong.

A stack of eighty bodies is piled up along the bank, ready to be recovered. Those that received direct hits while standing in their fighting holes are impossible to identify.

Sidney, Kendall and Hawthorne talk to a group of four German soldiers who look less tired and more alert. They are like an opposing cricket team who are accustomed to victory: proud and slightly embarrassed.

"Have you been to Germany?" one of them asks.

Hawthorne leads the answers. "Never, I'm afraid."

"We have beautiful countryside. Bavaria, the Black Forest . . ."

Not any more, Sidney thinks. Not if we have anything to do with it.

Another man interrupts. "I've been to London," he says. "The West End."

"Did you go to the theatre?" Freddie asks.

"My parents took me to *Night and Day* with Fred Astaire and Claire Luce at the Palace Theatre."

"I was in *Mr Whittington* at the Hippodrome at the same time," Freddie explains. "There's a scene at a Scout and Girl Guide jamboree . . ."

"You are an actor?"

"I was."

"Are you famous?"

"I'm afraid not. Although I do know famous people."

The German soldier laughs. What is the point of fame now? He takes out a picture of his wife, taken at Christmas 1942, with two sons and a new baby that he will never see.

People on both sides exchange cigarettes and pass round more photographs, eager to show that they have families, and if you took the uniforms out of the pictures you would not be able to tell anyone's nationality at all.

"Do you have a wife?" one of the Germans asks Freddie.

"I'm not really the marrying kind."

The soldier from behind the bush comes out to take more photographs. He speaks in German, discouraging friendship. "*Keiner wirds glauben. Dies ist verrückt! Wie können wir aneinander schießen wenn wir uns befreunden?*"

The stretcher-bearers carry the dead back to their lines. When the Germans run out of stretchers, the British lend them blankets to ferry the wounded. No shots are fired. A whistle blows to signify the end of the truce and Sidney salutes up the hill. They might as well have been playing football.

"What do you think they are saying?" he asks Robert.

"How do I know? Probably the same as we are. What are we all doing here? Wouldn't it be better just to go to the pub and sort it all out over a pint? What has any of this got to do with us, apart from the fact that our main job is to try not to get killed?"

CHAPTER EIGHT

On Burns Night, Harry Stamper, a short, wiry man from Kirkcaldy, asks Sidney why he fights with the Scots Guards since he lives in London and speaks with an English accent. Is he a proper Scot?

It is a while since Sidney has been asked this question and he doesn't know whether to give the polite answer or fire off with both barrels. He doesn't want to spoil the party. He explains how his father came to London from Melrose in the Borders to marry an English nurse and settle down. Alec Chambers had been a medical officer with the regiment in France during the last war, a war in which three of his brothers, all fighting with the Scots Guards, had been killed: at Marne, Ypres and the Somme. Sidney's grandfather fought with the regiment for the relief of General Gordon in Khartoum, and *his* grandfather had died on the ridge at Hougoumont during the Battle of Waterloo.

"Is that enough for you, Stamper?"

"Bet you're glad you asked him now," says Robert.

"I just wanted to ken. The question isnae a criticism. We're a' brothers here. It's Burns Night, after all."

They have found an abandoned farm that offers some level of protection and security, although they are careful to keep everything dark. It's too cold for a long celebration, but Stamper recites "A Man's a Man for A' That", Freddie is persuaded to sing "Ae Fond Kiss" and Robert makes up a "Toast to the Lassies".

"We all have mothers, sisters, wives, sweethearts — some of us may even have daughters, whether we know it or not! But sometimes I think that it's the women that we're fighting for. The lassies. Not so much God, or King or Country — although we *are* waging this damn war for all of those bloody things. But perhaps, more than anything, we're going into battle for the lassies in our lives, for the people who make our homes, who love us and give us children and who comfort us when we are weary — even though they are far from us now. There's nothing wrong with being sentimental about this. Perhaps it takes as much courage to admit the fact that we miss the ones we love as it does to fight in battle. We should not be ashamed. These are the people we want to get back to. The lassies. They are building a future as much as us. They make life worth living and our lives are nothing without them. We love them all — whether they be mothers, wives, sisters or sweethearts — we will love them all 'till a' the seas gang dry'. To — the lassies!"

The whisky has arrived courtesy of Rev Nev's father at Haig's in Markinch, along with a couple of haggis that are heavier on the oatmeal than they are on the offal, and although there are no neeps, there is sufficient drink and enough familiarity with Burns to create a corner of Ayrshire in the foothills of the Apennines.

Robert takes a swig from a hip flask and hands it round. "I wasn't expecting you to make a speech," says Sidney.

"Rev Nev asked me. I think that sometimes you have to say out loud what you feel about things. No point holding back. I hope it wasn't too mushy."

"People need to know that it's all right to think about home. It wasn't mushy, it was great."

Harry Stamper says he's planning on becoming a gardener when he gets back to Scotland. But the problem, if you live on the east coast, is the wind, *aye the wind*. The plants are exposed the whole time. They keep being rocked back; their roots get shaken no matter how much you try to protect them.

"I never thought I could imagine being a plant on the shoreline, but it's like that now for us, you know. The storm never lets up. The enemy never lets up. The sea and the wind come in time and tide again. Even the birds are scared."

The next morning, they are given their movement orders. This is the moment, Buchanan tells them, when audacity matters more than prudence. Any hesitation, delay or weakening of their assault will allow the enemy time to pull back and reassess the situation. They have to press on.

Outside Minturno, Allied tanks break through the barbed-wire barricades, exploding the minefields and threatening German positions with close-range shelling. Once they have softened the enemy up, the infantry follows on, using the tyre tracks to stay safe; the rifle group in tight formation, with the mortar and Bren groups to the rear. There is fire, smoke and darkness all around. Everyone knows the drill: a long opening salvo of everything that can tear flesh and shatter bone, then the rifle group has to drop to the ground ready for the Brens to take out the enemy machine guns.

"Go," Sidney shouts, "go, go, go, go."

Kendall leads the advance; Sidney is behind with the Bren, waiting to open up when the German defence has weakened. It is a sustained cacophony, rifles firing, blazes of illumination, silhouettes of movement, men stumbling, falling, shooting, killing, dying; a sustained attack and then a lull; a moment for replenishing, rearming, reconsidering before another opportunity to take the initiative while both sides work out what to do next.

Sidney calls, "Down," and the men nearby fall low, allowing him a clear line of fire. But a few soldiers in the distance either haven't heard or are confused about the battle orders and are scrambling back. In the darkness, it is hard to tell if they are Allied troops returning or whether it's an enemy attack.

Sidney keeps firing. He can't see Kendall, but then he can't see very much at all in the melée. He only stops when he runs out of ammunition. Then he realises how many of his own men are wounded. He calls out for the stretcher-bearers. Where is the Advance Dressing Station? How soon can they get help?

One man is unconscious, bleeding from the neck and chest, his head to one side, his eyes open in glazed surprise.

It is Robert Kendall.

Sidney calls out to Freddie and together they pull their friend back and out of the line of fire. As soon as they have done so, Sidney is given more bullets and returns to action, taking charge, issuing orders, stoked by anger and revenge. He doesn't care if he is killed or not. He fires until he runs out of ammunition. He throws his last grenade.

When he finally gets back to the bivouac area, out of artillery range, he lies down, exhausted. But he can't keep still. He is shaking. He cannot stop. He looks for his friend.

The eyes are closed, the body inert, the doctors absent.

There are bullet wounds across Robert's exposed chest and neck, earth and bruising on the right side of his head. Dried blood has matted his hair. His right arm has fallen; the hand is open and upturned. It could almost be waiting to catch a cricket ball. The skin is paler than before, with a faint tinge of yellow and, bizarrely, there is a slight smile across Robert's face, as if he has just finished saying, "I told you this would happen, you bastards."

"He was such a beautiful man," says Freddie and gently closes Robert's hand, holding it for a moment. Then he starts to cry.

"I don't think I can go on any more," Sidney replies, unable to comfort his friend. "He saved me when I was drowning and now . . . I can't . . ."

"Don't. There's nothing we can do. No worst. There is none."

Rev Nev conducts a brief funeral, invoking God's love, asking for mercy and the cleansing of Robert's soul.

> "I heard a voice from heaven, saying unto me, Write, From henceforth blessed are the dead which die in the Lord;
> even so saith the spirit; for they rest from their labours."

It is a hard, snowy day. Weather without hope of change. Few soldiers in attendance. No time. Other duties. Too many dead.

Nev speaks firmly and clearly. His voice can show no doubt, despite his own grief. His task is to proclaim the gospel and offer the hope of a life everlasting beyond an earth-bound, corpse-driven life of despair. A better life.

Sidney is moved by his steadiness. The time taken. The notice given. Even though the service is short it doesn't feel so. He gives Robert Kendall attention, respect, a gap in time.

He asks Nev how he is able to do it. The man is taking funerals every day.

"Where there is loss, there is sacred ground."

"I don't know what to tell the family. I keep thinking of his parents, his sister. He was such a force of nature."

"You don't need to say everything all at once, or anything too much at first, for that matter. In my experience, you do very little talking. After the parents have heard the news they will be the ones who want to speak."

Sidney tries to pray but he can't find the words. He has no idea what to think or say or what might happen next. He has surrendered his life to a void.

"Did Kendall write a 'just-in-case' letter?" he asks.

"Yes," Rev Nev replies, "and he gave it to me."

"What does it say?"

"I don't know. It's sealed."

"Did he ask for your advice?"

"Not in so many words."

"But you gave it anyway?"

"I told him he should never be ashamed of saying what he felt. You know he wrote to his mother every day?"

"There was one day he forgot and he was convinced it would bring him bad luck. He got into such a state. People don't know how superstitious he could be."

"Most men are deeper than we think. That's all I've learned. Not to predict anything. We behave differently because we never dreamt we would find ourselves in a situation like this."

Later that night, Sidney is alone in his foxhole and the absence beside him makes the space feel cavernous. He can hear people talking, smoking, someone writing a letter home and saying the words aloud. There is the odd cough, little bits of chatter, distant rumbling sounds that he can't place and he isn't sure if he is imagining them or not. He knows he should seek out company but he prefers solitude, the loneliness of memory and responsibility.

Sidney remembers Robert coming off the cricket field, in the Varsity Match at Lord's before the war. It is

July 1939. He had scored a fifty in the first innings and a century in the second, but Cambridge lost by forty-five runs.

"That's how it goes," he said at the time. "You win a battle but you lose the war."

He had been a forceful batsman, favouring the off side with his graceful cover drive, leaning back on his right leg to give himself room for a late cut, or skipping down the wicket to the spinners and lofting the ball over their heads for six. Robert Kendall saw every ball as an opportunity for attack, never worrying too much about protecting his wicket, or the state of the game. Defence had not come naturally; that is how he had lived his life and how he had met his end: on the charge.

The memories come in unexpected bursts: Robert knocking back a beer and setting the table at a roar; or sliding down the banisters of his home with Amanda behind him; or night-climbing King's College Chapel when they were students.

He brought a rope and torches, and they pulled themselves up by a drainpipe and then by the clamps of the lightning conductor on to the roof before an even more perilous ascent to the north-east turret. Robert had taken the lead, claiming to have done the climb before, though it was clear that he hadn't. He held on fast to the rope when Sidney slipped and he hauled him to safety, up past a crumbling gargoyle, over a buttress and on to the highest point of the chapel.

"Saved you there, Chambers," he said.

Then there had been the thrill of drinking half a bottle of port while enjoying the view of Cambridge under moonlight.

"Top of the world," Robert said. "No one can stop us. I feel like the devil showing Jesus everything he wants."

Afterwards there was the terror of a half-drunken descent that mixed joking with panic, and then the relieved laughter after the final drop to the ground and the escape back to their own college, having avoided both accident and discovery.

They polished off the port in their rooms and Robert had asked: "What's life without excitement?"

Sidney remembers him driving his open-topped car through country lanes after deciding, on a whim, that although they may have dined in Cambridge, they should breakfast by the seaside. They ended up in Southend on a cold foggy morning — it was February, for God's sake — and Robert insisted they ran naked into the sea before warming up with Guinness and jellied eels.

There is no logic to memory; the dreams come unbidden, whether it's Robert's laugh or smile or burst of mock anger, or the way he would wave at other motorists or shout out at canoodling couples in parks, encouraging them to "get on with it". Sidney remembers the way his friend shouted, "Have at you, Fritz!" as if he was starring in a war film rather than fighting a battle, and his own salvation from drowning when Robert had said, without meaning it at all: "Don't expect me to do that again."

It is impossible to conceive of him dead. Sidney has no idea how he will tell the Kendall family what has happened. The one thing that marked them out in the past was their positive outlook. They believed they could achieve anything to which they set their mind. Their home was a place of continual laughter, games, pranks and possibility. How can it be that now?

He thinks of Amanda and her parents. He cannot imagine their horror on hearing the news. To survive, with Robert dead, is abhorrent, even obscene. He wishes he could have died instead.

Two days later he is praised for his extraordinary courage, made a captain and given a medal for bravery, the Military Cross.

> On 26 January 1944 Gdsm. CHAMBERS was sent out as Bren gunner with a small fighting patrol in front of Point 141 west of Minturno. Throughout the day the company were subjected to heavy artillery and mortar fire, to sniping and attempted infiltration, and earlier in the day all the officers in the company were either killed or wounded and evacuated. Gdsm. Chambers then took command of the company and handled it with such outstanding skill that the feature was held despite determined and prolonged assault on it by the enemy, and in consequence the battalion was able to carry out its task of holding its objective.

> Gdsm. Chambers's personal bravery in walking about under constant fire, his coolness in action and his capability of making quick decisions at critical moments of the day are an inspiration to all ranks.

Robert Kendall is awarded a posthumous Distinguished Conduct Medal "for gallantry". It will help the family, Buchanan says.

Sidney tells Rev Nev: "I cannot stop thinking about what happened."

"You must try."

"I can't avoid it. I go over every moment. Again and again. The fire in the night. The gunshots. The confusion. The sounds. The bodies. I don't know how to speak about it properly, but I can't think of anything else to talk about. I don't see how it will ever leave me."

"It may not. But the pain will lessen."

"How?"

"Time."

"I don't know if that will ever help."

"You must also remember, Sidney, that this is not your story. It's Robert's. This is not your tragedy. It's his. And his family's. Yes, you are part of it, but you are not the central character."

"I should have done more."

"But you didn't, and you can't, and you cannot blame yourself."

"I don't seem to be able to do anything else."

"Would you like to pray?"

"I'm not sure if I can."

"Let me start for you."

Rev Nev bows his head. "Merciful Father, look down on this, thy servant Sidney. Accept his penitence, calm his fears, bring him your peace, in the name of your son, Jesus Christ, who suffered and died for us. Amen."

Sidney just manages to repeat the "Amen".

CHAPTER NINE

There is snow on the summits, rain and hard wind. The war cannot be won without an air raid on the monastery of Monte Cassino. It has become such a resilient position that the Allies are going to have to bomb it to bits if they want to crack on towards Rome. Rev Nev says it is the equivalent of destroying Westminster Abbey.

The attack begins at 9.45a.m. on 15 February, the day after Sidney's birthday. In the first wave, 142 B-17 Flying Fortress bombers drop their high-explosive and incendiary devices. The monks are at prayer. The sky turns grey. The mountain comes alight. The olive trees burn for days.

"That's cabbaged the bastards," says Stamper.

Not all of the bombing is accurate. It kills Italian civilians and Allied troops, who are bedded in so close that they are hit by shards of splintered granite. Forty men from one of the Indian divisions die. The monastery lies in ruins.

It is the first time that Rev Nev loses heart. All those years of prayer and simplicity of living, faith and tradition, fresco and architecture. Isn't the building worth more than human life, he wonders, surviving for generations beyond their own? How much should art and monuments be protected in wartime?

Buchanan tells him that they don't have the luxury of philosophy. The building is not a sacred space but a strategic position. Besides, the Germans have already obliterated Coventry Cathedral.

"And we bombed Munich."

Rev Nev goes over the ground that has been strafed and re-covers the exposed graves of the recently buried. The lull after the bombing raid is never silent; the stillness is punctuated by moving trucks, cries, bodies dragged either to medical stations or burial ground.

He tries to concentrate on straightforward, individual tasks. He cannot take in the greater horror.

"I'm amazed you can carry on," says Sidney.

"I have no choice."

"Don't you ever have doubts?"

"I think I have more doubts about myself than I do about God. If I don't have him then there's nothing left of me."

"I wish I had your belief."

"You *can* have it."

"In the middle of all this?" Sidney asks.

"The Christian faith is not based on anything you see here but on love — and its sign is not the clenched fist; it's the outstretched arms of the Cross."

But this is Golgotha without the Crucifixion, Sidney thinks; the place of the skull without hope of redemption, the bones not yet visible because there is still too much burnt and rotting flesh left behind.

When the fighting resumes it becomes clear that the Germans have evacuated the area around the monastery. The town stands. The battle is not won. The ascent is only possible along a narrow strip of land. The men move forward in single file towards the town of Monte Cassino, each one clinging to the battledress of the person in front, sometimes toppling into deep craters filled with water, worrying that they are going to drown rather than be shot. The forecasters have predicted three clear days, but what they get is torrential rain, making the going slow and soaking radio batteries so thoroughly they no longer work.

The leading company advances through a patch of chest-high gorse scrub. The Germans have filled it with tripwires linked to booby traps. Nearly every man in the front platoon is blown up by mines. As the rest of the company try to push on they are hit by grenades and machine-gun fire. The firing becomes so heavy they cannot lift their heads. Two Royal Sussex stretcher-bearers who get up to bring in the wounded are killed immediately.

The Germans drop leaflets suggesting that the Allies should feign illness to get out of fighting; anything from amoebic dysentery to hepatitis or tuberculosis. Sidney wonders what kind of home he'd be going back to; what kind of life.

"What's the first thing you're going to do when you get back to Scotland?" he asks Harry Stamper.

"Find someone to fuck."

"Do you have anyone in mind?"

"I don't care too much about that — as long as it has a pulse."

The code for the aerial attack on the town of Monte Cassino is "Bradman bats tonight". Sidney wants to tell his father. They once watched Don Bradman bat in Cambridge as long ago as 1934, only to see him bowled for a duck by J. G. W. Delaney, misreading a straight one from the renowned off-spinner.

On 14 March, in three and a half hours, the Allies drop 1,000 tons of high explosives on one square mile of land. They don't always find the target. Some of the fire extends to neighbouring towns and villages; sometimes they bomb their own men. Whole platoons and squads are obliterated by direct hits. Hot broken stone and granite rolls down the hill as lava until there is nothing but dust, smoke and the cries of those trapped in dark vaults of debris.

In Monte Cassino itself, not a single building stands intact. The rubble is over twenty feet high. Thousand-pound bombs hole out craters sixty feet wide and ten feet deep, filled with twisted steel and masonry. It is impossible to believe that anyone has survived.

In their slow advance, Sidney and his men meet with continual resistance. The Allied tanks are hampered by narrow streets and poor fields of fire. The arrangement of houses around courtyards and the heavy masonry of the buildings prevent them driving the enemy out into the open. Most of the fighting is hand-to-hand. It is contesting the next hundred yards all over again and without Robert Kendall beside him. Grenades are thrown back and forth. The enemy knows the territory, the layout of the town, and how quickly they can emerge from cover, fire off a few rounds and retreat to the shadows.

The standard form of Allied attack is to use five or six men against each house. Each unit is equipped with launchers and rifle grenades. Three leading men approach while the remaining two or three provide cover. They throw hand grenades into the lower rooms of houses and then rush through windows or doors. Surviving Germans flee upstairs, and the covering group fire rifle grenades through the upper windows to drive them back downstairs to be killed or captured.

They have it down pat now: Sidney, Freddie Hawthorne and Harry Stamper advance with Ford and Wallace as cover.

They move towards a triangle of buildings that look abandoned, but no one can be sure. The stone is solid; the small medieval windows offer sightlines and protection. They approach, fire, get down and wait for a response. There is none. Would this serve as a good position once they've taken it? Sidney isn't sure. The building he has his eye on, at the apex of two streets, looks out on to a small courtyard, but the Germans have retreated to a stronger position further up the line.

They walk in. They check each room. There are signs of an occupation but nothing too recent; shattered glass, a dusty table, abandoned ration cans, some broken crockery. It doesn't feel particularly Italian or even German. It is a building no one wants to live in any more and Sidney wonders if this is what the end of the human race might look like; old buildings, abandoned possessions, insects and rubble, all the achievements of humanity waiting either for the earth to cover them or the decay into dust.

On leaving the building and heading back to base, it is so quiet that he loses concentration, lulled by the absence of warfare, chatter or birdsong. It is like a Sunday afternoon silence. Children, he wonders. Where are the children and the elderly? Will they ever return? What was this town like in peacetime? Who lived in it and how would it ever be rebuilt? Monte Cassino is supposed to be at the heart of Christian civilisation. Now look at it.

He falls before he realises what has happened.

He is on the ground. What is he doing there? Has he tripped? Why is the sky so much brighter than he thought it was a few moments ago? Why do the buildings look so high? What is that iron crucifix still doing at the top of an arch that is on the point of falling? Someone should mend it.

Then comes the blaze of pain just below his right shoulder.

He has been shot by a sniper from 300 yards away.

Sidney thinks of raising his head to see where he is but knows that it will signal he is alive. It is better to pretend to be dead. He is annoyed by his lapse of concentration. He had anticipated death by mine or bullet, being caught by machine-gun fire or being hit by a mortar, but he never imagined he would make such an easy target of himself. He is tired — no, he is exhausted — but his lack of awareness of the dangers of his surroundings was such a mistake. How can he have been so stupid?

Ford and Wallace return fire, killing the sniper, and wait until it is quiet.

Sidney uses the time to think how he might crawl to cover. The ground is hard and rough and dry beneath his face. He feels thirst and also relief. All he has to do is lie here. He can't make choices. He will either live or die. It isn't up to him.

He hears Freddie's voice. "Bloody hell, Sidney."

They pull him away, back into the house they have cleared, and turn him over. There is blood high on the right breast, an exit wound. The bullet has gone right through him.

They put him on a stretcher and carry him to a dressing station where they cut him out of his clothes and take away his possessions, including the American combat boots he bought in Naples.

He looks up. "If you steal my boots, I'll shoot you."

"Don't worry, sir," says the orderly. "We wouldn't do a thing like that."

Sidney asks himself what he is doing, worrying about boots at a time like this? He should be concentrating on what has happened. Now he is unlikely to see out the war.

He is taken to a building just outside Subiaco. It had initially been a factory like the one they shelled when they first arrived: Battipaglia. So long ago now. This, too, became a barracks occupied by the Gestapo. Now it is a hospital.

There is little water and the wards are lit at night by single hurricane lamps.

Kitchens have grown up in the main corridor where the meals are served. Everything is mixed up and to hand; a nurse has to use a frying pan for a vomit bowl. Sidney is admitted on the dinner trolley.

His right lung is drained, the wound disinfected and packed with sulphonamide. The doctor is amused there is no sign of the bullet.

"Gone, leaving but a memory."

Sidney is given morphine and swerves in and out of consciousness. He has so many injections of penicillin (three-hourly, day and night) that he tells the nurse looking after him that he might as well sell himself when he gets home.

If he ever gets there.

For some reason, he can't think why, he pictures Amanda dancing to "*Bei Mir Bist Du Schoen*" before the war began. How is he ever going to talk to her about what's happened? By now, she will know that her brother is dead. He should have written but he still hasn't worked out quite what to say or if his words will ever reach her. London seems impossible.

Sometimes he feels guilty that he is not more seriously wounded. An Indian soldier has lost both legs and an arm but survived; a blinded Welshman has a little ritual rhyme going round and round. He keeps repeating it out loud.

"A sailor went to sea, sea, sea,
To see what he could see, see, see.

But all that he could see, see, see
Was the bottom of the deep blue sea, sea, sea.

A sailor went to chop, chop, chop,
To see what he could chop, chop, chop.
But all that he could chop, chop, chop
Was the bottom of the deep blue chop, chop, chop."

The nurses have developed an unspoken understanding of who to move on, who to stick with and who to ease gently out of the world. It is often the simple things that matter: the smile, the kind word, the turning over, the glasses of water. Thirst is almost always the first thing on a soldier's mind. If they can just ease the dryness then everything might feel possible once more.

Sidney starts to make lists in his head. He tries to remember all the men who were with him when they first arrived in Italy: the names of those who were killed, who are wounded and who have survived.

Aitchison (killed by a sniper outside Naples), Armstrong (*still alive*), Brennan (wounded in the chest), Campbell (drowned in the Liri River).

Carnegie (mortared approaching Nocera), Clarke (blinded by the Garigliano), Cummins (blown up by a mine).

Donaldson (killed by a mortar), Duff (*still alive*), Ford (*still alive*), Hart (mortar), Howe (sniper).

Gatchell (ambush), Gilchrist (*still alive*), Hawthorne (*still alive*), Kendall (shot at Monte Cassino), Lawlor (killed on landing), Logan (grenade).

Sidney doesn't know if he can bear to continue but he forces himself to remember, going back to the beginning every time he forgets a name. He needs a run-up to remember each one. At least he has the time to remember them now.

Macrae (never left his foxhole), McDermott (lost both legs), McDonald (blown to bits), Mackay (*still alive*), McKenzie (shredded in the face), MacGregor (lost an arm).

Naylor (machine-gunned by the Garigliano), Paterson (*still alive*), Quigley (shot in the neck).

Redmond (*still alive*), Reekie (desertion?), Robertson (shell shock), Ronson (ambushed).

Sweenie (don't know — disappeared?), Swint (*still alive*), Thomson (friendly fire), Thorburn (self-inflicted wound).

Wallace (*still alive*), Ward (blown up by a mine), Wichary (*still alive*), Wilson (last seen on a stretcher).

He is lucky to have got this far — or does luck have nothing to do with it?

His favourite nurse is a sweet-natured, red-haired, young Catholic girl from Belfast: Catherine McKenna. She is named after St Catherine of Siena.

"Had your parents ever been to Siena?" Sidney asks.

"No. This is the nearest I could get. They're probably worried I'll be martyred on a wheel like she was."

"There's not much danger of that, I would think."

"They probably joke about it because they're anxious they'll never see me again. People do that when they're nervous, don't they?"

"I can't think of anything funny."

"It's just as well. We don't want you splitting your stitches."

"I don't know what to say these days."

"You don't need to speak at all if you don't want to. There's plenty of entertainers in this lot. You just rest, Captain Chambers."

"I suppose all the men try to impress you."

"And why would they want to do that?"

"They want a beautiful woman to like them. We haven't seen one for a long time."

"Don't you have a nice young lady waiting for you at home?" Catherine asks.

"I'm not sure if I do. Do you have a nice young man?"

"I wouldn't like to say."

"That means there is one."

"He's called Niall but I haven't quite made up my mind about him . . ."

"You mean you might find someone better over here?"

"That would be telling. Have you ever been to Northern Ireland?" she asks.

"No, but I've been to the south. Cork . . . Listowel . . . Ballybunnion . . ."

"Did you go to the seaweed baths?"

"How do you know about them?"

"Everyone knows Collins's. Mighty cold in the water round there. Next stop's America. What took you there?"

"A wedding."

"I hope it was a good craic."

“It wasn’t what I was expecting.”

“All that aggressive friendliness take you by surprise?”

“Everyone talked all the time. I’ve never known such chat.”

“Well, that’s the Cork folk for you. And who did you have that bath with?”

“Someone I know.”

“That’s a bit vague, Captain Chambers. Was it a lovely colleen? Where is she now?”

“I’m not sure. I’m rather embarrassed about it all, if you must know.”

“Oh dear, I hope you didn’t behave badly.”

“I tried not to . . .”

“That doesn’t sound too good at all, Captain Chambers. I may have to take a very different view of you now that you’ve said all that. The poor girl.”

“I think she went on to marry someone else.”

“And you think that makes your behaviour acceptable, do you? She may never have recovered.”

“She’s quite resilient. She comes from a big family.”

“They don’t take kindly to disappointment down there. You’ll have to be more careful in future, Captain Chambers. I hope you’ll treat your next girl better.”

“Perhaps you could give me a few tips while I’m here?”

“That’s a bit cheeky.”

“No harm in asking.”

“And none in refusing. You lie back down. Have a good rest. Think of England or whatever you’re supposed to dream about that makes you go to sleep. We don't want you getting excited, do we now?"

As he starts to lose consciousness, Sidney hears Robert's voice again.

What's life without excitement?

After two weeks, he is able to walk, slowly and with a stick, into the garden and grounds. On Good Friday, he gets as far as the monastery where St Benedict set up his first religious community. It is housed in part of the Emperor Nero's old imperial villa. They are holding a special service in the Upper Church, a building dominated by a fourteenth-century fresco of the Crucifixion.

Sidney sits in the nave and remembers Nev telling him: Christ *descended into hell*. He can't fully understand the Good Friday meditation, delivered in Italian rather than the Latin he could have followed, but recognises the discussion of pain and suffering, that Christianity is not only about the joy of Christ's birth and the redemption of the Resurrection. It has to have the Cross at its heart. Even suffering is a gift. Blessed are those who suffer. Blessed are those who mourn, for they shall see God.

It is a clear spring day and, after the service, Sidney takes a moment to sit in the rose garden. There is a legend, the gardener tells him, half in Italian and half in English, that St Francis grafted the roses on to the thorn bushes into which St Benedict had thrown himself to avoid temptation. He is just beginning to explain the symbolism of thorns turning to roses, particularly on this Good Friday, when the nurse arrives and says she will see Sidney back to the ward just to "take the bare look off your face".

Sidney wonders what she means but likes the sound of it. The sun is high. It feels like the first proper day of spring.

"Let's enjoy a bit of the weather first," Catherine says. "We can sit here together for a while."

"I'd like that."

"As long as you don't start getting any ideas that you're some kind of favourite."

"I never assume anything. It's safer that way."

"Safer? And there's me having you down as a man who liked a bit of a risk. The odd flutter on the horses . . ."

"Well, if you ever invite me to Ireland . . ."

"You'd be welcome."

"Although it's a long way to go for a bath."

"Do you not have baths in England? You dirty lot!"

"Not with seaweed in them. They say it makes all the difference."

Catherine laughs and, for the first time since Robert died, Sidney laughs too.

"I'm glad you are recovered, Captain Chambers. Thank God for his blessings."

"I've needed this time."

"You should think of it as a gift."

"I don't think I deserve it."

"We cannot tell what we deserve and what we do not. And we cannot ever tell what God has in mind for us. That's what I've learned, being here."

He looks at the garden, the lavender coming into flower, roses already in bud, bees in search of nectar. "It's so peaceful. Who keeps it like this?"

"It's being well looked after. The gardener's been here since I came over. Look at him watering. He goes at his own pace, doesn't he?"

The man guesses that they are talking about him and gives them a little wave. He refills his watering can and returns to his geraniums.

"I wish I could take some of this back to England," says Sidney.

"And who is to say that you cannot?"

"I fear the noise of the world I'm going back to will destroy it."

"Then you must learn to quieten it."

"And how do I do that?"

"God will teach you, Sidney. He will show you what he wants; provided you don't put up a fight. You have to be open. And then the peace will come flooding in, I promise you that."

As she speaks she is almost a different person; dreamier, detached, halfway to another world. Sidney isn't sure whether he likes it or not. He can't quite understand it. He hears Robert's voice. *You don't need to listen to any of this, you know*. In his head, he tells his friend to shut up, to leave him alone.

"You have to pray," Catherine continues.

No, you don't.

"Every day. It doesn't matter how much. As long as you do it. Without prayer, without trying to listen to the

Holy Spirit, you may find that you are confusing your own will with God's."

Leave God out of it. Life's confusing enough as it is.

"Sometimes you just have to wait."

"In silence?"

"Perhaps."

Catherine sits still for a moment and they smile at each other. She has a smile that never comes to an end.

Oh God, here we go. You're a pushover, Chambers.

"Like this?"

"And you need to give it time; a change in your life need not be dramatic. It can be slow. We cannot all be St Paul on the road to Damascus. We are not all blinded by light. Sometimes revelation comes to us quietly. Sometimes it happens to us before we even recognise it."

"Then how will I know?"

"Have you read the story of the Supper at Emmaus?"

"In divinity lessons at school."

Crapper Crawley told us all about it. The chaplain. Remember him?

"Two people are walking — Cleopas and another, probably Mary, his wife — when they are joined by a stranger. In the paintings, it's normally two men, but I think it is a married couple. Christ did prefer to show himself to women after the Resurrection. He may have had male disciples but the women did the work. 'Twas ever thus."

"If you say so, Catherine."

He is not going to argue. He just wants the nurse to speak. He tries to think of a way of making this conversation last as long as possible because he doesn't want to be anywhere else or with anyone else. He just wants to hear this soft, slow and loving Irish voice on this warm Italian afternoon, protected by the shade in a garden used to peace and untouched by war.

"They don't realise that he is Jesus, after the Resurrection, until they sit down to supper. The stranger breaks the bread and their eyes are lifted. But I think the point of the story is that he is with them before they understood. He is *already* with them, just as he is *already* with us. We just have to recognise him by our side."

"And how do we do that?"

"We wait, we pray, we listen. He is with us before we know it. Waiting."

Are you really going to turn into Crapper Crawley? Robert asks. *You remember? He had a walk like he'd just crapped himself.*

Catherine wakes him up. "Have you thought about what you want to do with your life, Captain Chambers?"

"I think I'm supposed to be going into the Foreign Office. Something like that. What will you do?"

"I'm doing what I need to do here. Then I'll be home soon enough. But nursing's the thing."

"And will you marry when you get home?"

"Oh yes, probably, providing he hasn't run off with someone else. My Niall's a bit of a rapscallion."

"And do you like rapscallions, Catherine?"

He can't resist the tease and, at the same time, he wants to see if he can go further. Robert would have done so. In fact, Robert would have seen Catherine's virtue as a challenge. He would have kissed her by now. Charmed her with a bit of poetry and moved in.

"You're the devil of a fellow, aren't you, Captain Chambers? I can't see you having a career in diplomacy with cheek like that on you." She gives him a little punch in the arm that is harder than she means. "But you're all right, really."

He thinks about trying to kiss her and starts to lean in but, before he can get any closer, Catherine says, "Now let's the both of us be getting back."

He tries to make her stay longer but says the wrong thing. "I don't want to share you with anyone else."

"Well, I'd be a very poor nurse if I let you get away with that, wouldn't I, Captain Chambers? I'd lose my job soon enough."

"I'm sorry. It's just that on the ward, people keep talking about love and their sweethearts, as if it is the only thing that matters."

"And you feel left out?"

"Sometimes. But I can't imagine it."

"You've had too much time to think. But you'll be home soon. Then you'll have to decide how to find your way back from all this. It'll probably be the love of a good woman, or God — who knows, perhaps even both?"

"I can't imagine either."

"Don't try. Just wait."

"I've spent the last few years waiting, Catherine. I just don't know what for."

Her, you idiot. Get on with it.

"You have to welcome these things when they come to you. Remember how the disciples were with Jesus at the Last Supper . . ."

If you can't get her off this subject you'll never get anywhere.

". . . He died and they were in despair but he rose again and came back before they realised he had done so. I like to think of Emmaus as the *first* supper after the last. A new life. You do not have to die to be born again."

There are swifts darting round the bell tower, as if they can't decide whether to fly through the open lancets or not, or which they prefer — inside or out. Sidney tries to think what he finds attractive in Catherine. It is, perhaps, the fact that she seems to live between this world and the next, already halfway there. Perhaps she is an angel and he is dreaming her into existence or he is already dead, and all of this is an illusion?

He thinks of Rev Nev talking to him about patience; the sense that he accepted suffering, he took it for granted, he even expected it. Nothing surprises either him or Catherine. They look on human existence with a sad and loving amusement, patrolling the borders between life and death, believing that the best way to behave is with dignity and grace.

Grace, that was the word. This is what Sidney wants. How can he learn to have grace?

As they walk back to the hospital, Catherine takes his arm and they support each other. He tries to think what else might have made him feel so different. Then he realises. It is the first day, in a long time, when he has not thought that he might die.

CHAPTER TEN

He rejoins his regiment just before the end of the war. They have got past the Po Valley, seen off a rearguard action at Lake Comacchio and are now a few miles inland from Venice at Rovigo. Freddie Hawthorne and Rev Nev are still alive and old comrades ask Sidney if he has enjoyed his "hospital holiday". They are battle-weary but optimistic that the war cannot last much longer. Partisans have been blowing up bridges, taking retreating German soldiers prisoner, and the roadsides are filled with abandoned vehicles and empty munition boxes, dead horses and oxen. The Allies reoccupy enemy billets and push further north, covered by artillery and airborne attack.

Freddie has found an old tailor's shop just inside the city walls where they can sleep on the counters, surrounded by empty cabinets, a broken full-length mirror and a ripped poster displaying different suits for men; single- and double-breasted, plain and pinstriped.

"We're obviously too late for a fitting," says Sidney. "I prefer Savile Row, anyway."

Nev has somehow managed to commandeer some sparkling wine to celebrate their friend's return. They drink straight from the bottle. "I've still got a man in Edinburgh," he says.

"Have they seen much bombing there, do you think?"

"Oh yes. Leith. The docks."

"I hope you remember how to do all this?" Freddie asks Sidney.

"Fight, you mean? Don't be daft."

"We don't want you dying in the last push," says Nev.

"Or arriving at the last moment and taking all the credit."

"There won't be any of that, I can assure you."

They are ordered to take out a run of houses by a church that the enemy has been using as a munitions store. There have been reports of snipers in the campanile. The battalion approach cautiously, expecting a sudden last-minute attack, but there is nothing. Once they have blasted the buildings to bits they realise that no one is there. An elderly Italian woman emerges from a nearby shop and even though they can't quite understand what she is saying, it is clear that she thinks that enough is enough. Why are they attacking a House of God? Do they have no mercy? Are they no better than the fascists? Everyone is already dead — her mother, her father, her husband, her sons. Why is everyone still fighting? There is nothing left to fight for.

Sidney and Freddie scour the town for supplies and find an old wine store, some cheese and a few dried biscuits. It will help the rations go further.

"Not exactly the fine dining I'm used to," says Freddie.

"Are you still going on about that?" Sidney asks.

"I feel I have to. People feel more secure if there's a conversational routine. It's like my theatrical anecdotes. Others appreciate them because then they don't have to talk themselves or listen to Rev Nev's little homilies . . ."

"Charming . . ."

"We all need something to pass the time. And you've been away so long, Sidney, you must have forgotten most of them. I can regale you all over again. Have another stale biscuit."

Sidney tells Freddie and Nev about his recovery in Subiaco, Nurse Catherine, his memories of Robert and the Kendall family back in London. He has written at last, as his friends have both done, and now, it seems, there is nothing more to say.

They are just about to finish and settle down for the night, even though it's still early, when a boy bicycles past and shouts: "*È finita la guerra! È finita la guerra!*"

"Can this be true?" Freddie asks.

He gets up, pushes the tattered beaded curtain away from the front door and shouts out down the street: "*È vero?*"

The boy answers without looking back. "*Si, si, è vero. È finita la guerra! È finita la guerra!*"

People come out of hiding and into the streets. There's a burst of small-arms fire from the towns and villages around them and, for the first time in years, it's not directed at other human beings. The Italians are firing into the sky. Every church bell rings. People start waving handkerchiefs (Sidney remembers Robert's joke about the Italian national flag when they first arrived), play musical instruments (an elderly veteran has a trumpet, his grandson a small drum) and they hug, embrace strangers, and weep with grief and relief.

Freddie kisses Sidney on the lips and bursts out into the song "It's a Lovely Day". A woman falls to her knees, crosses herself, looks up to the sky and pushes back her rosary beads: "*Salve, Regina, Madre di misericordia, vita, dolcezza e speranza nostra, salve. A te ricorriamo, esuli figli di Eva; a te sospiriamo, gementi e piangenti in questa valle di lacrime . . .*"

Wine appears, enemies are friends and no one cares who is who any more. The woman who had shouted about attacking the church the day before produces a little cake with lemons, which she hands round with a bottle of grappa. Some people start to dance. There is more gunfire. Sidney sits down by the side of the road with his head in his hands. He has no idea what to think.

In the next few weeks they head further north. Sidney has a few days off with Freddie in Venice, where they drink in Harry's Bar and go out into the eerie grey light of the lagoon for a bit of duck shooting to remember Robert and their escapade on New Year's Day.

They walk through the deserted streets of the Dorsoduro and discuss the kind of world they will return to, how blessed they are to be alive, and how they can't think what on earth they are going to do with themselves when they get back home.

They are posted to Trieste, a hundred miles north of Venice, to stop Tito claiming the land as Yugoslavian. They are informed that this has always been disputed territory. Sidney is asked to join the Italo-Yugoslav Boundary Commission, working as aide-de-camp to the Head of British Delegation, Humphrey Waldock.

The roads north are bad and it's hard to cross the rivers because it's almost impossible to find a bridge that has not been blown up. They come into mountain territory, the karst, and it's so thickly wooded Sidney wonders if there could still be people hiding out and fighting there, unaware that the war has ended.

It doesn't feel like peace. There are blockades and sentry points and he is forever showing his papers and explaining where he is going and what he has to do, and it's a surprise when he finally comes to the top of a hill and his jeep stops for a moment to take in the view of the steep descent down to the seafront, with the Gulf of Trieste and the Adriatic beyond; the churches, squares, and bombed Renaissance buildings; the railway line leading to docks filled with transport ships. The bay is enclosed, and so far below them that it appears both vast and secret at the same time.

In the 1930s, his driver tells him, Trieste had the highest suicide rate in Europe. It is a town people only visit in order to leave, the gateway either to another life or to no life at all, a place of exile and departure in which those who stay live in dreamy quarantine.

Sidney wonders how long he will be in the city. The sea that surrounds them is so still it hardly makes a sound, as if it, too, has not resolved what to make of itself. The atmosphere is one of permanent transience.

"It's the Italian version of Liverpool," Humphrey Waldock explains. "All founded on shipping and insurance. At least, that's my way of understanding it."

He is a lawyer who could easily have become a headmaster instead, and he is dressed in a double-breasted pinstriped suit that ensures he couldn't look more English if he tried. Waldock believes that good organisation and a command of detail is the best insurance against calamity.

"People talk of law and order," he explains, "but they get them the wrong way round. Order has to exist before there can even be a soil for law to take root and grow. Re-establishing a clear administration is our primary task. You remember *Troilus and Cressida*, I am sure. 'Take but degree away, untune that string . . .'"

"'And hark what discord follows.'"

"Good, Captain Chambers. I can see we are going to get on."

The British officers are based at the Miramar, a grand but melancholy castle of Istrian stone that stands out on a promontory. It looks as if it is made of wedding cake. Inside, there is a Scots baronial-style staircase surrounded by so much wooden flooring and furniture — carved statues, free-standing globes, intarsia tables and lacquer cabinets — that Sidney is convinced the previous occupants must have run a school of marquetry.

They take a walk along the seafront and climb the hill up past the English church to the old castle so that Sidney can get his bearings. His job is to provide geographical clarity, to draw up maps, zones and boundaries, to work out where Italy ends and Yugoslavia begins in an area that has never been sure of its identity. It is historically Illyrian, Venetian, French, Hapsburg, Italian, and now both Yugoslavian and a grid-shaped limbo; a place defined by its lack of definition.

They retire to the Caffè degli Specchi on Trieste's Piazza Unità d'Italia. This is the magisterial square where, only seven years previously, Mussolini announced his racial laws. Then it was full of fascists. Now, no one has ever been one.

At the next-door table an elderly woman with voluminous grey hair and a fur wrap sips her coffee and picks her way through a slice of *torta Rigojanci* as if the war had never touched her. Her husband reads the latest news in *Il Piccolo*, only stopping to check the twist on a moustache that stands proud of his beard. How often had they changed their mind or switched alliances since the turn of the century? Sidney wonders.

Waldock buys Sidney Prosecco and coffee in a glass — a *nero in b*. He tells Sidney that he knows the Kendalls. He was Robert's godfather.

"I loved that boy like one of my own. The family's taken it badly, as you can imagine."

"I did write. It took me quite a while to think what to tell them."

"His was a gilded youth, like so many of your generation. It happened in the Great War too. Everyone told the Kendalls they wished they had a son like Robert. And now, of course, no one knows what on earth to say to them. Perhaps it's a punishment for all the luck they enjoyed in having him in the first place. Born in a leap year too — isn't that supposed to be fortunate? That's what some people think. I've always found that fate tends to correct itself. But there's no order to these things."

"No divine plan?"

"I'm not sure of the theology."

"I think Christians aren't supposed to have faith and believe in luck at the same time," says Sidney. "If you believe in God, then you must trust in his plans. On the other hand, we have to make an effort. We can't leave everything to chance. Machiavelli argued that it is probably half-and-half."

"Half God, half us?"

"I think so. Luck decides half of what we do in advance but leaves the other half to our free will. So, if a river is prone to flooding, we know we shouldn't just give up and accept our fate but build the defences to hold it back. We can still alter the course of the river."

"Flooding others instead of ourselves, perhaps?"

"Probably. This is Machiavelli, after all. But I don't know," Sidney smiled. "Perhaps it's different in the Italian."

"Then we must remain both prepared for all eventualities and, at the same time, in mystery about our fate. I'm glad to have you, Sidney."

"I'm sorry I'm not Robert Kendall."

"No, I can't have him, so you must be the next best thing. But I know you won't let me down."

Six soldiers walk through the square. They are on some kind of patrol. They pass a couple of jumpy *carabinieri*, a little boy taking his first steps and an old woman with a parasol and a determined sense of direction, hoping that no one stops or interrupts her on her way home.

A group of children are playing circle games; singing how the world is always turning, unaware of the insecurity around them.

"*Giro giro tondo,*
gira il mondo,
gira la terra,
tutti giù per terra!"

Sidney travels out to the villages, finding translators in Serbo-Croat, Slovine, Friulian and Italian. He eats pasta in one village but boiled meat and sauerkraut in the next. He makes longhand notes with a fountain pen as if he were a student once more, gathering evidence like a historian, working as part tourist, part politician. People tell him about how important it is that Trieste becomes an independent territory, with guaranteed principles of universal suffrage, democratic government, and the fundamental freedoms of language, schools, press and religion. Despite this similarity of ambition, everyone wants a resulting peace that suits them alone.

Up on the karst, Slovenians advise Sidney not to trust the Italians. The land is theirs. But the fascists have banned their language, closed their schools and thrown workers out of their jobs.

In the Serbian Orthodox Church of St Spyridon, a priest tells Sidney not to trust the Americans. Theirs is a country of jazz and decadence, noise and imperial brashness, without a soul, without a history, without any understanding of the spirituality of suffering.

In the Caffè San Marco, an old Italian lawyer eats a bowl of boiled eggs, cracking them on the wooden table, peeling off the shell and dipping each one into a pile of salt. He tells Sidney that the Slavs are human beasts.

In the remains of the vandalised synagogue, an elderly Jew tells Sidney about the rice factory at San Sabba, which had been turned into a transportation camp. There were 6,000 Jews in the city before the war; now there are barely 600.

They sit in the oratory, between its walls decorated with drops of water, citron trees and pomegranates, symbols of unity and fertility, and Sidney learns about the unreturned, those who left Trieste on transits for Auschwitz and Dachau. He is told of the cement sacks that were found after the war, filled with human ash and bone, the piles of shoes and spectacles left behind, the smell of burning hair.

Each time Sidney hears such testimonies he realises that he will need to listen to more. He is so daunted by the fierceness of the feeling and the passionate desire to own the future that he knows the process will take far longer than anyone has anticipated; and that if the Allies get it wrong there will be war all over again. Everyone wants a reward for surviving.

"I thought I was fighting for peace, but it's not the one I expected," he tells Humphrey Waldock. "Not that I ever imagined much in the first place. I was too preoccupied by the present. But now it's almost the same as it is in battle. Everything is so relentless. I don't know if anything I do will ever make a difference."

"We just have to perform to the best of our ability," Waldock replies. "But there's no harm in a bit of humility. Remember that it's arrogance, mostly, that got us into this mess in the first place."

They take a jeep up into the surrounding hills, past children on the roadside selling watermelon and home-made lemonade, past houses with Yugoslav or Slovene flags, or Italian flags with a red star in the centre of the white strip, and slogans pronouncing *Zivio Tito*. They find a sign with an upturned olive branch, a *frasca*, pointing them to a rural farmhouse next to a vineyard where they drink Prosecco and wine — so rough and red it looks like blackcurrant juice — and eat prosciutto, pork with fenugreek, bresaola with grated horseradish.

Villagers sit in the open air, under vines, at gingham-clothed tables. "We could almost be in a Cézanne painting," says Sidney and he thinks of Amanda Kendall talking to him about the pictures in the National Gallery. Will such days ever be possible again? "Those men over there should start playing cards," he says, without quite concentrating on the conversation.

A group of folk singers, too young for war, sing old Slovenian love songs — "Ripe is the Grain", "Where Are Those Paths?", "All the Wreaths are White" — in exchange for food and wine.

Waldock is almost tearful. "They are the future," he says. "We fought so that they could sing like that. Do you think their children will know what we have done?"

"I'm sure they'll have a few questions. They won't just be grateful."

"It's hard to imagine what the next generation might think."

As they drink bitter black coffee and eat a lemon sorbet, Sir Humphrey asks if Sidney has thought of marriage.

"Once or twice."

"Girl in mind?"

"Not specifically."

"A wife's a very good thing, provided you pick the right one — or even provided the right one picks you — and, as Benedick says in *Much Ado About Nothing*, 'the world must be peopled'. You've gone through all this hell," he continues. "The small matter of a romance should be a piece of cake for a man like you."

"I haven't quite decided on the right cake, though."

"Well, you know where to go if you need a distraction in the meantime. There's a place off the Via di Cavana. The streets are all named after fish, salt and bread. All man's basic needs. Apparently, James Joyce went there — not that it did him much good."

"I don't think I want that, sir."

"Then you had better learn what it *is* that you *actually* want. There's no point shilly-shallying. You can't have survived the war for nothing. Don't waste the reward of peace."

"Except it doesn't feel like peace, does it, sir? I can't quite trust it."

"Well, it's all we've got, Captain Chambers, so we have to make the most of it."

Towards the end of July, Sidney has a day off. He plans to visit the old Roman theatre, the castle of San Giusto and the cathedral. A small playground is being built outside, but the work has been abandoned for the weekend. It is a hot and airless afternoon with few people about. Freddie Hawthorne says that they'll catch up with each other later. Perhaps he'd like a spot of dancing in the Stella Polare? They have a very good jazz band. The Americans love it.

Sidney isn't sure. He thinks he prefers solitude. He has so little of it.

As he walks back down the hill towards the waterfront he looks in on the Anglican Church on the Via San Michele. It is next to a series of houses in which British and New Zealand troops are billeted. With its classical white façade it looks more like a Victorian temple or a Quaker meeting hall than a church.

The building is empty. He sits on a wooden pew halfway down the nave. He feels that he should pray but he isn't sure if he is ready. Instead he tries to think about the fierceness of Humphrey Waldock's sharp remark: *Then you had better learn what it is that you actually want.*

He remembers Nev's words: "The only truth that matters is that without God we cannot live. We can only take a longer or a shorter time to die."

How can he find the faith to understand this?

Prayer.

And how should he pray?

As Christ taught us.

Start with silence, his nurse had told him. The desire to pray is, in itself, already a form of prayer.

He wonders if he is scared of the consequences. Of what a changed life might mean.

He looks up the story of the Supper at Emmaus from the Bible in the pew in front of him.

"Read it slowly," Catherine had said. "You don't want to rush it. A bit like life, Sidney."

"May I kiss you?" he had asked.

"On the cheek. No nonsense."

"You can trust me."

"Then be quick about it."

"You told me not to rush things."

"We don't want to give the others any ideas."

He turns to Luke, Chapter 24. Rev Nev said it was the most important chapter in the New Testament. He works it out from the Latin.

> And they drew nigh unto the village, whither they went: and he made as though he would have gone further. But they constrained him, saying, Abide

> with us: for it is toward evening, and the day is far spent. And he went in to tarry with them. And it came to pass, as he sat at meat with them, he took bread, and blessed it, and brake, and gave to them. And their eyes were opened, and they knew him; and he vanished out of their sight. And they said to one another, Did not our heart burn within us, while he talked with us by the way, and while he opened to us the scriptures?

As he is reading, Sidney feels a flood of peace, of recognition. This is what he has to do, he knows. Study this. Acknowledge it.

He hears a door open, the rush of outside, traffic, air, unexpected interruption, the world pressing in.

"I thought I might find you here," says Freddie. "I've got tickets for *The Barber of Seville* in the Teatro Verdi. Do you want to come? You can't spend any more of your time in this place. You know how maudlin it makes you."

They have a box on the third tier. They look down on the soldiers and survivors of war, dressed in dinner jackets and evening dresses that have been kept in cupboards for years. The music is confidently played, the acting extravagantly bad. The singers hold a melodramatic pose at the end of every aria, demanding applause.

It is a story of love, comedy, money and deception in which Count Almaviva can only prove himself by pretending to be someone else: a soldier. Is this what he has been doing, Sidney wonders — disguising his own life in order to hide from it?

He thinks once more: what would it be like if, instead of dressing up as a soldier or training as a lawyer as Robert would have done, he became a clergyman?

Don't be ridiculous.

He remembers St Paul.

For to me, living is Christ.

After the end of the opera and its ludicrous but romantic conclusion — *Amor e fede eterna si vegga in voi regnar* — the two men go to the Caffè Tommaseo. They sit outside and drink cocktails of elderflower and Prosecco and discuss the nature of love.

Sidney asks about Henry Mortimer, a writer and theatrical impresario who is undoubtedly his friend's lover. Freddie's nickname for him is Henrietta — "because it's sometimes easier if people think I have a girlfriend".

"I'm not sure anyone's likely to believe that."

"It doesn't matter too much. He's probably traded me in by now."

"Haven't you heard from him?"

"Henry doesn't write letters. He says they're a waste of energy — time spent when he could have been working on his plays. He even views Christmas cards as unnecessary effort. You know what authors are like. They spend so much time writing about themselves they're not particularly interested in listening to other people."

"I'm sure they are."

"No, the irony is that they're not. They might behave as if it's all part of their art, that they're sensitive souls, always attuned to the needs of others, but they're quite selfish when you actually live with them."

"I suppose they have to be. You have to be alone to write, I would think?"

Freddie finishes his glass and asks for another. "Letter writing also means you have to put your thoughts down on paper. Evidence. Proof that you have emotions you might have to think about. It's easier to live without examining your conscience. Henry's rich and successful, and there are plenty of opportunities for distraction."

"You don't trust him, then?"

"I try not to mind. He promises me there's no one that *matters*. I don't find that entirely comforting. I know he can't resist a pretty boy."

"But when you're back home, and with him again, I'm sure he will."

"No, he won't. So we both have to pretend. Don't ask too many questions. That's how we've always been. Living a lie. It's easier than confrontation."

"But you do worry, Freddie?"

"For the moment, I try not to show any of my real feelings. That's what the war has taught me. And, as you know, I'm a very good actor. I have to believe Henry will always come back to me."

"You're very open about it when we talk in private."

"It's different with you. We can say anything to each other, don't you think? Besides, it doesn't really matter out here, does it? Everyone's been too busy trying not to die."

"But when we get back home you'll need to be more discreet?"

"I'm not sure what I'm going to do or say — being an actor is probably just one way of avoiding who you really are — but the whole thing is no one else's business. Once you've locked the front door of your own home that should be you. Remember, it's gross *public* indecency. In *private* you can be as indecent as you like."

"I'm not sure that's true, Freddie. Aren't you at all worried about it being a crime?"

"The full *thrust* of the law? No. After all this I'm not worried about anything. What's the worst that can happen to us?"

"Prison?"

"You're inside, there's food, plenty of reading material and a clean bed. It has to be nicer than war."

"But it's not better than Italy in peacetime, is it? I sometimes think, Freddie, that our stay here is not so much a kind of quarantine before we go back but a reward for all the hell we've been through. Look at us now. Opera, drinks, friendship, a beautiful view. It's like heaven after purgatory. We are very blessed."

"Oh dear me," says Freddie. "Either you've had too much to drink or you really have got religion."

They pay the bill and look at the sunset from the Molo Audace, a long stone pier that invites a promenade. It is full of lovers, children and the well-dressed elderly: men with dogs, ladies in furs. A foghorn sounds. There is cold in the bora already, wind set for home, the chill of return.

PART TWO

PEACE

CHAPTER ELEVEN

Back in London, it's hard for Sidney to take in how badly Britain has emerged from the war. The streets around Oxford Circus are pitted with shrapnel scars and pigeon dung. Bus tickets and torn newspapers blow down the pavements, broken glass remains uncleared and the destroyed buildings are so taken over by hollyhocks, buddleia and willowherb that they look as if no one will ever live in them again. There are queues for everything: food, clothing, paper, stamps, umbrellas. The older generation welcome the troops home but make it clear that, even though those returning may have spent months in a foxhole in Italy and buried so many of their friends, they cannot claim to have the monopoly on suffering.

Sidney's father has aged; his hair is now a silvery slate grey (how long until baldness?), his brown eyes diluted, watery and less bright, his nose sharper against hollower cheeks. Iris Chambers wears a new navy dress that has been bought to last and sports a powdery perfume that smells more floral than the one Sidney remembers. His sister Jennifer has a new hairstyle (she calls it "the pompadour twirl") and a delicate silver necklace — who gave her that? he wonders; she won't say — while his younger brother Matt talks about his intention to move to Manchester.

"There's a girl . . ."

"There's always a girl," their mother adds. No one quite knows what Matt does or how he earns his money or even his girlfriend's name but they have decided, by now, that it's best not to ask too closely about any of these things. It always sets him off.

Iris Chambers is keen to restore what she refers to as "normal family life". Sidney is given money for a smart new blazer and grey flannel trousers; proper civvies that fit a figure made slimmer by rationing and war. Italian food has not filled him out sufficiently and so his mother decides to serve up the familiar favourites — sausage and mash, cheesy toasts and jam roly-poly — in an effort to recreate the boy she remembers coming home from boarding school rather than the man her son has become. She tells him what he has always liked and what he does not, just in case the war has made him forget who he is. Her duty is to feed him and make sure he is warm, as if these two things alone will protect him.

"You've had enough excitement for one life already."

What's life without excitement?

She also believes in keeping busy, so she gets him out into the garden with his sister. Much of it has been given over to fruit and vegetables, and there are apples to be gathered, runner beans to be picked, the last of the raspberries and the first blackcurrants. Some mornings there's a blackbird trapped under the net and

Sidney makes sure he is out first to free it. He wears old corduroy trousers and a loose Viyella shirt, carries a trug and dons a floppy hat of his father's that reminds him of the gardener in the monastery at Subiaco.

He enjoys being with his sister. Jennifer tells him stories of her war rather than his, working as an ARP warden during the Blitz, going out with a tin hat, whistle and respirator to direct people to the nearest public shelter and to check on the old, the infirm, children and those who were either too stubborn or too afraid to move.

"It was the unpredictability that got to us all. That, and the uncertainty as to when it was ever going to end," she says. "But there was also so much kindness and compassion, the sort that you never see in peacetime. It was strange, Sidney. People almost miss it now."

"I thought of you all," her brother replies, "because it was important to treasure what we might be returning to. But, at the same time, you couldn't let the homesickness get to you."

"'You mustn't dwell', as Mother would say."

"Yes, well, I'm certainly dwelling now, I'm afraid. Don't tell her."

"She *has* noticed, though she's pretending not to. But if you play along and do things 'nicely', you'll be fine. Lay the table for supper, deadhead a few roses, pick her some special pinks and you'll be favourite again."

"I thought I was always the favourite?"

"Not any more, Sidney. I've done quite a lot of catching up while you've been away."

"Devious."

"Necessary. And there wasn't much competition."

"I see Matt's still hopeless."

"I think it's called 'making your own way'."

"What does he actually do?"

"He's 'self-employed'. It's mainly property. Buying and renting out flats. Talking to builders. I'm not sure how much he uses his bank account. It all seems to be cash. Sometimes he's quite flush, at other times he's stony broke, but we're not encouraged to discover the details. All I do know is that he's got plenty of slack from the parents, so you should get some too. You can mope around here for weeks if you like."

"I don't 'mope'."

"No. Of course you don't. You reflect and you think, even while you're lying down. Nobody could possibly call that moping. You're different from us mere mortals . . ."

"Oh, stop it."

"You should be grateful there's someone to tease you. But I should finish sorting out this bed. Some of the weeds are remarkably stubborn . . ."

Jennifer is kind, but there are moments when the family seems to have forgotten what it's like to have Sidney at home. Every time he enters a room they feel they have to put him at ease or entertain him when what he really wants, if he is honest, is to be left alone. At one point, he overhears his mother's raised voice behind a closed door: "For God's sake, Matt. He's depressed. Show some respect."

He considers the quality of family conversation and wonders how well they listen to each other. Each one has to work out how much truth to tell and how much to keep private, how to balance present fears and old injustices, how to avoid being unnecessarily thoughtless and remain kind, thankful that they have made it this far through life without illness or early death.

It might be easier if he told them to stop trying so hard to be nice to him, but Sidney knows that if he says this it will be too hurtful. Instead, he reads: poetry at first, but too often it makes him weep, especially if it is Scottish or reminds him of absent friends:

When I last rade down Ettrick,
The winds were shifting, the storm was waking,
The snow was drifting, my heart was breaking,
For we never again were to ride thegither,
In sun or storm on the mountain heather,
When I last rade down Ettrick.

He starts on George Eliot's *Middlemarch*, a book he has never managed to get around to reading. He stays in his room or finds a sofa and, in the end, his gardening duties are reduced and he is allowed a deckchair on the small sunburnt patch of lawn in front of the potting shed.

His family bring him lemonade and cups of tea, and he only comes back inside to shell peas and string beans in the kitchen. The wireless plays in lieu of conversation — *Workers' Playtime, Shipmates Ashore, Harmony Hall* — and all this normality feels like a world in stasis.

Life's different when you don't think that you can die at any moment, he says to himself, before hearing Robert's voice in his head once more: *You still can*.

Jennifer asks when he's going to visit the Kendalls. They know he is back. She told Amanda herself. She could hardly not. She was so pleased to have Sidney home, she said. It was her best news in weeks. Her brother nearly asks whether this was the most tactful way of putting it but decides to remain silent. Jennifer tells him that he can't put it off for much longer or the family will take his failure to pay them a call as cowardly.

He remembers Humphrey Waldock: *Everyone told the Kendalls they wished they had a son like Robert. And now, of course, no one knows what on earth to say to them*.

Amanda arranges to meet him in advance so she can help him prepare. Her parents can be a little unpredictable. Some of their friends have already said the wrong things — about how proud they must be, what a son they had — he lived seven lives — or even how the good die early: God takes those he loves most back into his bosom sooner than the rest. She knows Sidney won't make the same mistakes, but she wants to be as helpful as she can and, besides, it will be wonderful to have him to herself for an hour or two. He doesn't mind, does he?

On his way down Highgate Hill, Sidney sees an agitated old man under a street light. He is using a walking cane to poke at the pavement, clearing away leaves that aren't there.

"Can I help you?" Sidney asks.

"I've lost something."

The man hasn't shaved for days and has a face that has grown into the idea that most people will ignore him.

"What is it?"

"A pen, I think."

"Shall I help you look?"

"It doesn't matter." The voice is a little firmer as the result of the attention. "I keep losing things. Soon I'll have nothing left. Then I won't expect anything any more."

"You can't live without hope," Sidney says, not knowing if he believes this.

"I've been living without it for years, son."

Sidney catches a bus and passes a bombed-out cinema. He remembers going to see a comedy there with Robert and his sister before they left for Italy. It had Alastair Sim in it and was about a small town that banded together to try to save their music hall from closure — what was it called? It was based on a book by J. B. Priestley. Amanda had rejected *In Which We Serve* and *Went the Day Well?* She hadn't wanted to see anything depressing, patriotic or warlike.

Let the People Sing. That was it.

Amanda spent the early part of the war helping with her mother's charity work, surviving the Blitz by sheltering underneath the Hungaria restaurant in Lower Regent Street. You could dance and dine and book a shelter place in the cellar all at the same time. If a raid lasted all night they even served breakfast.

"It's a home from home," she says, as she shakes his hand and welcomes him inside. It is curiously formal, this gesture from the little sister, a girl who has turned into a woman while he's been away. Her features are thinner than he remembers, both sharper and sadder. Perhaps the word is "pinched"? Sidney realises she is now old enough to be the same age as the widows of friends killed in Italy.

"They look after me here," she says. "We can have a quick lunch. I hope you don't mind. I thought it would be easier."

The restaurant is dark, even in daytime, with few customers and tired linen tablecloths that the owner tries to make last for three or four days if there aren't any spillages.

"There's not much choice, I'm afraid. They'll bring us soup and some kind of fish if they have it. It's taking such a long time for everything to get back to normal. I sometimes think we'll never be so again."

"I suppose they said that after the last war."

"Well, let's hope there's never another." She puts down her handbag, arranges her things, and adjusts hair that she can't check. "I hope you won't disapprove, but I'm not sure if I can do without wine, Chambers."

For a moment, he has forgotten that she calls him by his surname. "Do they have any?"

"There's a rather thin Beaujolais, probably from the Vichy region. You won't think that's a betrayal?"

"I don't mind. There are worse things than making wine during a war. I'm just relieved."

"Relieved?"

"That I'm here, that no one is shooting at me and there's food on the table. I should count my blessings."

A small, pale waitress in a black pinafore dress takes their order. Sidney is so solicitous that Amanda accuses him of being too attentive. "She's hardly more than a schoolgirl."

"Then she's probably terrified of getting things wrong."

Sidney smiles as Amanda raises what is intended to be a quizzical eyebrow. She is dressed soberly in a dark woollen utility dress with little jewellery. It could almost have done for a funeral. It doesn't feel right for summer.

"How are your parents?" Sidney asks. "It must be so hard for them."

"You'll find them much changed. I hope you'll be able to cope with that."

"I have already written to them, of course."

"They appreciated your letter. Thank you for mine too."

"They were hard to write."

"And hard to read. But you said the right things. *He was a born leader and fighter. You must be very proud of having such a son — stroke — brother* . . ."

"Yes, I did use the same words to both you and your parents . . ."

"It doesn't matter. I think we all know your letter off by heart. You wrote the best one. *It's a tragedy that England has lost such a fine man. His is the type that make our country great.* You made it sound noble. You didn't have to take so much trouble."

"I did."

"Although you didn't go into very much detail about how it happened. I know it must have been vile, but they'll want to know. Mummy, at least."

"I am sure they will. I think there was another letter for the family . . ."

"You mean the one Robert wrote? The chaplain brought it. Do you know him?"

"He's a good man."

"It was just to Mummy. She won't show it to any of us. I've no idea what it says. But it makes her feel special. Did you write one to yours?"

"I didn't, no."

"Were you worried that if you did then it would all come to pass — that you would be killed?"

"I think it's more the case that I didn't know what to say."

"And you're the one with the words at your command. Robert may have thought it was tempting fate but he still did it. It's weird, given the fact that he was so superstitious."

"He loved you all very much." Sidney doesn't know if there's anything more he can say on the subject.

Amanda looks round, perhaps hoping that the food is coming, but there's no sign of it at all. "It's good of you to see my parents. You were always a kind man."

"I try to be. I'm not sure I always succeed."

"It's what I've always liked about you. Robert was so loud. You are more thoughtful. None of us quite know what you think. Still waters . . ."

The soup arrives. The waitress gives Sidney a special smile that Amanda interrupts by asking for salt and pepper. She gives her friend a warning look. *That's enough politeness*. Then she laughs.

"Sorry. I know I shouldn't be so fussy. But they always forget that I like it properly seasoned. They should remember. I come here often enough. Perhaps you've distracted the waitress?"

"I don't think so."

Sidney tastes the soup. It is hard to tell what it is: a variant of leek and potato. It certainly needs spicing up. "I'd like to know how *you* are, Amanda."

"Me? No one ever asks about me."

"Well, I'm asking you now."

"There's not much to say."

"I'm sure there is."

She tells him that she is studying the History of Art at the Courtauld. She wants to work in an art gallery one day. She has kept up with most of her girlfriends from school. They've all lost somebody. But she's convinced that you have to have something normal to hang on to and you have to keep busy. She's been to a couple of Proms, heard Vaughan Williams's "London Symphony" conducted by the composer himself, and gone to some recitals at the Wigmore Hall. She still plays the clarinet. Does Sidney remember? One day she wants to be good enough to get through the Mozart concerto but she's a long way off at the moment and she can't always concentrate.

"You've done so much," he says.

"There are good and bad days, Chambers. You know how it is. You can't live in the past but sometimes it's hard to imagine a future. But I study as hard as I can. And I try to look at my best, to put on a brave face to the world."

"You do . . ."

"I want to work in museums, amidst beautiful objects; things that last and don't die on me. I've lost so many friends. But what am I saying? Why am I telling you all this? You must have seen so many dreadful sights. I can't bear to imagine them."

"There's not much beauty in war."

"It's a wonder there are any men left in the world, Chambers. I hope I can rely on you . . ."

"Of course . . ."

". . . to put me right about things. Robert said that you were always good at advice."

"Not that he always took it."

"No. He had his own way of doing things. We're lost, as a family, because there's never been anyone like him and never will be again. I could always rely on him for an opinion even if it was wrong."

"He gave you something to think about. He couldn't stand dithering."

Sidney can hear Robert's voice in his head now, rallying in the midst of battle: *Come on*.

Amanda abandons her soup. "What's on your mind?"

"I was just thinking about him."

Never mind me. Just talk to her.

"I know it's going to be hard," he says.

"But I'm with you, Chambers, and I'll look after you; as long as you promise to look after me too?"

"Always. I can promise you that."

"Thank you. I'll remember that promise."

Sidney finishes his first glass of wine. It has gone down far more quickly than he expected. "I suppose I'm worried they'll think, however much they try not to, that they wish I had died instead of their son."

"You can't help what they might think — and neither can they. There's so much grief and rage. Most of it unspoken. Which makes it worse."

"And you must feel it too."

"Not about you, Chambers. Only fury at the dreadful loss — and shame for all the unfair thoughts I have."

"Unfair?"

"I can be selfish too. I shouldn't tell you."

The soup is taken away. The fish arrives in a white sauce to make it look better than it is. There are a few potatoes and three or four carrots. Amanda asks for more wine.

"Please do. If you would like."

"It's the fact that Robert was always the favourite," she continues. "I might as well come out with it, since we're being honest with each other. I hadn't expected to be able to say all this . . ."

"You can say anything you like when you're with me, Amanda."

"I've heard people say the secret of parenting is to disguise your real feelings and make each child think they are the best. Mummy had a damn good try at that but Daddy couldn't manage it at all. Robert was going to do everything he had never done — win a gold medal at the Olympics, score a century at Lord's, become prime minister. He was going to achieve anything he wanted. No one could stop him. He never failed at anything."

Except staying alive.

"I know."

"And now he has achieved one thing with which I cannot possibly compete."

"He has become your parents' favourite for ever."

"Simply by dying. He can never disappoint them. Why didn't I think of that?"

Clever, eh?

"Don't."

"I'm sorry. It's been over a year and the grief just gets worse and worse. Will it ever get any better? How much do you think about him?"

"Every day. I imagine what he would say. Sometimes he even makes me laugh. I probably won't tell your parents that."

No, don't. They'll think you're very odd.

"You should. I don't think they've laughed since he died. I assume they see it as a failure to mourn properly; even though Robert's mantra was to keep cheerful. We should get the bill. This food is ghastly. I don't know why I still come. Perhaps it's just for the wine."

"It's nice enough."

"No, it isn't. There's no need to lie. It's horrid."

"I promise it is perfectly acceptable. Well, the wine is, anyway."

"I hope it's given you a bit of Dutch courage. I wonder if that phrase is fair these days? They must have been courageous enough with the Nazis. I can't imagine. If we'd had to put up with what they went through; if the Germans had won and taken over London. I wonder how many of us would have killed ourselves and how we would have done it. Thrown ourselves in the Thames, I suppose."

Sidney remembers the young girls driven to prostitution in Naples and Robert's remark. *For God's sake. They're younger than our sisters*.

"I hope you'll be all right, Chambers. I know it's daunting."

"If I can't manage the next hour or two, then I can't get through anything."

Amanda says she must go to the bathroom to powder her nose. She puts on lipstick. Sidney wonders why she needs to do this before a meeting with her parents. Does she have to put on some kind of show, even for them?

She insists that they take a taxi rather than the Underground. It won't take long. Has Sidney been down Piccadilly and seen Hyde Park Corner yet? Perhaps he'd like a detour to reacquaint himself with the capital?

"No. We can't put it off any more," he says.

Amanda squeezes his hand. He is surprised by the gesture and thinks that it should have been the other way around.

There is little traffic and they arrive early at the house in Chester Row, just behind Sloane Square. They pull at the brass bell (Amanda has forgotten her keys) and Alice, the maid, opens the door to reveal a stately London hall with its late-Victorian staircase curling up to the drawing room. It is decorated with English landscape and Dutch seascape paintings, Victorian mahogany furniture and objects from Sir Cecil Kendall's travels: rugs from Iran, Japanese woodcuts and even some Austrian porcelain. Sidney is surprised to see it still on display: the art of the enemy.

The Kendalls no longer have a butler. There have been the necessary economies of wartime, but the maid has survived; she is family, inherited from a previous generation, and besides, she lost her sweetheart in the last war and was so brave about it that no one has the heart to dismiss her.

She's smaller than he remembers and her face is as lined as a walnut. She holds on to both of Sidney's arms and bursts into tears. He can smell furniture polish and rose water. She wants to talk about Robert.

Yes, yes, Alice.

"Please don't," says Amanda.

"It's all right," Sidney replies. "I understand."

"He was always such a kind boy. You're so like him."

"It's a tragedy. I'm very sorry."

Sir Cecil Kendall has been waiting with his wife Lavinia in the drawing room but he comes downstairs to help with the commotion. "Now then, Alice. Let the poor chap escape. We'll have some tea, if you don't mind."

Sidney remembers Robert talking about his father. "Decent enough man, of course, but sometimes he thinks rather too well of people. He's far too prepared to give them the benefit of the doubt."

Sir Cecil had taken part in the diplomatic process in 1919, after the Great War, arguing all the way into the thirties that the conditions of the settlement had been too harsh and would inspire revenge. He'd only stopped when the accusations against him went from "appeaser" to "Nazi sympathiser".

It wasn't true, Robert said, it was never true and his father had no truck with fascism. He just wanted to ensure that such a terrible war never happened again. But the rumours went on and Robert was determined to volunteer and fight; in part to make up for his father's perceived weakness. Let no one say that this was a family of appeasers.

They climb the staircase, which needs illumination, even in summer, but the lights are off. "It's not as if we need to save money," says Lady Kendall, "but we don't want to appear extravagant."

She is Sir Cecil's second wife and fourteen years younger, a handsome woman with high-piled hair that has been coiffured into submission. She organises the Red Cross sales and goes with her daughter to encourage aristocratic friends to hand over their heirlooms for charity auctions — old masters, books and manuscripts. Some recent acquisitions are piled in the corner of the drawing room, waiting for Christie's to pick them up: *A View of Westminster* by Samuel Scott, a sampler worked by Charlotte Brontë at twelve years of age, the fountain pen used by Earl Haig throughout the First World War, Kipling's gold cigarette case.

Lady Kendall gave birth to Robert at twenty-three; the same age at which her son died.

The grandfather clock is no longer ticking. She sees Sidney notice. "We didn't stop it deliberately. We just don't have the heart to wind it up."

The three sofas in the drawing room are arranged around the fireplace. There is no wood or coal waiting. The brass needs a clean. Clearly there is only so much Alice can do.

Lady Kendall is in the middle of embroidering a sampler. *I thank my God upon every remembrance of you.*

"What time of day did he die?" she asks.

"It was in the afternoon."

"Dark?"

"It must have been at about four o'clock."

"He always liked to stop for tea. When he was studying for exams I used to bring it to his room and he would break off and look up and say: 'You're so good to me, Mother.' He was polite even when he was thinking of something else. I like to think we brought him up well. Manners are so important, don't you think?"

She is wearing a plain black dress, with no jewellery apart from her wedding ring and a pair of pearl eardrops. Her skin is too pale, her lipstick too pink for her to be an Italian signora, Sidney thinks, but add a veil and she could fit into any Sunday Mass in Trieste.

Sir Cecil has recently been knighted but the honour doesn't mean much now. "We try not to think about it, but it's hard not to blame ourselves for failing to prevent the war in the first place. The sins of the fathers, you know. I spoke to Cadogan about it. Humphrey Waldock feels the same. I had a letter from him the other day. He spoke very well of you, Sidney. Thinks you could have a career in the Foreign Office if you put your mind to it."

Robert's father doesn't want too much detail about the death. His mother does. She wants to know how it happened, if it could have been prevented, how much her son had suffered and how long it took him to die. She wants Sidney to tell her exactly what happened to the body, who tended it, how her son had been buried, what prayers were said, how easy it might be to find the grave.

Sidney concentrates on the basics: that they were on the charge and there was a blitz of enemy fire. In fact, there was fire all around them. Robert fell. He wasn't wounded for long; he couldn't have been too aware that he was dying.

"Too aware, you say? So he knew?" she asks.

She is not going to let him get away with any vagueness.

"I don't think he was conscious."

She waits before asking him the next question. There is no sound in the room apart from her husband's awkward breathing and the little chinks of teacups raised and lowered on to saucers. “You didn’t speak to him?”

“I managed to pull him out . . .”

“And they gave you a medal for that?”

“They did.”

“It was good of you to go,” she concedes. “You risked your life in order to save his.”

“He would have done the same for me.”

I did. He hears Robert’s voice. *I bloody well saved you from drowning.*

Sidney wants to laugh at the memory and at the conversation in his head.

“Why are you smiling?” Lady Kendall asks.

“I was just remembering him.”

“How long did it all take?”

“The end, you mean? It’s hard to tell. Nothing lasts the same in war. Time stops and then jumps. Fifteen minutes, perhaps?”

“Between being shot and dying . . .” She says these words faster than anything else, wanting to say them but also wanting to get rid of them as quickly as she can because to linger will only be more painful.

“I don’t know. I wasn’t with him when he died.”

“Why not?” she asks, staying on just the right side of politeness, but with enough aggression to make Sidney hesitate and consider the power of her two-word question.

Why not? Sidney thinks. Why not? Because I was in the middle of a battle. People were dying all around me. Have you any idea what it was like? Do you really want me to tell you what actually happened? Would you, yourself, have been able to survive five minutes of what I've been through?

Instead, he says, "I'm sorry."

"Was he in a terrible state?"

Well, of course he was. "Not too bad."

"I'm sorry to ask. I know it must be difficult for you to go through it all over again. Do you have the most terrible nightmares?"

"Sometimes."

"Where was he shot?"

"In the chest." *As well as everywhere else. Six bullets, if you must know*.

"So, his face was all right?"

Not really. "Yes."

"He was always such a handsome boy. You remember his eighteenth birthday? He had such a glow of health. You danced . . ."

"That's enough, Mummy," says Amanda.

"I'm sorry. The War Office hasn't been very helpful. You were there. It's so different talking to you, Sidney. I know you'll tell us everything."

"I'm sorry if I've upset you."

"It's not your fault."

Sidney is worried how much more detail Lady Kendall requires. He wonders if this is the only conversation they will have on the subject or if she will ask him to come back for more over the ensuing years and how he might cope with that. Will they have to find some kind of shared story that they can all agree to keep telling each other?

"Would you like to see Robert's room, Sidney? We've kept it just as it is."

Amanda jumps in. "He doesn't have to."

Sidney knows he must fulfil the entire obligation. "No, I'd like to."

He is shown up a further flight of stairs into Robert's bedroom with its high window, old oak furniture, single bed, side table and lamp. There is a bookcase with its legal texts and unread volumes of Gibbon's *Decline and Fall of the Roman Empire*; a college scarf over a chair; an Aquascutum raincoat on the back of the door; two glass tumblers and a decanter of whisky resting on a slate taken after the successful ascent of King's College Chapel; a print of Turner's *Fighting Temeraire*; a photograph from a climbing expedition to the Isle of Skye; an oar commemorating his cricket blue in 1939.

A diary for 1944, which can't have been Robert's (he left before the year began), is kept open on the day that he died: Wednesday 26 January.

Behind is a photograph in a silver oval frame, of him in his first army uniform with his light moustache, the suggestion of a smile, as if joining up and having his picture taken was just another lark. No one would ever have been able to persuade him not to enlist, and there was no danger of him failing on the grounds of health. Sidney had never known anyone so fit and strong. Besides, as everyone keeps saying, Robert never failed a test in his life.

Lady Kendall sits on the edge of the bed, resting a hand on the top sheet folded over the blankets.

“My husband doesn’t like to come up here,” she says. She tries to smooth away a crease. “It’s because if he doesn’t enter the room, then Robert might still be in it. He can pretend. We all have to have our illusions, don’t we, Sidney?”

CHAPTER TWELVE

So, what to do now? He has been so preoccupied by the past that he has hardly considered his future at all. Sidney can't work out why peace is so much harder than war. He can't think of a purpose or a career or something that will pay him enough money to settle down and do — what?

His old Classics teacher has written to say that he is retiring. Might teaching be an option? He could put a word in.

Sidney takes the train down to Marlborough College. He dreads seeing his former teachers and listening to the stories of their favourite pupils who have died. But he has always been fond of Mr Pyatt. Whenever pies are on the menu for lunch the boys still sing: *Who ate all the pies? Pyatt ate the pies. He's so fat. He ate his cat. Pyatt ate the pies*.

The Head of Classics is a kind and portly man, most often found in a loose tweed jacket and a colourful bow tie. He wears handmade shoes inherited from his father and, if a voice could sound like well-worn corduroy, then his would be that voice. His party piece is to recite the whole of the funeral oration of Pericles in ancient Greek.

"So many boys gone, Sidney. I'm glad we didn't lose you as well. Remember how Pericles describes it? 'The youth who have perished in the war have vanished from the city just as if someone had removed the spring from the year.' That's how I feel now. I was used to a new crop of boys every autumn. You send the old ones out into the world to become leaders of men and you expect to read about all their exploits in the newspapers — but not under 'deaths'. Not at eighteen, nineteen and twenty. You were with Kendall, weren't you?"

"And several others."

"Everyone loved that boy."

"I know."

"Although I wasn't so sure, if you'd like my opinion. A bit cocky, if you ask me. Of course, I can't say that now he's dead."

"No, you can't."

"You were always my favourite, Sidney. I always prefer a horse that no one's quite spotted coming up on the rails."

"I'm not sure about that."

"We should order."

They are having lunch in the White Hart Hotel in the high street: beef consommé, scampi and chips, apple pie. Pyatt wants to spare his former pupil the school food and talk in confidence. What does Sidney think about taking over from him? There are many rewards to teaching and he can do what he likes in the holidays.

"I haven't done any training."

"That doesn't matter. You'll soon pick it up. That's one of the advantages of public school. No experience required. You remember Jonesy?"

The Head of History, Roddy Jones, hadn't had any teacher training either. He was an old army friend of the headmaster from the Great War, the possessor of a Distinguished Conduct Medal, who had saved the lives of his comrades by sitting on a grenade and getting his bum blown off.

Greater love hath no man than this — that he lay down his arse for his friends.

Sidney can't imagine a similar career but wants to remain tactful. "I'm just not sure I'd be any good at teaching."

"You've been in the army," Pyatt replies. "You've given orders. You know how to make men follow your commands. You're a natural communicator. And think of the opportunity. All those wonderful texts. All that scholarship. You'll be introducing a new generation to the classics, giving them an intellectual foundation for the rest of their lives."

Sidney notices the future tense, as if he has already agreed to the job. "I do want to do something of value, Victor." (It's odd to be calling a teacher by his Christian name.) "But I'm not sure if teaching's the thing for me."

"You are more ambitious?"

"I'm not sure if it's that. Everyone assumes I'll end up in the Foreign Office. But I've found diplomacy rather distant from everyday life. You're negotiating with representatives without meeting the people they claim to be speaking for."

"Have you thought about journalism? You could always turn in a good essay."

"I've got a friend on *The Times*. But I don't know enough about it. I'm not sure I know enough about anything, to be frank."

"Then you should do some more research. People can never make decisions if they aren't in full possession of the facts. You need to start making a few lists, Sidney. All the pros and cons. Let's start with teaching; a good salary, job security, long holidays, a proper pension, if you live that long — there's a lot to be said for it, you know?"

On the train back, Sidney considers careers. What can he do best? What would constitute the worthwhile life? Perhaps he should pray about it all? He closes his eyes and leans his head against the window. It's a hot afternoon. There's a wasp in the compartment but he's too tired to do anything about it. What he wants, he decides, is relief from expectation.

He opens his eyes to see houses and back gardens. Mowing and watering. A man sawing a bit of wood outside his shed. A child on a swing. A thatcher coming down off a ladder. Chores and hobbies. Simple tasks. None of this has much to do with him. He can't imagine how he can ever belong in the world of everyday routine. What is all this compared to what he has seen?

"Are you all right, sir?"

It is the ticket collector. He is genial and sweaty and probably should have retired, but he needs the wages. "You seem a bit lost."

Sidney notices the dandruff on the shoulder of the man's uniform and can't quite work out where he is. "I was dreaming."

"I hope it wasn't a nightmare. You've not been back long?"

"How can you tell?"

"I've seen enough lads like you this last while." He punches the ticket, leans over, slides open the window and lets the wasp escape. "You look after yourself, sir."

CHAPTER THIRTEEN

Sidney's first social outing since his return to London is a ball at the Caledonian Club. He arrives with Freddie Hawthorne because Amanda has been fearful that there won't be enough men to go round and has asked him to "scrape up as many of them that you can find. If they can dance they're invited. Most of my friends are desperate."

However, it turns out that there are more than anyone has anticipated. This comes as something of a relief. Sidney had imagined being on his feet, dancing the quickstep with Amanda all over again and even partnering her mother (he has heard her say how "it's vital to spread the men"), but there's a complement of confident fresh faces sprucely dressed in kilts and dinner suits, too young for war and knowing that this is now their turn at youthful possibility, love and flirtation — the kind of faces Sidney last saw at Robert's eighteenth birthday. The ball is in the same venue.

Freddie Hawthorne remarks that "there must be more kilts in this room than anywhere south of the Highlands" and he jokes about the inevitable dilemma: the wearing or absence of underwear. He is on the border of inebriation, just sober enough to be charming but only an hour or two away from being drunk.

"Who is that divinely androgynous creature?" he asks.

"You mean, Amanda?" Sidney replies.

"She moves so gracefully. Such style. Like a ballet dancer."

"You know that's Robert Kendall's sister?"

"That would explain it. She's so like him when you look closely. You know, if I met her properly I do believe I could be turned."

"Even you, Freddie?"

"I'm serious. She's utterly heavenly."

"She's barely out of school."

"Nonsense. She could play Cleopatra."

Amanda catches Sidney's eye, is sure they must be talking about her, and introductions are made. "I *loved* your brother," Freddie begins, "and now I'm completely ready to *adore you*."

"Oh, Mr Hawthorne, there's no need to flatter."

"Call me Freddie, please . . ."

"Very well, if you wish: Freddie . . ."

"Let me be your slave for the night."

"There's no need for that. All I ask is that you come over and meet my parents. They're always glad to meet a friend of Robert's."

Sir Cecil and Lady Kendall are in different parts of the room. Amanda chooses her mother and, as she escorts them over for the meeting, she whispers to Sidney, "Is your friend drunk?"

"Not really," Sidney replies. "I'm afraid he's always like this."

"You will keep an eye on him, won't you?

Introductions are made and Lady Kendall asks Freddie how long he's been back from the war and what he is doing in London. There are some vague answers about the West End, his glamorous theatrical friends and his weekends in the country before they go on to talk about the Italian campaign and how well he knew Robert.

"Like an elder brother who could do no wrong," Freddie replies. "He was, and remains, the perfect man. Even his faults were beautiful."

"Faults?"

Sidney chips in, "I'm sorry, Lady Kendall, he doesn't really mean that," but Freddie keeps going. "Your son's only fault was one of abundance. Of energy, beauty, courage and talent . . ."

Stop there, Sidney thinks, but Freddie is in full flow.

"To me, he was a god. Like Apollo. Or Zeus. There are others. I can't remember all their names, but I can imagine him on Mount Parnassus even now. Your son was perfection incarnate."

"I don't know about that," Lady Kendall replies, unsure whether to be amused or not. "Isn't that supposed to be the job of Jesus Christ?"

"Oh, dear me, no. Robert was *beyond* divinity."

Other people are hovering around them, waiting to be introduced. "It's lovely to be here," says Sidney, taking his friend by the arm. "Thank you so much for inviting us, Lady Kendall. We should honour our obligations on the dance floor."

"Ah yes," their hostess replies. "I can see the orchestra getting ready. Do call on us at any time, Mr Hawthorne. Amanda will tell you where we live. I am always glad to listen to people talking about my son. So many of our friends are embarrassed to do so. They don't know what to say, whereas you don't seem to suffer from embarrassment at all."

"Oh, you never need to worry about me," says Freddie. "I am beyond embarrassment."

"How fortunate."

Freddie gives a little bow. "It's been an honour to meet you, Lady Kendall. Now I know why Robert was so marvellous. It all comes from you."

"Enjoy the dance, Mr Hawthorne. And do come and see me when you have the time. I mean it."

"I have all the time in the world."

"Extraordinary," Amanda says to Sidney as Freddie leaves in search of "a little sharpener to keep us all going". "How does he get away with it?"

"People think he's ridiculous but most of it's an act. Your brother adored him."

"Was he in love with Robert?"

"A little. But he does have a special friend of his own."

"Will I meet him?"

"I imagine so. But they are very discreet about it."

"I can't imagine your friend being discreet at all."

"He is when it matters. That's what you have to remember. He'd lay down his life for any one of us."

There follow the introductory dances so that everyone can get to know one another: the Gay Gordons, the Britannia Two-Step and the Eightsome Reel.

There's a man dancing who looks as much like Robert as his sister, only a younger version: the shock of dark hair, bright blue eyes, the defined jawline and confident posture. He's clearly used to attention; admired by men, adored by women. Is there a ready supply of such people? Sidney wonders. What gives them such assurance?

The memories returns: of his bloodied friend, bodies in mud, dark water and charred landscape, the cries of the wounded, the dead unburied, Robert on the charge.

Sidney can't help but think how many ghosts there are in the room. What if all this was a dream or a strange Scottish version of the dance of death, mixing the quick and the dead?

Slow, slow, quick, quick, slow.

He thinks of the Epistle to James: *Know my beloved brothers, let every person be quick to hear, slow to speak, slow to anger*.

He's dizzy for a moment, uncertain where he is and whether he can keep himself together. Amanda notices, comes over and asks: "Are you all right, Chambers?"

"Sorry. Funny turn."

"We don't want you fainting. Can I fetch you some water? Sit down."

"I don't want to make a fuss."

"Nonsense."

She escorts him to a chair at the side, gives him as cold a glass of water she can find. He takes a sip and then presses the glass against his forehead.

"It's very hot," he says.

Her hand is on his shoulder. "One more dance and it's dinner. Don't worry. You're next to me. I made sure. Talk to the person on the other side first. Then, after the turn, I get you for longer."

There's supper for sixty. It's too soon for game — the Glorious Twelfth is this coming weekend — and so they have pea soup, smoked trout, Atholl Brose and a final savoury, devils on horseback, before the loyal toast, *Floreat Caledonia*, and the post-dinner dancing.

Sidney takes it as slowly as he can and only sips at the wine. Afterwards, he asks Amanda for a waltz. It's what he finds easiest but, even so, he knows he has to be nimble in the turns and that he mustn't lose time or tread on her toes. He holds his friend with what he hopes is gentle strength, persuading her round the dance floor with a seriousness that she finds amusing. "You know this is supposed to be enjoyable?" she asks.

"I am enjoying it. I just don't want to embarrass you."

"There's no chance of that."

"I'm frightened of making a mistake."

She comes in closer. "Let me sort you out. Stop. Hold me properly. Now let's start again. *One*, two, three. *One*, two, three. Perhaps you're just out of practice."

Sidney remembers learning how to dance at prep school and having to take the lady's part for the tango because Robert refused to do so. Then there were the balls at Cambridge, with Caitlín Delaney insisting that they practise beforehand because she didn't want to make a show of herself, and how he'd once abandoned her, at Trinity, in order to take pity on a tall woman who had burst into tears after someone had said that she looked like a horse.

Amanda holds her head high and smiles as she dances, showing off her pale, thin neck and victory rolls. She's in a dark red silk dress that's designed to give and fall with the flow and movement, and Sidney remembers a word he learned when reading poetry at university: *liquefaction*. He knows that she is beautiful, despite her anxieties about her "Roman nose", and that he should appreciate this moment more than he does, that this is pleasure, and life doesn't get much better than this, but something holds him back.

It's the right to happiness, he decides. He doesn't deserve it.

CHAPTER FOURTEEN

On the eighth Sunday after Trinity, Sidney tells his family that he'd like them to come to church with him. They are not regular worshippers, attending services only on high days and holidays. They regard the Church of England mainly as a balance of national heritage and social cohesion rather than the crucible of universal salvation. It does not need to be taken too seriously, does it?

St Michael's, Highgate is a nineteenth-century building whose main claim to fame is that it is where Coleridge worshipped for the last eighteen months of his life. It stands higher than any other church in London, the entrance all but level with the Cross on top of St Paul's Cathedral. The congregation is healthy but much reduced after the ravages of war. The spire is still being repaired after bomb damage.

Alec Chambers enjoys some good-humoured grumbling about why they need to be doing this at all when they could be at home with the papers or pottering about in the garden (picking the sweet peas, for example) and he is keen not to sit too close to the front, making sure that his family surround him and that he is not exposed to the concerns or ailments of his patients hoping for some off-duty diagnoses.

Iris and Jennifer are content to see old friends and enjoy the music, singing the Trinity hymns with gusto:

> "Tell out, my soul, the greatness of the Lord!
> Unnumbered blessings give my spirit voice."

But Sidney is quieter, still thinking through the implications of pursuing a more devout, contemplative faith.

"O God, whose never-failing providence ordereth all things both in heaven and earth: we humbly beseech thee to put away from us all hurtful things . . ."

The gospel reading is St John's account of Jesus appearing on the other side of the sea after the feeding of the five thousand; the Saviour of the world encapsulated as the bread of life: "he that cometh to me shall never hunger; and he that believe in me shall never thirst."

Sidney's father mutters that the good Lord didn't have to put up with rationing, and Jennifer giggles before Mrs Chambers intervenes with an elbow jab to the ribs.

The sermon is addressed to the children of the parish. The elderly vicar tries to explain the symbolism of bread as manna from heaven but when he goes on to describe *that meat which endureth everlasting life*, Alec Chambers can't resist the rather-too-loud summary that it all sounds like a divine version of a corned-beef sandwich.

"It is extraordinarily hard," he says afterwards, "to take all of it literally, don't you think?"

"The feeding of the five thousand has always struck me as problematic," Sidney replies.

"Five loaves, two fish. Even your mother would struggle with that."

"It's just as well that lunch is already in the oven," Iris Chambers points out. "I bet you're all hungry. Nothing like a good sing-song to raise the appetite."

Even though it's summer there is still a roast lamb with new potatoes and garden peas followed by a lemon syllabub. The children are asked all over again about who they danced with at the ball, who else was there, what people talked about and whether there were any memorable moments.

Jennifer is teased about a man called Hugo Channing who served with the Grenadiers and is thinking of going into parliament.

"Oh please. He only asked me to dance."

"Three times," Sidney reminds everyone. "That shows he's keen."

"I'm surprised you noticed. You were the centre of attention with a certain young lady."

"Really?" Iris Chambers asks. "With whom?"

"The usual suspect," Jennifer replies.

The family are cautious on the subject of Amanda Kendall. They ask about her parents, or the Foreign Office, or what concerts Sidney might be going to in the near future, but the answers given are vague and only just graced with the necessary smile. In the kitchen, mother and daughter still worry that Sidney is depressed, that he needs activity, a proper job, and they decide that Alec Chambers should have a serious conversation with his son, but the two men are more preoccupied with the safe subjects of cricket and even contemporary politics (relations with Russia, the Paris Conference, the future state of Palestine and the match between the army and navy at Lord's).

"I don't think you have to rush into a career," says Sidney's father, "but I've got all manner of patients I could call on for a bit of advice if you need them. I seem to look after most professions and it's unlikely you're going to want to go into medicine, unless I'm mistaken . . ."

"No . . ."

"In any case, I'm sure Humphrey Waldock can find you something, or even Cecil Kendall."

"I don't think I'd like to ask him for any favours, Dad. It would be pretty awkward."

"You were his son's best friend."

"Exactly. I have disappointed the family enough already."

"What? You mean, by surviving? It was war."

"I feel I've let them down. I've not done as much as I could have done."

"It's hard to see what more you could have done, son."

It is a warm, airless afternoon. They go for a walk in the open plains of Hampstead Heath, amidst families with dogs and younger children, makeshift games of cricket, and football with jumpers for goalposts, the swimmers out in force. Despite the pleasing views and the expanse of landscape, Sidney still finds London claustrophobic. It's the return to a family that sees him as a child, he thinks, that any change in his behaviour is an unnatural break from the patterns his parents hope to have set.

Or perhaps it's even simpler. They just don't know who he is any more.

That night, he does something that he has not done since he was a little boy. He kneels at the foot of his bed and says his prayers. It is just about the only thing that makes sense to him. It feels secret, private, illegal and right.

"O God, from whom all holy desires, all good counsels, and all just works do proceed: give unto thy servants that peace which the world cannot give; that both our hearts may be set to obey thy commandments, and also that we, being defended from the fear of our enemies, may pass our time in rest and quietness . . ."

CHAPTER FIFTEEN

Amanda telephones and says she's keen to cheer Sidney up. She asks if they can do something normal, just the two of them, to prove that it's possible to resume the life of peacetime. "I thought you were a bit gloomy at the dance. Especially after that funny turn."

"I was hoping no one noticed."

"I wouldn't worry about it too much. I think I'm the only person who can tell when you're out of sorts."

"I'll have to get better at disguising my feelings."

"Please don't, Chambers. You're inscrutable enough already."

"Not to you, Amanda."

"Not to me, *so far*. But if you're going to worry about improving your behaviour, I wouldn't start by hiding your emotions."

"Weren't we brought up to believe that it's bad manners to show them?"

"Not in private. Come and meet me at the National Gallery. Let me take you round a few paintings. It must be a while since you've been."

"We went to that Myra Hess concert, remember? You showed me a couple of Cézannes. Otherwise I think it must have been when I was at school."

"The gaps in your education must be quite shocking, then."

"I'll have to rely on you to fill them in, Amanda."

The gallery is in the process of recovering works of art from wartime storage and some of the rooms are still closed. Amanda plans to avoid the Renaissance rooms because she believes that it's better to study ten paintings in detail rather than look at a hundred like a tourist. Besides, she doesn't want Sidney having troubling memories of the Italian landscape or the violence of war. As a result, they skip past Uccello's *Battle of San Romano* and the martyrdoms and crucifixions of Pollaiuolo and Raphael. Sidney's seen quite enough of that kind of thing recently, she says.

What she wants to show him instead are some of her "old friends": Dutch still lifes and summer paintings filled with pearly light, eternal verities, normality and beauty. There are interiors of domestic simplicity: a young woman seated at a virginal, another drinking a glass of wine with a couple of admirers, a housekeeper sweeping her front step, a maid hanging out the laundry. They are performing uncomplicated daily actions that will continue despite war and interruption and across the generations, because people will always need to eat, drink, wash and play music. The sun will rise, and light will travel and fall and never quite rest as the shadows finally appear, lengthen and descend into darkness. There is a repetitive nature to transience, Amanda says. It fades and yet it returns. Paintings fix people and their activities in time and, even though particular moments are lost, light and beauty remain.

"How do you know all this?" Sidney asks.

"I hope you're not surprised? Men can feel a bit threatened by a woman's expertise, but there are times when it's important to be serious. To stop and say what you really think rather than witter away. That's why I don't want you to look at too many paintings. Let's concentrate on a few that matter."

"I'm in your hands."

They look at landscapes and seascapes, dappled light and swaying trees, roads stretching away and people with warmth on their faces: Eugène Boudin's paintings of the harbour and beach at Trouville, Camille Pissarro's *View from Louveciennes* and then, finally, Georges Seurat's *Bathers at Asnières*.

"I want to show you, Chambers, that this is what peace looks like."

She guides him through the rhythm of Seurat's composition, the balance of colour, how the heat haze of a summer afternoon by the riverside is achieved.

"Roger Fry said this painting has a 'tremulous sensitivity', which is rather good, don't you think? The whole thing shimmers."

"Like you on the dance floor."

"Steady on, Chambers."

They sit down next to each other and Sidney feels a wash of calm. She rests her hand on his, and offers him a quick nervous smile, as if the moment is stolen, too nice to last. "Are you happier now?"

"When I'm with you, yes. I think I am."

"But something's still not right."

"I'm enjoying this."

"But you're still not entirely with us, Chambers, are you?"

"It's not just Robert."

"Oh yes, my brother . . . he's never far away."

Sidney thinks of his friend lying dead before him in the darkness, the noise of war blotted out, just the faint smile, the shock of hair, the blood and dirt around the ear.

"Then what is it?"

"I don't know. I think it's the feeling that I have to make things right."

"You can't take on such a burden. What's happened has happened. It's fate. War."

"But we're not at war any more. In a funny way, I could deal with that. There were rules. Orders. Everything was outside my control. It's the peace I find hard."

"You don't have to decide on things just yet."

"But I'm not doing anything . . ."

"This is something. This is not nothing."

"I know."

"Let's look at something else," she says. "I can tell you're restless."

They study an arrangement of tulips, roses, carnations and lilies by Jacob van Walscapelle. Amanda tells him that, as the flowers bloom at different months in the year, the artist must have painted it over a period of time or after drawings from nature. Complementing them are strawberries, blackberries and a few golden ears of wheat. She shows him the artist's command of minute detail in the tiny insects and butterflies that hide amidst flowers and foliage, and the glistening droplets of water that kiss the surface.

"Every brushstroke matters."

They look at the reflections of light in the glass vase. It's so hard to paint glass and reflection at the same time, she says, to track light and fix it. She describes each work with such fluent affection. Sidney thinks she is more involved with art than she is with her friends. Perhaps this is her version of faith.

They stop before a Chardin still life: a broken loaf of bread, a tumbler of red wine, with a knife and a bottle resting on a newspaper. Amanda shows him how the complex is made simple, how a tactile balance is created in the rendering of wood, metal, glass, dust, liquid, paper.

They find themselves in front of Caravaggio's *Supper at Emmaus*, Christ with outstretched arms in blessing, the two strangers suddenly realising who is with them, light in the darkness, the simplicity of bread and gesture, its distilled meaning.

Amanda points out that there's another still life on the table at the centre of this painting too. There's the carafe of wine, the loaf of bread, a jug of water and, in this case, a bowl of fruit. But not just any fruit; a worm-eaten apple to remind the viewer of the Fall, the bunch of grapes that represents the new vine of faith and the blood of Christ. Sidney wonders whether the white linen cloth over Christ's shoulder could be the grave cloth from the empty tomb after the Resurrection, and Amanda talks through the difference between this painting and Seurat's *Bathers*. There, the recumbent figure in the foreground frames the painting and leads you in. Here, the outstretched arms of Christ, and the stunned realisation of the dinner guests, open the picture out. The fall of light concentrates and illuminates. It is a fable of invitation and blessing in paint.

Sidney wonders if Amanda — or God, even — has planned this day to arrive in front of this painting and make it complete. He remembers Catherine in the monastery of Subiaco and looking up the Emmaus story in the church in Trieste.

How faith can arrive like the dawn.

And he went in to tarry with them. And it came to pass, as he sat at meat with them, he took bread, and blessed it, and brake, and gave to them.

"What are you thinking?" she asks.

"No thoughts. Just a few memories."

"You're a dark horse, Chambers."

"I don't mean to be."

They study the picture in silence. It is an image of commanding serenity, perfectly proportioned in its beauty and stillness. He feels the painting is calling him. Christ is calling him. This is the peace that the world cannot give.

CHAPTER SIXTEEN

A few days later, Sidney takes a bus to Trafalgar Square, alighting near the National Gallery once more. He walks down Pall Mall to the Athenaeum Club, where he has arranged to meet Rev Nev for a drink before dinner.

It is a warm evening, with office workers returning home, men heading for the pubs and newspaper boys calling out news of Stalin's latest demands. As he passes the bottom of Haymarket, Sidney witnesses a near miss between a taxicab and an absent-minded bicyclist who is the right age to have fought in the war — imagine surviving all that, he thinks, only to be knocked down in the street. He steadies himself in front of the imposing Palladian façade of the Athenaeum and remembers Humphrey Waldock's words: *You had better learn what it is that you actually want, Sidney. You can't have survived for nothing*.

Rev Nev greets his protégé in the hall and tells him to "come on up" the grand staircase, graced by its statue of Apollo and stately portrait of George IV. The clergyman is nattily dressed in a light grey summer suit, wears a white carnation in his buttonhole and smells of a musky aftershave. Sidney has never seen him looking so spruce and compliments him on his appearance.

"I needed cheering up."

"Aren't other people supposed to do that for you?"

"I thought I'd save you the bother. If you look better, you feel better, don't you think?"

The drawing room on the first floor is a regal expanse of sofas and chaises longues, desks, card tables and bookcases, with fireplaces at each end. Men come here to escape their lives and their families, leaning forward to share an animated secret or back to read newspapers and periodicals. The clientele is the elderly, the great and the remains of the good: lawyers, academics and, principally, clergymen. The most frequent sight in the room, Sidney has been warned, is of a sleeping bishop.

It is a spacious and privileged space, and he wonders how his friend can afford it.

"It's my only luxury and it's rather naughty of me, I'm afraid. The trick is, you get someone else to pay the subs."

"How do you do that?"

"Ideally you have an aunt."

Sidney thinks of his father's sister, an intimidating ruddy-faced farmer's wife from the Borders who is careful with her accounts and has little time for the contemplative life. She considers reading a book to be the height of indolence and is never going to fork out the cost of a heifer on a London club.

"You wanted to see me?" Rev Nev asks.

"There's something I need to ask you about. But I'm not quite sure how to put it."

"Then you need a drink. They'll come in a minute. Let's have some gin. It's so difficult for all of us these days, isn't it? I always think of George Herbert's words, 'soldiers in peace are like chimneys in summer'. We don't know what to do with ourselves."

People around them are speaking with the kind of relaxed confidence that Sidney doesn't know if he can ever achieve — or if he even wants to do so.

"I don't read fiction any more," one man is saying. "I can't abide the stuff. Such a waste of time."

There is laughter from the far end of the room, between the swagged curtains and under the illuminated busts of Roman emperors. Sidney wonders how soon they will get on to the subject of what he is going to do about his career. There will probably have to be some small talk first. Men are writing letters on tables in the windows. Others, closer by, are enjoying drinks and joviality, and uttering sentences that seem to bear no relation to each other.

"I can't say my life has become boring, but nothing matters after Anzio."

"My daughter's twenty-seven already. I can't think who on earth is going to marry her."

"You can't stagnate, Marcus. You just need to discover a more amusing way of living your life."

"Cornwall can be rather desolate, even in summer. And there are never any decent parties."

The gin and tonics arrive on a silver tray. Sidney's host acknowledges the waiter, who has an obvious limp, a legacy from the Great War. "Thank you, Vincent. On my account, if you don't mind." He leans forward. "Auntie Flo pays that as well, but I don't like to take liberties. Cheers."

"Cheers."

There is a moment of silence that lies between companionability and expectation.

"Well?" Nev asks at last. "Are you going to come out with something or not?"

"I'm slightly embarrassed," Sidney begins.

"I thought we could say anything to each other."

"We can."

"Then please carry on, unless you'd like to talk about the price of onions."

"No, I wouldn't. Why onions, Nev?"

"It's just something to say."

"I think it is normally 'fish'. The price of fish."

"Fish, onions, Brussels sprouts. You get the idea."

Sidney shifts forwards in his chair. It doesn't feel right to be sitting back while he says this. "I haven't ever spoken out loud about this to anyone, Nev, and you may find it all rather extraordinary, but I wonder if we could talk about what it's like to be a priest?"

"Are you asking because you are thinking about becoming one?"

"I'm not sure. You don't think it's rather implausible?"

"No, I don't."

"That's helpful. Reassuring."

"And neither do you, otherwise you wouldn't be suggesting it."

"I know. But I don't want to be thought a fool."

"As Christ was . . ."

"I don't know much about that."

"You do, Sidney, and you've always struck me as a very serious young man. Too serious, sometimes. You think things through —"

"I'm not always good at coming to a conclusion."

"That doesn't matter."

"So you don't think it's mad?"

"I do not. And I have to say that I think you might be rather good at it. But you have to be going into it for the right reasons. Being a priest is not so much a job as a vocation, a desire to live differently. There's no clocking off. It's with you all the time."

"That's how I feel at the moment. I thought it would go away but it hasn't. Sometimes it's all I can think about."

"And how would you describe this feeling?"

"It's that I have to do *something*. I have to make more of my life. I can't be merely ambitious. I want to do something of value. The right thing."

"And many priests would argue that there is nothing more important than what we do."

"I'm not sure I'm up to it, of course."

"Yes, well, that self-doubt never quite goes away either, I am afraid. Apparently, it's the same in other professions, but I never believe it. I haven't met that many money-men afflicted with conscience."

"I suppose doubt is part of faith."

"You trust in the Lord but doubt in yourself. Better that than the other way round."

"Trust in yourself and doubt in the Lord?"

"Christianity is very much about the future, Sidney; it's not so much who you are now but the man you might become. There's an optimism at the heart of faith. Always remember that."

Nev finishes his drink and offers another, making a little joke. Sherlock Holmes relished his two-pipe problems. This could be a two-gin problem. He is buying time, changing the subject before coming back to it, giving his friend a moment of respite.

"Well, Sidney," he says at last, "it's a brave thought."

"It's more than a thought. I think it's the most momentous thing I can possibly imagine."

"It is. And that's a good sign."

"It's completely terrifying."

"It's meant to be. But you don't have to do everything all at once. People don't become marathon runners or surgeons or concert pianists overnight. You need training. And you can always apply and see how it goes. If it is not right for you then you'll know soon enough. You can always go on and do something else. Olympic swimming, perhaps . . ."

"What?"

"I'm joking. But if it feels that you should be doing it, then you must carry on and see where it takes you. It's almost impossible to know what God has in store for us or who we are going to become. That's part of life's journey. If we knew all along, life would be so predictable that it wouldn't be worth living."

"I just want to lead a better life, Nev."

"And you think you need to be a priest to do that?"

"I'm trying to work it out."

"And you wouldn't be doing this out of guilt?"

Nev is aware their second drinks have arrived but makes sure that they are looking straight at each other.

"For Robert. For surviving when he did not."

(As if Sidney needed the name.) "You're very direct."

"I do not think it helps if we are oblique. Not with friends. Not in the times we are living. You cannot sacrifice your life for his. One loss is enough. You must be doing this because you want to do it, not because, in some warped way, you feel you must, or that your life no longer matters. It cannot be a punishment. Your life matters just as much as his."

"You gave the letter to his mother. The 'just-in-case' . . ."

"I did. And you have been to see the family."

"I have."

"So, you'll already know a little of what it's like to be a priest. To sit beside those who suffer. To understand pain."

"I don't know if I understand it exactly . . ."

"I'd like you to remember, Sidney, that you can atone, if that is what you feel you must do, in other professions."

"I can't think of any other means of finding my way back from the war."

"I hope we're not considering the Church as a last resort?"

"Not at all."

"The need must be absolute."

"Do you not think, Nev, that faith sometimes comes when people no longer have the energy or the willpower to deny it?"

"You have to want it with all your heart. Like love."

"I wouldn't know about that."

"You will. Eventually. You have to open yourself up — make yourself vulnerable. As my tutor once told me, 'Yearning makes the heart deep.' "

Rev Nev stops for a moment, perhaps wondering whether this is all too much for a conversation in a gentlemen's club.

"Would you like to stay on for dinner? We don't have to decide anything now. We've probably said enough. The idea has been raised. The subject is out. We can return to it once we are ready. There is no hurry. God is not going to go away. That's one of the advantages of eternity."

"But 'strait is the gate'."

"And you can see it ahead of you. All you have to do is decide when you want to walk through it."

"I'm expected at home."

"Another time, then."

"Thank you for listening to me. I do appreciate it."

"That's my job, Sidney. And soon, perhaps, it will be yours."

"I know it's a big step. I can't run before I can walk. 'The race is not always to the swift.' "

" 'Nor yet battle to the strong.' You are getting the idea."

"Will it take long, Nev?"

"A lifetime. But then, Sidney, if you are not always learning, what on earth are you doing with your life?"

"So you approve?"

"I approve of your beginning the pilgrimage. We'll just have to see how you get on during the journey. But I promise to keep you company on the road as much as I can. We don't want to take any wrong turnings."

So this is the start, Sidney thinks: to say it out loud. To proclaim an intention that forces you to follow it. The conversation doesn't feel momentous but ordinary.

Is this how people decide to become doctors or teachers or politicians? When they look back in old age, if they ever get that far, how much do they wonder if their entire career has been some kind of arbitrary accident rather than planned and judged accordingly?

He takes the Tube home and tries to guess the profession of everyone in his carriage. There are RAF uniforms that help, and giveaway signs (a lawyer's briefcase, a red-cloaked nurse, a bag of tools). There's even a young woman from the Salvation Army who smiles at him encouragingly. He decides this is a coincidence rather than some oblique message from God.

CHAPTER SEVENTEEN

Like Amanda, Alec Chambers is also worried that Sidney has become introspective since the war. He tells his son he needs to watch a bit of cricket to take him out of himself and so they go to the England v India game at the Oval. Iris Chambers provides bottles of beer and sandwiches — white bread with caramelised onions together with a bit of pork left over from the Sunday roast.

"Your mother has some kind of relationship with the butcher," his father begins. "I think it's innocent — he knows she won't let anything go to waste."

"You can eat all of the pig but the squeal," Sidney remembers.

"I've had trotters and ears in my time, but I find the intestines difficult, which I shouldn't for a Scot who's so used to haggis."

"We had some of that at the front. The padre's dad sent some from Markinch along with the whisky. It was extraordinary that the supplies and the mail got to us faster than we could advance."

India are batting on a placid wicket, but England bowl well, restricting the opposition to 331.

"If we still had Hedley Verity playing, then it would have been a different story," Alec observes. "He'd have polished off the tail before tea."

"Such a loss," says Sidney.

He knows how this conversation will go. His father worshipped the cricketer who died of wounds suffered in the Eighth Army's first attack on the German positions in Sicily.

"He was a marvellous bowler. You do know, Sidney, that he is the only cricketer who has taken fourteen wickets in a day in a Test match?"

"Wasn't it against Australia at Lord's?"

"It was 1934. I wish I'd been there. So much of my life has been spent in places where I would rather not have been. I suppose that it's the same for you."

Sidney realises that, in going over the fate of Hedley Verity, his father is rehearsing what it might have been like had his son died instead.

Perhaps he should have been a cricketer? He had given up when the bowling got too fast for him.

"Are you all right?" Alec Chambers asks. "You seem to have been very maudlin recently."

"I keep thinking about everything that's happened. Was it like that for you, Dad?"

"Yes. But we don't talk, as you know. It's our way of coping. If you dwell on it too much it stays with you all the time."

"I never expected to have to bury so many friends."

"I know. But you mustn't let the past ruin your future."

"I'm trying."

"Just enjoy the game, son. Concentrate on that. Think of it as an escape from life. You don't have to say or do anything at all at the moment."

Sidney understands that cricket is the perfect backdrop to difficult conversations. It allows men to imagine that they are not awkward with each other. They can pretend they are not really talking about war or an impending death, the state of their marriage, the possibility of a looming bankruptcy or a terrible betrayal by a friend or employer — because they are "watching the cricket". Yet, at the same time, they *are* saying these things; but they are talking while looking at something else, within the protection of a ground, a boundary, a world in which there will always be another day, alive with possibility, when everything can be different.

And that is why, in the middle of an innings, with Walter Hammond batting, Sidney tells his father that he is thinking of becoming a clergyman.

"Really?" Alec Chambers asks, shocked by the seriousness of the subject matter and surprised by his son's quiet intensity. "Have you considered this properly?"

"Not yet. That's why I'm raising it with you now."

"Well, I'm not sure what to say. I wasn't expecting this *at all*."

"You hadn't guessed?"

"I knew there was something. But this is a turn-up for the books. I thought it was more likely to be some kind of romance, like when you nearly married that Catholic girl."

"I didn't 'nearly marry' her . . ."

"What was her name again?"

"Caitlín."

"I was worried we'd lose you to the Irish. Now, it seems, we might lose you to the Church. Was that why we all had to go the other day? I thought it was a bit odd."

"I found it comforting."

"Yes, it's always reassuring. But have you got enough faith for it, son? You've never struck me as being particularly religious. Has something come over you all of a sudden?"

"There was a war."

"But people don't all come back on their knees, do they?"

"It's not a joke."

"I'm trying to come to terms with it, Sidney."

"And so am I. It may not work out. You have to apply for training. They may reject me before I've even begun."

"You've never failed anything in your life. Just like that friend of yours. They'll take you. Good heavens, what a cover drive! Hammond really is the most marvellous batsman."

"I was hoping you'd be pleased for me, Dad."

"Yes, I am, Sidney, of course I am, and all I can do is to wish you luck, and remind you that you have our support. I suppose there will be quite a few stages to go through before you become a saint. Will you tell your mother, or shall I?"

"I'll do it."

"Better coming from you. She can think she's the first to know."

England reach 95 for 3 by the close, with only one day of play remaining. With rain forecast there is little chance of a result other than a draw. But then, Alec Chambers points out, glad for a resumption of normal conversation, no matter what your expectations are on the field of play, anything can happen.

"I remember one of Verity's most extraordinary deliveries. The ball seemed to hang in the air. The batsman knew it was there for the taking so he advanced down the pitch and *at that moment, and in those few seconds*, there could have been any number of results. The batsman could have hit it for six, he could have hit it and been caught, he could have missed and been bowled, he could have missed and been stumped. There were at least four different outcomes, all distilled in that second before he played his shot. And do you know what happened?"

"He ran his partner out."

"A straight drive, grazed the bowler's fingers, ball deflected on to the stumps, the other batsman backing up and out of the crease. Impossible to predict. How did you guess?"

"I didn't guess, Father. You've told me the story before."

"You've spoilt it now. You could have pretended not to remember."

But Sidney is already somewhere else, thinking of Robert as his father rattles on. If the conditions had been different, if they'd had a better understanding of each other, like two batsmen at the crease, knowing when to call for a run and when to stay put . . .

Yes! Go, go, go.

Down.

They could have saved each other's lives.

"I was just thinking," Alec Chambers says on the bus home. "The Victorians used to send either their youngest or their dimmest sons into the Church. Aren't you a bit too intellectual for them?"

"I'm not aware that being clever is a clerical disadvantage."

"Perhaps it isn't. I'm sure they could do with you. Maybe chaps like you are supposed to redress the balance?"

"I don't know. I have no idea what the others may be like. But there's no such thing as being 'too clever' for them, don't you think? I must make the best use of whatever gifts I may have."

"And the Church is the best place to exercise those gifts?"

"I don't know, Dad."

The bus heads north through Camden and up towards Highgate. Two drunks are swinging at each other outside the Bull and Gate, staggering without ever falling over, missing their punches. A man crosses the road in his dressing gown, appearing to wear his medals from the Great War. They overtake a woman on a tricycle carrying a basket of sunflowers. It is a surprise of colour amidst the impending dusk. Perhaps she is on the way back from her allotment?

Sidney's father is still thinking. "Has God spoken to you about it all?" he asks

"I don't think so. Not yet."

"Isn't he supposed to? You haven't had a Damascus Road moment?"

"No. But perhaps I don't need one." Now is not the time to lecture Alec Chambers on the theological significance of the Supper at Emmaus. "I just need to acknowledge the kind of peace I can't find anywhere else."

"Ah, so it's peace you're after?"

"Not world peace, although that would be good, but a kind of quiet, a solitary striving: a need to be still, to listen, if that doesn't sound too pious. I want more of Christ in my life, and, even more than that, to give my life to him. To live in Christ and Christ in me."

His father looks to the side and behind them. He isn't sure he wants people overhearing the conversation. It isn't the kind of chat you have on a bus. You're supposed to talk about the weather, the cricket and what you're going to have for tea. God is best kept for Sundays and inside a church.

An elderly couple smile encouragingly, as if to say that Alec Chambers is lucky to have a son at all.

"You are aware of what you will be giving up, Sidney? A priest has to set an example, be examined and judged. You'll have to sacrifice your private life."

"As you have done."

"I'm not on call all the time. A priest is."

"I don't know about that. I think they do have time off."

"In which they pray, meditate, reflect. It's a calling. A whole life. It won't be like anything else."

"I know, Dad."

"And won't you get bored, have doubts, wonder if it's all been worthwhile?"

"I think that is part of the job. I'd have more doubts if I went into the Foreign Office."

"And what about money? What will you do about that?"

"The Church does pay."

"Not very much, I imagine."

"I think that's the idea, Dad. Jesus didn't have much time for money — or moneylenders for that matter."

"And will you have the common touch? I suppose the army has given you a bit of that."

"I don't know. All I know is that I have to do something. Why did you become a doctor? Perhaps it's the same thing. St Luke was a medical man. We have to be more than ourselves. What did your parents say when you told them?"

"They didn't approve. Imagine, your mother and father not supporting your desire to be a doctor? They thought I should have worked on the farm."

"There you are then. Imagine your mother and father not supporting your desire to be a priest?"

A bell rings. The bus slows down and pulls to a halt. "Very good, Sidney. This is our stop. I think you might call that checkmate."

CHAPTER EIGHTEEN

Rev Nev has organised a two-week religious retreat so that Sidney can think his decision through.

"There's no need to tell people what you are doing. You can keep it a secret," he advises, "and if questioned you can just say that you are going on holiday with friends."

But when Amanda asks directly, "Who are these people, Chambers?" Sidney can't quite answer. He bluffs and says something about an army reunion that he doesn't really want to attend and that he won't be gone for long.

The monastery is situated in Northumberland on a hill overlooking the North Sea. Sidney takes the Flying Scotsman and the train is filled with soldiers still returning from Europe and businessmen on their way to meetings in York and Newcastle. There are families with children off for a last, cheap, end-of-season holiday weekend in Scarborough, as well as the nervous elderly, with sandwiches in greaseproof paper, worried about missing their stop. Sidney is alert to those around him, but once he has had his ticket checked he settles down by the carriage window, determined to finish

Middlemarch. He looks forward to discovering what George Eliot means by "the other side of silence".

He is met at the station by a member of the community in a Morris Bullnose. Sidney smiles because he hadn't expected to see a monk in a motor car. It feels too modern and yet it is also reassuringly unpredictable.

Brother Martin offers him a peppermint from a brown-paper bag (they are home-made), asks him about his journey and sets off on a winding road and up a hill that tests his ability with double-declutching. There's a close encounter with a tractor and a few other vehicles, and Sidney closes his eyes as they round a sharp blind corner, but Brother Martin is unperturbed. He even whistles.

"Such superb weather," he says. "I think it's a day that calls out for the poetry of Gerard Manley Hopkins, don't you think? 'Glory be to God for dappled things . . .' "

The monastery looks like a late-Victorian public school and, approaching the heavy oak door at the end of a gravel path lined with ageing lavender, it reminds Sidney of the Michaelmas term at Marlborough, of muddy playing fields, cold hands and damp scarves, of bonfires and turning leaves, the withdrawal into winter.

He is shown into a small single room with a bed with a crucifix hanging above it, a lamp, chair and desk with a copy of *The Rule of St Benedict* and a Bible. On the wall is a reproduction of Fra Angelico's *Annunciation*. Little is expected of him apart from silence and prayer. He arrives in time for a simple supper of vegetable soup, bread, cheese, an apple and a bottle of beer, which surprises him. He had thought there would only be water. Afterwards, there is Compline, the final service of the day, in the chapel.

The Abbot, mid-fifties, businesslike and less saintly than Sidney had been expecting (he might even use Brylcreem), waits in the porch and tells him that he doesn't have to attend all the offices if he doesn't feel like it. Nothing is compulsory. He can come and go as he pleases. It will take him a bit of time to get used to what they do. It's best just to observe the silences and come into the study if there is anything in particular that he needs. The weekly shop is tomorrow if he has forgotten anything.

It takes Sidney three days to adjust to the routine of this new life; the benign acceptance of his presence, the lack of inquisition.

His room has a narrow view of the Northumbrian coast and, twice a day, he walks down a steep bank and along the rocky shoreline in solitude; at first light and at dusk.

Lighten our darkness, we beseech thee, O Lord.

He adapts to two new and unfamiliar rhythms: the tides of the sea and the monastic timetable of Vigils, Lauds and Mass before lunch; Sext, None, Vespers and Compline before bed.

The days stretch and the solitude gives him freedom. He borrows a pair of binoculars and a book on bird-watching from the library and takes delight in picking out the differences between ruffs, oystercatchers, stilts and sandpipers: the bright orange and yellow thinness of their beaks, legs and feet; the trilling of their cries; the manner in which they hop and dart across rocks or burst into flight or the way in which the sun lights up their underwings as they turn in the sky.

He sits on cold boulders, inspects rock pools and takes off his socks and shoes for a paddle on the edge of a North Sea that is too cold for a swim even at the end of summer.

He follows the path of the sun across the water from left to right, sometimes waiting and watching one complete movement of disappearance into cloud and its re-emergence half an hour later, or even longer, depending on the force of the breeze and the thickness of the haze.

Landforms are revealed as the tide goes out: sandbanks, outcrops and dark forms that he cannot discriminate between. Is that a rock or a buoy, a porpoise or the head of a man? He is reminded of distance training in the army. They were taught the importance of not wasting ammunition and knowing when it's safe to shoot. At 200 yards, all parts of the body are distinctly seen; at 600 yards the head is a dot. There's no point firing if you can't be sure of a hit.

The monks wait until he is ready to join them. Then, when Sidney starts to get involved, he finds he cannot skip anything at all. If he remains in his room or wanders by the sea all day then he might as well be staying in a hotel.

He works in the laundry with Brother John, hangs out the sheets on a line in the back yard, attends a service, has lunch and collects them when they are dry.

They spend a quiet afternoon folding and ironing and putting everything away. One day, this is all he does.

He helps Brother Simon in the gardens, lifting the potatoes, dividing the perennial plants, preparing the ground for winter. He washes his hands under an outside tap and uses a hand-towel that is hanging just inside the back door. As he returns the towel to its place he realises that he is doing so far more thoughtfully and carefully than he has ever done before. At school, they just threw their towels on the floor. In the army, if towels existed at all, they were damp and dirty. He has a memory of sharing the tin bath with Robert: *This is about as useful as a eunuch in a brothel*.

He hasn't thought of his friend for several days, not even when the sea has become such a dark and lustrous blue that it could easily have been the Mediterranean. In fact, he hasn't really thought about anything deliberately at all. Instead, he decides on this surrender to simplicity, only dealing with what he can manage.

In the kitchen, he prepares vegetables with Brother Luke, shelling the last of the peas, stuffing apples with cloves before baking, chopping carrots and dicing the first turnips.

The monks show him how to make bread and soup to monastery specifications and Sidney falls into a routine of prayer and silence that makes each sound stand out: picking up a plate, scraping a bowl clean, putting down a spoon, pouring water into a glass, arranging flowers in a vase. The silence amplifies the sound around it. Everything, he learns, has to occupy its own space and time. He has to slow his life down completely, not rushing or predicting anything about the future but waiting for what comes. Time has been suspended between life and death, and with the silence and the contemplation the days lengthen. He has more space to be himself, to think without interruption, to let the life of the mind recover and grow. In abdicating from his former life, he realises, he finds a new existence. He can, perhaps, be healed: clearer about the man he wants to be.

There are readings at mealtimes, not only from scripture and the work of the Church Fathers but also from the outside world: the locked-room mysteries of John Dickson Carr, the detective fiction of Dorothy L. Sayers, even a bit of Dickens. The monks inhabit a silent world of gesture and acceptance, offering food, holding open doors, pointing out steps ahead that might cause a fall. There are times in the day when they can speak, but words are few, quiet and gentle.

In the chapel, they genuflect, pray and make their devotions in speech and plainsong but, even here, the main quality is one of silence. They arrive together, processing in pairs, but leave separately after each service, whether it be the first or the last of the day, allowing time for quiet contemplation as they ready themselves for work, food or bedtime.

Sidney does not imagine that he could ever join such a community. He is too mindful of the world and the work he has to do, but he begins to think that he could carry back some of the peace that he has found here, and that he might possibly be able to offer at least a part of what he has discovered in Rev Nev, Nurse Catherine and the monks around him: a selfless grace.

It might all prove overwhelming, and he is not entirely certain he can live in two worlds, one of faith and one of everyday reality, or even if he can bring the two of them together; but, when he leaves, he is surer than ever that he will be unable to do anything else.

CHAPTER NINETEEN

Telling his father is one thing. Confessing his plans to Amanda is another matter. He chooses the Mayfair Hotel, even if it is going to cost him more than he can possibly afford.

His friend says she is dreading another autumn of tired greens, root vegetables and rissoles made with grated potato, oatmeal and hardly any meat. There is no joy or sparkle to London. Robert would have hated it, she says. Everything requires rationing coupons. Apparently, you need eleven for a dress but she has such a lavish wardrobe Sidney is sure she has an arrangement with Norman Hartnell. There is certainly nothing cheap about today's outfit: a V-necked chiffon dress in pale pink. It is only just warm enough to wear and needs a navy cardigan.

"You look wonderful," he says.

"I like to make an effort for you, Chambers. And I don't come here every day. I hope the prices aren't too shocking."

"Not at all," Sidney lies as he considers the menu.

Consommé 3/0
Mushrooms on toast or pâte 3/6

Oysters 4/0
Honeydew melon 5/0

Roast Sussex chicken with artichokes,
tomatoes and beans 7/6
Lamb with Sarladaises potatoes and truffles 7/6
Pheasant in a Perigourdine sauce 7/6

Small decanter of wine 8/0
Large decanter of wine 15/0

"We save a shilling by having the large decanter of wine," Amanda observes.

"And we spend seven more than having a half. Not that I'm complaining."

"I see you're adjusting to thrift. Are you short after your little holiday? I'm longing to hear about it."

"I'll come on to that . . ."

"I could lend you a bob or two to see you through if you need it."

"I'm all right."

"Good." Amanda picks up her napkin and spreads it out on her lap. "I've been so looking forward to this, Chambers. It's been ages since we've had a proper chat. I want to know what's been going on in your busy little brainbox."

"Yes, of course. Shall we order?"

She picks up the menu again. "Oh dear, you seem distracted already. Have you something to tell me?"

"It's not that serious."

"I bet it is. I know you far better than you think I do."

The restaurant is full and, even though Sidney has been back from the retreat for just over a week, he still finds it hard to adjust to the noise of London. It's not just the traffic. It's the calls to the kitchen, the stacking of plates and the dissonant chimes of cutlery, the opening of windows to let in more sound, the hum of conversation, the relentless need to be heard. A heavyset waiter with dyed black hair takes their order. ("You'd think he might have lost weight with all the rationing," Amanda observes, "but I imagine if you work in a kitchen you'll always find something to scoff. I don't suppose he's fussy.")

Sidney doesn't want an aperitif and insists the waiter brings the wine straight away. After it has been poured he listens to his friend's London news and gossip, and holds off for as long as he possibly can before confessing to his religious retreat. No, his holiday wasn't an army reunion at all, but he didn't know how to tell her where he was going as he knows she would have thought it rather ridiculous, but he thinks the whole thing may have changed his life.

Amanda is as silent as the monks when he describes his days of contemplation.

She waits for a few seconds after he has finished and then says: "I know you may have wanted to get away from us all, but it's a bit drastic, isn't it?"

"I suppose so."

"You lived your life as a monk?"

"I did."

"Then you must be starving. I don't suppose there was any booze."

"They have a glass of beer or wine when there are guests."

"And you were a guest?"

"Yes, I was . . ."

"Why are you hesitating?" Amanda asks. "You're not thinking of joining them, are you?"

"No, of course not."

"Well, that's a relief."

"But there is something else . . ."

"Intriguing. What on earth can it be?"

He's not sure if this is the right time or place, or even if he wants to tell her at all, because he doesn't want her to dismiss what he has to say as something he doesn't really mean, or that it's just a phase he's going through, or that it can't be a serious proposition. He wonders whether he should wait, put everything down clearly in a letter or even let someone else break the news, but he has got so far into his confession that he can hardly back out now, and it would be cowardly not to tell her face to face.

And so, when she presses him and he finally confesses that he has every intention of training to become a priest, Amanda laughs out loud.

"I don't believe it."

"I thought you'd be surprised. I didn't expect you to find it amusing."

"I'm sorry, but really, Chambers. You?"

"I'm completely serious."

She can tell he is hurt by her reaction but requires more information before she can deal with his feelings. "Will you be going back to some kind of university?"

"Theological college."

"And you'll get into one of them, will you? Is there an exam?"

"I think there's an interview. I do have a first-class degree. I haven't gone into all the details but I've got someone to help."

"I bet you have."

"It's quite straightforward, apparently."

"Well, I imagine they're grateful for anyone they can get."

"I don't think they're desperate."

"How long does it take?"

"Eighteen months, I think. Perhaps two years."

"In London?"

"No. Somewhere else. Cambridge."

"So, you'll be abandoning us?"

"Not for long."

"You've only just come back." She sighs as if Sidney is too thick too understand what she is saying. "I can't imagine you in a dog collar at all. Do you think you'll change?"

"I'll have to."

"And give up your former life? Renounce the world, the flesh and the devil?"

"I imagine so."

Sidney thinks about making a joke about giving up the devil and keeping a bit of the world and the flesh but worries she'll take it the wrong way.

Amanda looks around the room, checking either to see if no one has been listening in or to find out if anyone else can share in her amazement. "And what's brought all this on, Chambers? Can't you just go to church like the rest of us?"

"No, I don't think I can."

"It's rather a melodramatic thing to do, don't you think?"

"No. It's the most natural thing in the world. To try and understand God's love."

"Is that what you want to do with your life: 'understand God's love'? Why didn't you tell me before?"

"It's not been easy, Amanda."

"I'm sure it hasn't. But it's not that straightforward for my family either."

"What do you mean?"

Up until now her tone has been cautiously measured. Now her voice drops. "It's difficult. You must realise . . ."

"What?"

She looks away from him for a moment and Sidney thinks she is biting her lower lip. It's what she does when she is wondering whether to speak or not. "I think I probably have something to say too but I'm not sure you'll want to hear it."

"I thought we could tell each other anything, Amanda. That's why we're here. That's the whole point of our friendship."

"So, there's one thing I'll have to say now that you've come out with all this and since we are being so candid . . ."

"Then say it."

"I don't want to do this at all . . ."

"What is it?"

"I was going to keep it to myself but you give me no choice."

She finishes her first glass of wine. She sees that Sidney is waiting and realises that there is nothing else she can say other than this:

"I suppose what I really think is surprisingly obvious when you study it carefully. I find it very hard to believe in a God that killed my brother. And I don't see how you can either — let alone become a priest. There. I've said it."

Sidney waits. He will not react to the word "carefully" but he decides to reply with caution and denial. "He didn't kill him."

"He didn't spare him. He spared you."

"We can't always know the reason for these things."

"Well, I don't think much of God's will."

"That's what I'm trying to explore."

"It's a bit late, don't you think?"

"So, you disapprove?"

"I don't disapprove. I can't imagine it, that's all."

She pushes her chair back and tenses her hands, uncertain whether to fold her arms or leave them out in front of her. Her upper row of teeth covers her lower lip ready to bite — either in anger or to stop tears, Sidney can't be sure.

"I'm sorry you think like this, Amanda."

"I don't know what to think. You've taken me completely by surprise. I could have anticipated almost anything except what you've just said."

"I didn't expect you to feel so strongly."

"But what *did* you expect? It seems a complete and utter betrayal of everything that's happened to us. There. I've said it. That's what I think."

"A betrayal, Amanda? That's very extreme. It's not meant like that. Quite the opposite."

She replies quickly, unable to countenance interruption, wanting the conversation to end or the mood to change but neither of them knows how to stop everything getting worse. "I don't know what the opposite of betrayal is, Sidney. I can't help what I think, even if I didn't know I thought it until you forced me to come out with all this. But we have to be honest with one another."

"That's what I've been trying to be too."

"Well, I don't know if you've been trying very hard. It's all a bit last minute."

"I've given it a great deal of thought."

"On your own. In a monastery."

"Where else was I supposed to do it?"

"I don't know. Perhaps I should go off and decide to become a nun? Except I already know that it would be ridiculous. I don't need to go to a bloody nunnery in the middle of nowhere. I've got friends. I'm not cut out for it and I can't believe you are either."

"Certainly not to be a nun."

"Don't joke about it, Sidney, even if you're nervous. It really doesn't help. The whole thing is ridiculous, isn't it? Telling me you've made a decision like this. I can't imagine how you've reached it. Are you sure you're not having some kind of nervous breakdown?"

"No, I'm not."

"It's just that I'm not sure that you're being entirely yourself."

"And I'm not clear what that means."

He should have thought harder, known her better. Perhaps they could abandon the lunch altogether, but some stupid etiquette demands that they both stay. "I'm sorry you feel like this," he repeats.

"And I'm sorry you've been completely unable to anticipate my emotions, Sidney. You can't know me very well at all."

He knows her sufficiently to recognise that Amanda only calls him "Sidney" when she is upset.

"And what do you think I should do instead?" he asks, rather more aggressively than he had intended.

"I don't know. Don't ask me. You haven't before."

"I've been away."

"In a monastery, for God's sake. *Literally*, it seems. We all assumed you'd become a diplomat. Humphrey Waldock told my father you were first rate, but that you'd discovered God. I didn't count on it being this bad."

"You make it sound like a disease. It's a calling, Amanda." He says her name, hoping it will make her take him more seriously. "A vocation."

"You think it is?"

"I cannot think of anything that matters more. It is the only thing I have to do."

Amanda leans back. "I just cannot understand why . . ."

He had thought she might talk about how all this might change their friendship and how they were going to behave from now on. What he hasn't anticipated at all is her philosophical disapproval, her denial of the very existence of God. He is about to continue the conversation, not quite knowing what his friend is thinking or even what words might come out of his mouth, when the waiter arrives with the mushrooms and the melon.

"I don't want that, thank you," Amanda says. "Take it away. In fact, I don't want anything at all." She pushes back her chair and stands up. "I think I'd better leave."

Sidney realises he has been silent, ignoring her while he thinks things through, dreaming away. How much time had passed? It can't have been that long, can it?

"Don't, Amanda, what are you doing? Stay."

"How else am I supposed to behave? I just don't know what's come over you."

The waiter makes a little bow and retreats, not wanting to intervene. The food is on the table. Amanda is waiting for Sidney to speak in response. He looks at her and he can only see her brittle aggression.

"I need to change my life," he says. "I can't go on like this." He doesn't know if he should stand up or stay where he is. Manners dictate that he stands but he is too nervous to move.

"What is wrong with you, Sidney? What is this really about?"

"I've told you."

"Everything?"

He looks at the untouched melon, the abandoned mushrooms. Where to begin? Or, rather, how to continue?

* * *

She puts her handbag down on the chair and folds her arms, the gesture meaning nothing less than *Is that all you can say?*

"I'm sorry if I've upset you."

"If?"

Amanda picks up her handbag again. She appears to be annoyed with it as much as with Sidney. She shouldn't have put it down in the first place. The waiter returns to the table, anxious that Amanda is still standing and that a scene is developing in his well-mannered, and now silent, dining room. "Is everything all right, madam?"

"No, don't worry. I'm leaving. It's not the food that's disappointing. It's my 'friend'."

"I'll fetch your coat, madam."

Sidney thinks he can hear someone cough. He doesn't want to look up and see Amanda or anyone else. People might know them, recognise them, even, but if he doesn't see them he can pretend, like a little boy putting his hands over his eyes, that they're not there. A man clicks his fingers to summon the waiter. In a different situation, Amanda might remark how rude that was, but not now. These people might be friends of her parents. They could have heard everything.

The couple at the next-door table have ordered a bottle of champagne. It sits beside them in an ice bucket. Perhaps Sidney can concentrate on that? Have they been listening to all this? he wonders.

A bus passes outside, a blur of red, traffic and heat. He knows he should say something more but he cannot think what.

"I'm going," Amanda concludes. She looks down at their table of food and wine, avoiding all eye contact. "I do so hate a scene. Perhaps God would like the mushrooms?"

PART THREE

FAITH

CHAPTER TWENTY

Sidney's New Year resolution is to start the process of becoming a priest. He applies to be an ordinand at the theological college of Westcott House in Cambridge. The training will last eighteen months.

He secures a recommendation from his local priest, is briefed extensively by Rev Nev and prepares with an intensive burst of prayer and Bible study that removes him from his social life and reminds him of his finals. The application form asks him to concentrate on three things: the glory of God, the pain of the world and the renewal of the Church.

The interview is on the Feast of the Ascension. Sidney is given lunch, a tour of the grounds and attends evensong in a chapel that is more High Church than he has anticipated, with plenty of bells and smells. After singing one of his favourite hymns ("Alleluia, Sing to Jesus") with enough volume to demonstrate familiarity without drawing attention or showing off, he reflects on the lesson from St Paul's Letter to the Ephesians, expecting that he will be questioned on it later in the day: *I, therefore, the prisoner of the Lord, beseech you that ye walk worthy of the vocation wherewith ye are called*.

He is shown into the Principal's study, a book-lined room that's too dark, even in early summer, with low-wattage light bulbs that seem dimmer through the pipe and cigarette smoke that fills the air. There are two other clergy in attendance, sitting back in well-worn armchairs and holding clipboards with Sidney's application form in front of them. The atmosphere is a strained mixture of the relaxed and the intimidating and he wonders if the whole process is more like joining a club than applying to become an anointed intermediary between man and his Maker. The first thing he has to do, he realises, is to prove that he is the right sort of chap.

"When did you first think that you might like to take holy orders?" the Principal begins. "Is it a recent decision?"

Sidney fears that if he answers in the affirmative then this will lessen his chances of admission; on the other hand, he knows he has to speak the truth.

"It has been a growing realisation for the past few years," he replies, his voice still not quite steady. "I think it's also been a question of knowing when I might be ready. I've wanted to wait. I didn't want to rush things. So, it is a relatively recent decision, but I hope it's not an impetuous one."

"No," the Principal states firmly. "We wouldn't want that."

"At the same time, I think perhaps the feeling has always been with me. It seems inevitable."

"Does it now? And how can you be sure of that, Captain Chambers?"

"Because any other choice of career feels inadequate in comparison."

"And what makes becoming a priest so much more interesting than anything else, do you think?"

"Because we are called."

"And you are convinced that you *have* been called to do this?"

The Principal smiles and Sidney cannot tell if it is a smile of amusement, recognition or forgiveness.

"Yes. I am."

In the past, when he has sat exams, Sidney has known that there are either necessarily right or wrong answers, or tests of intellectual capability, but this interview is a matter of character as much as anything else, and he is not entirely sure what these men are looking for and what he might need to say to convince them that he is, indeed, the type of man they want. Nev has told him to "be himself" and "speak from the heart", but he feels exposed and even slightly fraudulent.

The youngest of the three men has an engaging friendliness that Sidney fears may be manufactured to lull him into making a mistake. "How would you describe your relationship with Jesus?" he asks.

"That's a hard question to answer . . ."

"It's why I'm asking it."

"I suppose it's one of awe, and gratitude. There's a sense I can never live up to his teaching, but I am filled with wonder when I realise it's there."

"Wonder?"

"Yes. It is the most astonishing event in the history of humanity."

"And which particular event do you have in mind? His birth? His teaching? His death on the Cross?"

"The Resurrection. I am thinking of 1 Corinthians 15, which is, for me, perhaps the most important chapter in the Bible."

"And if you were to preach on that passage, what would you say, Captain Chambers?"

The opportunity to speak about a specific text rather than his own character gives Sidney a moment of confidence in which he can expand his thoughts on the inspirational nature of St Paul's teaching and the thrill of the risen Christ. He remembers something Amanda told him when they were looking at Caravaggio's painting of *The Supper at Emmaus*, how the central figure was filled with an "inexorable serenity". There is power in the idea of triumph over death, and yet there is also a selfless grace. This is, perhaps, what a priest's life should be like, he suggests: a mixture of confidence, reassurance and generosity.

The more elderly interviewer, who is wearing a grey flannel, double-breasted, pinstriped suit that might be considered too flash for a cleric, writes the answer down with an expensive-looking fountain pen and returns to the subject of Sidney's character. Does he have the temperament to be a priest rather than an ordinary, God-fearing believer? What is the difference?

"Sacrifice," Sidney answers.

"And what will you be sacrificing, do you think?"

"Normality."

"You think that being a priest is abnormal, Captain Chambers?"

"I mean to say that a priest can't be like anyone else."

"And how is that defined?"

"By thinking of others before himself. By putting Christ first."

Sidney detects a smile as the suited man nods — *that's the right answer* — and he wonders how his interrogator might have responded to similar questions when he applied for theological college himself.

The Principal taps and refills his pipe. "What is the one quality, in particular, that you think a priest requires above all else?" he asks.

Rev Nev has warned Sidney about this question.

"Steadfastness," he replies.

"And where can you find reference to this in the Bible?"

"The same chapter: I Corinthians 15: 58. 'Therefore, my beloved brethren, be ye steadfast, unmoveable, always abounding in the work of the Lord . . .' As a priest, people have to be able to rely on you. You cannot let them down."

The clergy want to know more about Sidney's personality and relationships. What's he been reading? What are his hobbies and who are his friends? Is he romantically "unencumbered"? Has he thought of marriage?

"Not exactly."

"But it has crossed your mind?"

"I imagine myself being married to someone eventually, yes, of course."

"You just haven't met the right woman?" the younger cleric asks helpfully.

"Yes, I suppose it's that."

"Or there is someone and you can't make up your mind?"

"I thought that I had better sort this out first."

The Principal is about to write something down but lets his pen hover over the page before judgement. "Then we must be glad of your priorities." He puts the pen down again. "What will you do if we don't think you're suitable for the priesthood?"

"I'm not sure. Perhaps I'll just have to keep trying to show you that I am."

"You can't imagine an alternative career?"

"It's the only thing I want to do."

Sidney has never spent so long talking about himself. It so blurs the private with the professional that he is not sure if the questions are entirely fair. He is being asked to demonstrate a sincerity and seriousness of purpose and, at the same time, prove that he is neither naive nor lunatic.

He hears Robert's voice: *You're both*.

He knows his friend would think this ridiculous and he wonders how long he will be haunted by imaginary conversations in his head that come unbidden. Would a limited amount of forgetting be a betrayal, or might it simply enable him to survive and get on with the rest of his life?

The Principal concludes the interview with a final, inevitable, question. "Is there anything you'd like to ask us, Captain Chambers?"

"I'm sorry if I haven't given you all the right answers," Sidney replies.

"That is not a question."

"What is the most helpful prayer you know?"

"Apart from the Lord's Prayer?" The Principal considers his response. "I think it must be St Anselm. 'O Lord my God, teach my heart this day where and how to see you, where and how to find you . . .' Do you know it?"

"Thank you," Sidney answers. "I do. I shall remember it on the train back to London."

A masterstroke, says Robert. *Well done. Absolute genius. You're in*.

Sidney walks out into Jesus Lane and follows the road up towards the station. It's a warm summer afternoon, with students bicycling back to their colleges, shoppers heading home, and a few picnickers still out on Parker's Piece. One day, Sidney thinks, people such as these might be his parishioners.

He boards the train to London, takes out a copy of *The Times* to finish the crossword and says his prayers as he promised. When he finally gets back home to Highgate he finds that his family are remarkably uninterested in what he has been through.

"All go well?" his father asks without quite waiting for an answer. "England are 180 for 7. They'll have to bat a lot better in the second innings."

"I've got some plaice on special offer from the fishmonger," says Iris Chambers. "It'll make a nice treat. Jennifer should be home soon."

There's a letter waiting from Lady Kendall. She has written to say that Sidney is welcome to visit at any time and they look forward to hearing more about his intriguing "news". She mentions Amanda, saying that her daughter is hoping to get a job at the National Gallery. Art has always been her first love.

Ten days later he is accepted by the theological college ("We expected no less," his father observes) and he writes to Amanda to say that he'd love to see her. She can come up to Cambridge any time she likes. He keeps the tone friendly and neutral. He doesn't want to apologise and he doesn't want to say that he misses her, but he tries to be kind, even Christian. They could have a bun at Fitzbillies, he suggests, take a punt on the river when it is warmer, go to the museum. They have some very good English paintings that are slap bang in the middle of her field of expertise — but she probably knows that. He doesn't want to trouble her, but he sends his love.

There is no reply.

CHAPTER TWENTY-ONE

Westcott House was founded in 1881 to provide training in theology and the devotional life for graduates preparing for ordination. The buildings have an unpretentious, mock-medieval feel to them but need young men to give them life. As well as concentrated bursts of Bible study, Sidney attends lectures and seminars on Christian ethics, the Church and the law, the meaning and celebration of the liturgy, Church history, and pastoral care. There are singing lessons once a week, and the ordinands are encouraged to create their own musical theatre, revues and concert parties.

They eat together as if they are in an officers' mess, but the men are divided between those who have seen war and those who have not. Sidney knows that the ministry has to be open to all, but he is surprised by the unquestioning acceptance of his colleagues to pastoral instruction. He can't see how his more naive contemporaries, who have never fought in battle, will ever be ready to counsel the dying or comfort the bereaved. They are a long way from the quiet but practical holiness of Rev Nev. Instead they behave as if they have been admitted to a secret club, chatting confidently away with in-jokes and knowing looks.

Sidney had expected seriousness, scholarship and ascetic discipline, but Westcott House is more of a home to gentleman amateurs. When he tentatively confesses to this anxiety, one of his tutors remarks that the word "amateur" with its root in the Latin verb "to love", *amo, amas, amat*, should hold no embarrassment. They are all "amateurs" who love what they are doing. The "professional priests" full of certainty and efficiency are the ones that need watching.

Sidney isn't so sure.

The tutors have their own interests, ranging from lepidoptery to jazz and model railways. One of them, Simon Opie, like a latter-day St Francis, keeps his own aviary. But there is a quality of camp, even an affectation, in some of the ceremonial behaviour; so much so that one of his colleagues, a no-nonsense Lancastrian who has worked in a bank and served with the Royal Artillery, rails against "southern effeminates" during a lesson on clerical vestments. Some of the students get the giggles while practising their processional walking and he shouts out: "This is not a bloody pantomime. Christ didn't die on the Cross for this."

Freddie Hawthorne would be more at home here than he is. Sidney remembers being with him at his parents' house in Hertfordshire and how, as they proudly showed off the roses and the apple orchard, his friend had whispered, "I'm the only pansy in the garden." Cyril and Daphne Hawthorne know nothing of their son's other life.

The training at Westcott House might have been cleansed of the Victorian patriotism of his childhood, but Sidney wonders what alternative is being put in its place. There are woolly dialogues about the nature of grace and the workings of the holy spirit, but there doesn't seem to be much thought given to what kind of country Britain might become in the future; how the clergy can help build a better society, or restore a sense of selfless nobility and moral ambition to a damaged world.

Sidney makes a special study of the Book of Job and tries to address the problem of pain. How can a loving God have given up the character of Job, a man of blameless life, rooted in the fear of God, to the wiles of Satan? How could he have allowed such an avalanche of misery?

Suffering, he argues in seminars with Opie, is a test of the quality of a man's religion. If there is a point at which it will cease to stand the strain, then it is hollow and without value. Religion, to be worth anything, has to be worth everything. It is only worthwhile if it enables human beings to endure to the end.

While impressed by his dedication, and appreciating the earnest nature of his endeavours, Simon Opie worries that Sidney is in danger of becoming too serious. He has to understand not only the problem of suffering but also the joy of worship and the importance of praise. He should recite the psalms. Sing with a glad voice. Give thanks.

Opie introduces him to the delights of jazz, and Sidney finds himself relishing the music of his namesake, Sidney Bechet, which, he is told, has its own improvisational theology.

"You take a theme and 'riff' on it," Opie explains. "Think of a sermon as a solo. As long as you get back to where you started from, you can go anywhere. Listen to 'Preacher Man Blues' or '*Si tu vois ma mère*'. Get the joy and energy, the celebration and surprise."

Sidney thinks that, if he did this, he might be shedding too much of his old life, becoming almost unrecognisable, denying past sorrows, but his tutor reminds him of Cardinal Newman's words. *To live is to change, and to become perfect is to have changed often*.

In any case, there is plenty of the old life to come hurtling back into the new. One cold February evening, Freddie Hawthorne arrives after Vespers and insists that Sidney accompany him to the pub. He suggests the Mitre in Bridge Street because he finds it amusingly appropriate.

"I can imagine you as Bishop already, Sidney. You suit purple. What'll you have? It's my treat." He's clearly had a few already.

"I can't drink, Freddie."

"Why ever not?"

"It's Lent."

"Oh, you don't need to worry about that, do you?"

"Yes, I do."

"And who will notice?"

"God."

"He gets everywhere these days."

"That is rather the point of him. But come on, Freddie. You're not just here to say hello. You came to tell me something. What's troubling you?"

"It's Henry." Freddie drops his voice. They are still at the bar, and even though it is noisy enough for them not to be heard, he leans in to be sure. "He's left me." He raises his voice as the barman approaches. "Just have a pint, will you?"

"I'll have a tomato juice. You have the pint."

"And I'll have a whisky to go with it. I can't tempt you, Sidney? You could just have a wee dram?"

"If I can't do this, I can't do anything."

A couple of students, newly in love perhaps, vacate a corner table at the front of the pub and leave in one another's arms. Then, once the two friends have settled down with their drinks, Freddie continues.

"I've put up with quite a few of Henry's little episodes in the past, but now he says he's fallen in love and there's nothing he can do to stop it. It isn't love at all, it's lust, and he could have avoided it perfectly well. It's just that he doesn't want to. He's always been able to do whatever he wants, the selfish bastard, and now I've been cast out, just like Adam and Eve. We can't even be friends as the new boy is 'jealous'."

"You can understand that, Freddie."

"Jealous? I should bloody well hope he is. He'd be better off working down at the docks than in the theatre. The boy's only nineteen. The age gap must be nearly thirty years. Imagine that."

Sidney declines to point out that it has been at least fifteen with Freddie. "Do people know about it?"

"I know about it. That's what matters. Henry's pretending this boy, Frank, is his nephew. I don't expect anyone will believe it, but he's so well connected that people aren't going to ask any questions — at least they're not going to do so in public. But I can't imagine that boy passing muster when the going gets posh."

"So, you could wait until Frank's limitations become clear?"

"I could. But I'm not going to be all nicey-nicey and take Henry back when it's over. I've done that before. You can forgive a man once but if he keeps straying then he's telling you something. I could kill him. In fact, I could kill both of them."

"I don't think you mean that."

"I do, actually: I've stolen Henry's duelling pistol. I've been thinking about it quite a lot."

"Don't be ridiculous."

"But I am ridiculous."

Sidney looks round to check that they can't be overheard. There is enough noise for privacy. Two men at the next-door table are playing backgammon, others are standing at the bar and talking about their rowing training. "You need to give it back, Freddie. The pistol's not yours and it's dangerous."

"I know it's foolhardy. That's the point. I want to give Henry a few sleepless nights — just like the ones he's given me. It's only right."

"Only right? What on earth do you mean? Two wrongs don't make a right."

"Is that what they're teaching you, Sidney? No wonder your course takes so long. Can I really not tempt you to a proper drink? I think I need another."

"No, you can't, Freddie. You've said and drunk enough. How much did you have before we came out?"

"Only three or four whiskies. I'm fine. You know me: soft heart, hard head. It's you we need to worry about, Mr Goody Two-Shoes. How are all your new friends?"

"Rather too serious and a bit too sure of themselves, if you must know."

"I suppose that's only to be expected. It's a rum business, religion. All doom and gloom."

"No, it's not, Freddie, it's quite the opposite. It's sublimely optimistic: the salvation of mankind, eternal life."

"My definition of eternity is the time the bus takes to get from the railway station to my aunt's house in Lacock. That's a disappointment, let me tell you. No lays and precious few cocks."

Two years ago, Sidney would have laughed indulgently, but in his new life he cannot engage in army banter. "Promise me you won't do anything stupid?"

"I promise I won't do anything stupid — without consulting you first."

"You are impossible, Freddie."

"That's what Henry says."

"Perhaps that's why he's ended it?"

"Don't you dare take his side."

"I'm not. Sometimes it helps if you see the other person's point of view, that's all."

"Honestly, Sidney, this religion of yours is an absolute disaster. How can anyone survive such selflessness? No wonder they got rid of Jesus."

"They didn't get rid of him, Freddie. He sacrificed himself and rose again. He lives now."

"Well, where is he then? Perhaps *he* could have a word with Henry?"

"I don't know, Freddie. I imagine he's busy with bigger problems."

"Bastard."

"Now then . . ."

"Well, he probably is when you think about it. Joseph wasn't the father, was he?"

Sidney returns to Westcott just in time for Compline. He kneels down in the chapel and prays, trying to calm down, asking God for patience. Even though Freddie is his friend and in trouble, he is irritated.

Afterwards Simon Opie tells him he has to "embrace interruption". He must be glad to see people even if he is in the middle of something important.

"But how will I ever get anything done?" he asks.

"An interruption may be God's way of telling you that you are concentrating on the wrong thing."

"Well, it's still bloody irritating. I find myself feeling angry and resentful."

"You are allowed to be angry with God," his tutor continues. "He doesn't mind. He expects it. It's how we find out who we are."

CHAPTER TWENTY-TWO

Sir Cecil and Lady Kendall ask if Sidney can come down to London to commemorate Robert's birthday. Even though it is a Sunday, they hope he might be able to get a train after the morning service in time for a late lunch. He can hardly refuse but thinks he should telephone Amanda to see if she minds.

"It's all right now," she says. "I've calmed down. I can hardly forget that you were Robert's best friend — even if you haven't always been mine. It's taken almost a year but we can't be on 'no-speaks' for ever. Will you be coming in a dog collar?"

"Not yet."

"Have you tried one on? What do you look like?"

"It's a little more sober than army uniform. But just as uncomfortable. It brings your neck out in a rash if you're not careful."

"I'd have thought the word 'rash' to be rather appropriate for a man like you, Chambers — all those impulsive decisions."

"I like to consider all my judgements with care, Amanda."

"I remember. I'll be interested to see if you've changed."

"I'm still the same old Chambers."

"I hope so. If you are, then I'll know what to expect. And if you're not, then heaven help you."

Robert's room still looks as if he has just left it. Sidney remembers his friend reminding everyone on his twenty-first birthday that he was born "a leaping" and so he was not yet six years old.

Then the battlefield.

Do you think we'll make our next birthdays? It's a leap year so I'll be six. Still too young for anyone to propose to me. Not that there's any chance of a woman round here.

There are fresh spring flowers by the bed, books Robert might have read but never did. A few more photographs in silver frames have been added to the display.

Lady Kendall says that she changes the sheets once a month. "I find it comforting. Sometimes I even have a lie-down."

Sidney sees there is a white towel and flannel laid out for a visitor. In Westcott House, they are just about to start their preparations for Easter. It reminds him of the linen cloth left in the tomb at the time of the Resurrection. The calm and the neatness; leaving things ready to be returned to.

Lady Kendall continues: "I want the room to be serene. I like to feel that Robert can come back and that we will always be prepared for him. I hope you don't think that's foolish, only . . ."

She stops.

"Forgive me . . ."

"There's nothing to forgive. You loved your son. You always will."

"Yes, I will, but . . ."

Again, she breaks off. Sidney does not know whether to help out or let the silence fall. He looks at Amanda, whose smile assures him that all this is perfectly normal.

Her mother starts up again. "It's difficult for both of us, isn't it? Every time I know that you are coming, Sidney. I feel such trepidation. I'm grateful but worried. I can't . . ."

"Explain? You don't have to."

"I rather think I do, if you don't mind. Then at least we can be clear. Seeing you is a reminder that Robert is no longer here. I know I don't need 'reminding'. Also, perhaps, in another life, you could have been my son, part of the family. But, of course, you're not . . ."

"No."

"And never can be. Forgive me if that sounds harsh. I know how awkward it must be for you. Mr Hawthorne told me how courageous you were in battle. People probably forget that, especially now that you're about to become a clergyman."

"Freddie's been to see you?"

"I invited him. We're firm friends these days. He was very fond of Robert too, you know."

"We all were."

"All the bright young things together . . . you 'lived, felt dawn, saw sunset glow' . . . isn't that how the poem goes . . . I can't remember how it ends. It's good of you to come."

"I can visit whenever you want, Lady Kendall. Or I'll stop if it's too upsetting . . ."

"No," she replies quickly. "Don't ever stop. I'd rather have the pain than nothing. It keeps him alive. If you live, in a strange kind of way, I can still believe that Robert lives too. I know that's —"

"Enough, Mother." says Amanda.

". . . foolish."

Even though it is a cold, dark afternoon, and they are due a frost that night, Amanda wants to get out of the house and walk in the Chelsea Physic Garden. They can see how the hellebores and crocuses are coming on.

Sidney takes her arm as they cross Belgrave Square, but switches every time they have negotiated a crossing or find themselves on a different pavement. He must stay on the outside of her, and he does this automatically, but after a while Amanda cannot help but comment.

"Sometimes, good manners are rather absurd, don't you think? I can manage perfectly well. It's not a dance. You don't need to keep your sword arm free."

"It's what your mother would expect from me."

"But I'm not my mother, am I? You don't need to satisfy her. You need to please me. And I want to talk in a way that's free of etiquette and expectation. As pals."

"And as we always do."

"I hope so. Just as long as you don't deliver any more bombshells."

"No, I'm not planning on any more of them just yet. I think you're safe."

Amanda tells him how she spent New Year on the Isle of Skye. She needed an escape after the claustrophobia of Christmas. The Kendall family used to holiday there every summer. A local fisherman took the children out to catch mackerel. He taught Robert how to gut them, make beach fires, and find secret caves along the coast from Elgol. It was the time when her family had been at its happiest, Amanda admits, and whenever she is depressed or in despair, she knows that she can go back to Skye and find herself again. The mountains make her feel small and yet they are consoling. They have permanence, a sense of the eternal. Is that what Sidney's faith is like? she wonders.

"Perhaps."

"I'm still trying to understand what took you away from me. Sometimes I think I've lost you as much as I've lost Robert."

"You haven't, Amanda. I've come. I'm here, aren't I?"

"But can't you see? You are not the man I used to know. Sometimes, when we're talking, it's like speaking to the man in the moon. Despite what you say, I can't help feeling that there are two different versions of you, the old and the new."

"Everyone changes."

"But the new Chambers has this invisible friend with him all the time that he has to consult before he can declare an opinion."

"It's not like that at all."

"What is it like then?"

"It's hard to describe. Perhaps, if I could do that, it would be less of a mystery; and the mystery is part of the attraction. Trying to solve the question of what life's really about."

"Are you enjoying it?"

"It's not easy. And it's hard to explain to people who regard it all as a bit of a joke."

"I don't think that, Chambers. You're being unfair. I'm just not clear that what you are undertaking is really 'you'."

"But what if I think that it is — that I have found myself at last? This is what faith is about. You lose yourself in order to find yourself."

"I'm always rather distrustful of people who have discovered themselves. They become so self-assured that they're quite incapable of listening to anyone else."

"Then I'll try to be different."

They sit down on a wooden bench at the end of a gravel path, with a view back over the garden. For a moment, Sidney remembers being next to Amanda in the National Gallery before he finally decided to become a priest. They are in the same configuration but now, outside, it is so much colder.

"I suppose I should say that you don't have to see me if it upsets you," he begins once more.

"You've already said that to Mummy. Are you trying to get out of coming to see us altogether?"

"Not at all."

"There's no escape, you know."

"What do you mean?"

"You are *in my life*. You *are* family, despite what my mother tells you."

Before Sidney can reply, a lady in a scarf and with bright red lipstick comes out and warns them that the gardens will be closing soon. Sidney dislikes her for interrupting but is charming and polite. As a result, they can have fifteen more minutes.

"I have been thinking about it quite a lot," Amanda continues. "How much is your decision to become a priest connected with Robert's death? Mummy's convinced it's some kind of atonement, that there's more to know, but you've seen how she goes about everything."

"It's not just about that."

"But it wouldn't have happened if Robert was still alive. I can't imagine that he would have let you become a priest."

"Perhaps not. But he isn't alive, and now I can't envisage anything different. I'm sorry to put it so brutally."

"You do still think of him, don't you?"

"Every day."

"I'm glad I'm not the only one."

"He'll always be with us."

He thinks of putting his hand on hers. It would be a brotherly, or even a priestly, thing to do but Amanda keeps talking before he can give it any further thought.

"Or even between us. But, perhaps, no matter how much we try to avoid each other, Chambers, or whatever you do to me, and whatever I do or say, I think you'll find we're going to be stuck with each other for ever and ever."

"You make it sound like a hardship."

"Then you must make it easier. Perhaps we're both running away. I look at art. You turn to God. We try to find something to counteract the horror."

"Beauty for ashes . . ."

"What?"

"It's from the Book of Isaiah."

They stand up without saying anything more, knowing that it is time to go. After they have walked a few yards back towards the entrance, Sidney risks a correction. He doesn't want their relationship to be one in which he can never be anything less than guilty.

"I'm sorry if you think that I don't always say the right thing."

"You don't. But I forgive you, Chambers."

"Although you could say that we are both to blame when we have our little differences."

"Is that what you call them?"

"I wouldn't want to exaggerate, Amanda."

"Is this your attempt at teasing me?"

"It's not my attempt. I am actually teasing you and yet I am also being serious at the same time."

"Are you implying that there are times when I don't say the right thing either?"

"I'm not implying it. I'm saying it out loud."

"That's very foolhardy, Chambers."

"I like to live dangerously."

"Not with me, you don't. The rules are very simple. You once promised to look after me. I remember that you even used the word '*always*'. Don't tell me you wish you hadn't?"

"No, I don't. But 'looking after you' is not the same as 'agreeing with everything you say'."

"Is it not? It's certainly quicker."

"No, Amanda, it's not."

"Never mind. Now that you're a priest —"

"Not yet, I'm not."

"Don't interrupt. Now that you're nearly a priest you have to keep your promises. You also have to forgive people's faults. Not that I have too many of them, I'll have you know."

"I wouldn't be too sure of that either, Kendall."

"Please don't feel the need to point them out."

"I won't."

"Good."

"As long as you refrain from drawing attention to mine."

"I don't need to refer to them, Chambers. Sometimes your faults are so blindingly obvious you can see them from the moon."

"As bad as that? Have you ever been to the moon?"

"And back, as a matter of fact."

She walks him to the Tube at Sloane Square and holds out her cheek to be kissed. He does this lightly and proficiently and returns to his parents in Highgate. As he heads up Dartmouth Hill he remembers Robert Kendall as a child and their respective families playing a makeshift game of cricket in the park. They brought their own stumps and, after he had been bowled out, Robert refused to walk, insisting that his friend had been guilty of a no-ball. He couldn't believe that he, himself, had made a mistake, that he had failed to make a connection, and he did not give up his bat until his father had made him do so.

Had Amanda been there at the time? Sidney thinks he can picture her now, the little sister crouching down behind the wicket, but perhaps he is imagining it?

He rings the doorbell of his family home before he quite realises he has arrived. He has been dreaming. Now it is time to wake up and be a dutiful son to his parents; a son who, at the very least, is still alive.

CHAPTER TWENTY-THREE

One way of making his friendship with Amanda a little more balanced and carefree, Sidney thinks, is to take her to a show in the West End. Freddie knows one of the actors in a revival of J. B. Priestley's *Dangerous Corner* who gets them cheap seats. They meet in the stalls bar of the Lyric Theatre just before the matinee.

"It's supposed to be wonderful," says Freddie. "Apparently, it changes your whole attitude to family and friendship over time."

"I'm not sure I want my attitude changed," Amanda replies.

"But it's boring to remain the same, don't you think?"

"Not if one becomes a completely different person. You have to replace all your friends, for a start."

Sidney chips in. "Or stick with those who still understand you."

"No sermons, please, Chambers."

"I was thinking, Sidney, only the other day, how you're such a loss to the theatre," Freddie continues. "It gives you all the delights of not having to do a proper job without the tedious business of faith."

"Faith is not tedious."

"Responsibility, then . . ."

"I prefer to call it 'purpose'."

"Call it what you like, darling, it's still costume and performance."

Freddie's playful mood is interrupted by the appearance in the bar of his former lover, Henry Mortimer, with his "nephew" Frank.

"Oh, my giddy aunt and bloody God, excuse me."

The new arrivals are dressed in sharply tailored grey flannel suits, with artfully draped scarves that serve no purpose other than decoration. They have spring flowers in their buttonholes and sport toning ties in salmon pink and pale yellow. Frank has sleek hair, pale skin and is wearing varnish on his manicured nails.

Henry is charming but keen to ensure that they are all sitting in different parts of the theatre (he always has an aisle in the stalls). Just before they part he says, in what is meant to be an aside, "I got your note, Freddie. There was no need to say what you did."

"I think you'll find that I will say whatever I like, Henry duckie."

"Then much good may it do."

Sidney buys a programme while Freddie orders the interval drinks. Amanda says she hopes the play isn't going to be too long. She has a dinner that night and needs to go home and change first. "That couldn't have been the man's nephew, could it?" she asks. "He's from the wrong side of the tracks, don't you think? The boy must be out of his depth."

"I think Freddie behaved rather well under the circumstances."

"That's probably because he hasn't had anything to drink yet."

"He can get rather oversensitive, I must say. But that's partly why I love him. He wears his heart on his sleeve."

"Unlike you, Sidney."

"I don't think that's very fair. If you ask me something, I tell you."

"Perhaps I shouldn't have to ask?"

"Here we are." Freddie returns with some white wine to "cheer us on our way. Theatre's so much better after a sharpener."

"What did you say to Henry?" Sidney asks. "I didn't quite catch it."

"Nothing too melodramatic."

"That means it was, at the very least, dramatic."

"Honestly, I didn't expect to see the two of them here. Perhaps they think they're less likely to meet anyone they know in the afternoon, but Henry abhors matinees. He always says they're full of old people from the country."

"Not guilty on both counts," says Amanda.

"And they're so much slower on the laughs. Not that there'll be many in this, I imagine."

People start to take their seats. "They're certainly looking very stylish," says Sidney.

"Honestly, I could kill them both."

"For pity's sake, Freddie. Stop it."

"It would be so easy to do it. Shut them up for good."

"I hope you gave the duelling pistol back?"

Amanda puts her hand on Freddie's arm. "You've got a gun?"

"I know everyone thinks I'm being a right royal pain in the you-know-where, but I really could kill them."

"Oh, Freddie, you don't mean that, do you? This is even more thrilling than a play."

"No, it's not," says Sidney. "Keep your voices down. What do you mean by 'everyone', Freddie? How many people have you told?"

"It doesn't matter. Who cares?"

"I care . . ."

"Why can't you and Henry just talk to each other?" Amanda asks.

"We're long past reasonable behaviour. I have been humiliated and I refuse to let Henry behave as if nothing has happened. We were together for six years. Not that anyone's aware of that. We don't live in your world, Amanda, where everyone knows who's in love with who and what each other's prospects are . . ."

"In Sidney's case, there are none, now that God's got to him."

"Don't be rude," her friend replies.

"I was joking."

"No, you weren't."

"Stop squabbling," says Freddie. "I'm doing the talking. In my world, because everything has to be discreet, people can behave like absolute bastards and get away scot-free. No one ever knows *what's* going on."

"Scot-free," says Sidney. "I wonder about the origins of that phrase . . ."

Amanda picks up Freddie's point. "That can just as easily happen with us."

"Not really. Your parents and all your friends get involved and then there's a society wedding. With people who are considered 'abnormal', it's all vile and underhand, no matter how much we try to pretend that it's not."

Amanda touches Freddie's arm. "Has it been horrid?"

"There are moments when I think I'll never get over it — and there are other times when I think I've been such a fool. It's dreadful how a life can be ambushed by love."

"Things may seem impossible," Amanda replies. "But we're all young enough to get over a disastrous love affair, aren't we? Everything changes over time."

"I don't know. They say time heals all wounds but I think they just fester."

Sidney is intrigued by a play that involves acting out the first scene twice; once when Robert Caplan asks a series of direct questions about his brother's suicide — with terrible consequences — and the second when he decides not to "disturb the truth" but "let the sleeping dog lie". He bets that Amanda and Freddie will delight in a discussion of the nature of secrets, truth and revelation afterwards.

Back outside, in Shaftesbury Avenue, Freddie asks if they'd like a snifter to recover from "that terrible encounter and that gloomy play". They climb a set of stairs in Dean Street to arrive in a private drinking club with four or five tables, an upright piano, indifferent food and a well-stocked bar. Little attention is paid to anything other than drink. People sit round bitching about recent exhibitions, dreadful theatre shows and what might have been if only some bastard publisher hadn't made the wrong decision and the BBC wasn't staffed by Oxbridge arseholes. Freddie, like many of the male clientele, has been given a girl's name, *Winnie*, derived from Wini*fred*.

"All right, Winne?"

"Good to see you, Jemima. Keeping well?"

"Keeping swell and making hell."

It's a familiar exchange. They pass a man in a bright green floppy hat and velvet smoking jacket who is drinking a brandy and eating what appears to be a tin of cold ravioli. Sidney cannot help but notice his nose. It is like a giant strawberry.

The hostess brings them the standard house cocktail with gin, vermouth and pastis. Amanda tells Sidney they should make the most of it.

"You won't be able to come to a place like this after you've been ordained."

"I don't know about that. Why wouldn't I?"

"You'll have to be on your guard everywhere. Your reputation will be sacrosanct."

"And sinners like us," Freddie adds, "will be ruthlessly discarded in your new life. Cheers! I will be Falstaff to your Henry the fifth."

"You're not fat enough."

"And I shall be Mistress Quickly," Amanda cuts in, "although I can't remember anything about her."

Freddie leans back in his chair with his hands on his hips and bellows: "'Dost thou think, because thou art virtuous, there shall be no more cakes and ale?' Actually, I think that's Sir Toby Belch in *Twelfth Night*. Such a wonderful name, 'Belch', don't you think? I wish I could play him."

"You're far too young," Amanda replies. "And much too beautiful."

Freddie puts one hand to his face in a coy eighteenth-century gesture. "You think I'm beautiful? Why, madam, I thank you. Please be so good as to accompany me in my chaise through the park this afternoon."

"But, good sir, my reputation . . ."

"I will even show you my china . . ."

"Women of quality can never have enough good china —"

"Oh, stop it," Sidney interrupts. "This is nonsense. I shall never be rid of you both."

"Charming," says Freddie.

"I mean that with the greatest affection. I'll always want your company."

"Of course you will, Chambers. We only want to make sure you don't become an impossible prig."

"I don't expect everyone to appreciate the seriousness of what I am doing."

"We understand you perfectly well." Amanda giggles. "After all, you go on about it often enough . . ."

"Only because you ask."

"We're being polite. We know how you appreciate good manners."

"Good manners do not include ridicule."

Freddie is tempted to go further but can see that Sidney has had enough. "We just don't want you to lose your sense of humour, Sidney. It's what Robert would say if he was here. 'Imagine, my best friend becoming a bore. I can't think of anything worse.' "

The mention of Robert sobers them all up.

"I will try to remain entertaining," Sidney replies, "and I will always love you both. That's all I can say."

"And we will help you to keep that promise," says Freddie, "no matter how irritating you find us. Let's have another drink. This is all going so terribly well, don't you think?"

CHAPTER TWENTY-FOUR

Before he finishes his training, Sidney is asked if he wants to take part in a service of post-war reconciliation near Monte Cassino. Representatives from all sides of the conflict are to attend a ceremony to commemorate the fallen and reflect on the creation of a new Europe. Rev Nev offers to go too but Freddie Hawthorne says he never wants to visit Italy again either in this life or, if there is one, the next.

They proceed by boat and train. It takes two days to get there and three to get back, crossing the Channel from Dover to Calais and then on to Paris, where they change stations and board for Turin. Sidney had travelled up through Italy before he went to Trieste but has not witnessed the devastation and the battlefields from this, and even the last war: Amiens, Flanders Fields and the Somme. As they enter the Vichy region, he sees graffiti all over a house, accusing its inhabitants of collaboration. He wonders what it might have been like to have been a priest in such a place; the secrets he would have had to have held, the compromises and sacrifices he would have made, the people he might have needed to hide or protect.

In Turin, they switch trains once more, moving down towards Milan, Florence and Rome. Italy itself doesn't seem to have changed since Sidney worked in Trieste. The main roads have been cleared, but what strikes him now are the piles of abandoned rubble and machinery; the rusted jeeps and windowless factories; the sight of people sitting outside their homes doing nothing but watch travellers pass, as if they have already decided that the task of cleaning up a country is too much for them.

After all the ruined landscapes they've seen, the cemetery at Minturno is surprisingly trim. The newly laid grass and headstones are arranged in perfect rows, which either means that the corpses have been moved from the bomb craters and foxholes or that there are, in truth, no bodies in the places that have been assigned to them, but only empty spaces.

Sidney decides not to ask too many questions in front of people who have made the journey from England with flowers and rose bushes and the memorials they want to leave by the graves of their loved ones, but he feels that, even though the dead have been remembered, there is no sense of the terrors of war, no images of destruction, and that the horror is, if anything, remote.

Only the number of victims, this great assembly of the dead, has the power to shock.

He stands by Robert's grave and looks at the simple headstone.

LT R. W. KENDALL
2ND BATTALION SCOTS GUARDS
26 JANUARY 1944

He prays for those whom God has gathered "from the storm of war to the peace of his presence": *May that same peace calm our fears, bring justice to all peoples, and establish harmony among the nations . . .*

During the service, the survivors pray for reconciliation in their own words, in English, French, German and Italian. They remember the dead with a minute of silence. The Last Post sounds.

After the ceremony Sidney goes back to the monastery at Subiaco. Catherine has long gone, but he sits in the garden on the bench where they talked together four years ago and where, perhaps, he first decided to change his life. He should find her and thank her, he tells himself, bring her back a pressed flower or herb: rosemary for remembrance.

The same tall, deaf gardener, with the stoop and the floppy straw hat, is watering a row of red geraniums. He turns, stares and breaks into a slow smile. He either remembers Sidney or is pretending to do so.

"*Signore, vecchio amico, sei tornato*."

His mixture of Italian and English is convoluted but Sidney understands words from Latin: *pace, speranza, la remissione, amore*.

The rose garden is, as it always has been, untouched by war, with thyme and camomile between the paving stones; lavender, basil, rosemary and oregano edging the beds; bay, orange and eucalyptus trees in the distance. Sidney wonders how long it will take the surrounding landscape to recover from the ravages of battle and find a similar serenity; to heal itself with grass, vine and olive grove and become a place of pilgrimage once more.

He listens to the bees as they gather the last of the pollen from the orange blossom, finishing the work of the day, returning to the walls and roofs and hives they know well, reproducing without courtship or lovemaking, renewing themselves in their wax palaces, unaware of war or death.

That night, over a bowl of spaghetti with ragu, some rough bread and rather too much red wine from a Castelforte vineyard, Sidney tells Rev Nev that he has been humbled by the experience of returning to Italy. At the same time, he isn't sure if he can ever be a good enough priest.

"Perhaps you won't be, Sidney, and you may have to accept that. But then none of us are good enough in the end. We all fall short. That is part of being a Christian, acknowledging our failings and our weaknesses."

"It's a bit depressing, isn't it, to have to face up to all of that?"

"Listen, Sidney, how can anyone measure whether they are successful in any chosen career? A businessman might have a large house in the country, with a happy family and a tennis court, but will there ever be a time when he feels he can stop making money? A surgeon might think of the lives he has saved, but he is more likely to remember those he has lost. A cricketer, to refer to your favourite sport, might recall a very fine hundred, but will always regret the times he's got out. Our failures gnaw away at us, Sidney; but without our setbacks there can be no desire for success."

"So I've heard."

"Can you swim?" Rev Nev asks.

"I can. You were there when I nearly drowned."

"I suppose it is a rhetorical question."

"It didn't sound like one."

The patron pours them a limoncello on the house. And he brings them a little almond cake as well. The two men don't need to worry about the bill, he says, and he shakes them by the hand.

"I think there is a similarity," Nev continues, "between faith and buoyancy. I met a man the other day who has spent part of his life teaching adults to swim. He found it very frustrating at the beginning. Those in his charge are so impatient to succeed early on that they fail to understand the first simple rule of staying afloat.

"He pointed out that when you *can* swim it is difficult to sink. You have to make a deliberate effort to go down underwater. But many of his pupils started to drown. He would show them the strokes, get them to practise holding on to a rail, give them tips about breathing and tell them to launch out. Immediately they would sink. It seemed perverse. But then, he says, he realised what was happening. In their anxiety to get the strokes right, in the concentration on what their arms and legs were doing, the trainees would tense their bodies, and through this tension they were denying themselves the support of the natural buoyancy of the water around them."

"I see."

"You have to let the buoyancy of faith do its work, Sidney."

"Yes, I understand."

"Do not resist it. Do not fight against it. So many things will keep you afloat."

"Yes, yes, yes, I did get the metaphor, Nev . . ."

"Trust in the Lord, Sidney. Remember the words of the responses. 'I believe and trust in him.' No one ever says this is going to be easy. That's why it's called 'faith'. It's not a science. You have to give yourself up to it."

"I suppose I'm still scared of sinking."

"You can't cling to your former life."

"Perhaps I feel it's my lifebelt."

"Well, in reality it may be the chain that weighs you down. Persevere in the Lord. May he bless you, and keep you, as he has always done."

Keep you? Then why didn't he keep Robert?

Sidney knows that both his faith and his reason are limited, and that there are things beyond his comprehension. When he wrote to the Kendalls after the death of Robert he said that *a great purpose is being fulfilled that is beyond our understanding*.

He may still believe this, or even hope to believe it, but he is not sure he can teach it.

CHAPTER TWENTY-FIVE

After his son's return to London, Alec Chambers insists that Sidney join him on a trip to see the Australians at the Oval. It is Don Bradman's last game before his retirement and neither of them has seen him bat properly. The great man was dismissed for a duck in the previous game they attended, at Cambridge in 1934. Now it is time to make amends.

It is a damp morning. Sawdust covers large patches of sodden turf and play is delayed until midday. England win the toss and decide to bat. Sidney's father thinks this is an odd decision.

"In these conditions? It's mad. They should have had a bowl."

"Perhaps they're expecting more rain?"

"It rather lessens our chances of seeing Bradman, I'm afraid."

However, England are dismissed in two and a half hours for a paltry 52, and after the Australians have put on 117 in response, Sid Barnes is caught behind. And so, just before six in the evening, the crowd rises to give Don Bradman a standing ovation as he comes out to bat. The England players doff their caps, shake his hand, and give him three cheers as he arrives at the wicket for the final time.

Alec Chambers is one of the last men to sit down as Eric Hollies, the England spinner, prepares for his first delivery. "This is going to be one of the finest moments in any sport that we will ever see."

The first ball is a leg-break that the batsman pushes away. The next is a good length. Bradman comes forward to defend. The ball turns past the edge and hits the middle and off stumps.

That's it. The greatest cricketer in the world is out. He has lasted two balls. No one can quite believe what has happened. There is silence, then applause.

"Honestly, Sidney," says Alec Chambers, "we've jinxed him. We are surely the only people to have watched him twice, only to see him get out for a duck both times. It's ridiculous. Do you think it's you or me?"

"It could be both of us."

"Or fate or, I suppose, an act of God."

"No, Dad, it's an act of bowling. A googly rather than a leg-break. You can't call that dismissal an 'act of God'."

"Call it whatever you like, it's a damned shame."

They watch the final overs of the game as the light dwindles. There is little tension now that Bradman has gone. Alec Chambers remembers to ask about Sidney's trip to Italy — he has forgotten amidst all the cricketing excitement of the day — and then wonders if the Kendalls have had a report of the visit.

"Not yet. I am planning on seeing them soon."

"Quite tricky, I imagine. You have to go and yet you will always remind them of their son."

"I know."

"Is it easier now that you're going to be a priest?"

"I don't think it will ever be easy, Dad."

The two men return to Highgate, expecting a quiet family dinner, only for the telephone to ring as they start to lay the table. It is Henry Mortimer. His voice is no longer suave and assured but higher, quicker and caught at the back of the throat.

"Sidney, I don't know what to do. You have to help me."

"What's wrong?"

"Frank's dead. I'm not sure how it's happened but he's been shot. I just got home. The flat's a mess and my housekeeper's away. I was out . . ."

"How long for?"

"I don't know. I had lunch at my club and then I looked in at the theatre, ran into a few chums and came back to this. I don't know what to do."

"Have you called the police?"

"No, not yet. I don't want a scene and, the thing is, this whole ghastly business may be about to get much worse."

"What do you mean?" Sidney asked.

"Well, I assumed Freddie must have done it, so I phoned him . . ."

"You confronted him?"

"He was drunk. Then he went mad. How dare I accuse him of a crime he couldn't possibly have committed even though he'd been threatening that selfsame thing for weeks? He said he was going to come round straight away. I'm expecting him at any minute and I'm so afraid of what he might do. He sounds so angry."

"He often makes vague —"

"This wasn't vague. It was completely specific. I'm so scared that I telephoned Amanda because they've seen each other quite a lot recently but she's out at a dinner. Her father said he would try and get a message to her. I'm not sure that's going to be enough. Frank's still by the fireplace. I don't know if Freddie's shot him or not, or if we've had burglars or God knows what's been going on, but I'm terrified Freddie might try and kill *me*. He's still got my duelling pistol."

"I told him to give it back to you."

"Can you come down, Sidney? You know how to speak to Freddie."

"He doesn't always listen . . ."

"And when the police do arrive it'll be helpful to have a clergyman with us."

"I'm not actually ordained yet."

"It doesn't matter. You look the part. And you'll know what to say."

"Have you called them or not? I thought you said you hadn't."

"I can't remember what I've done. It's all a bit of a blur."

"What's your address?"

"It's Albany, Piccadilly. Ask the porters when you arrive. But don't tell them there's anything amiss. You need to act as normally as possible."

It will take half an hour from Highgate. "I'll be there as soon as I can," Sidney replies.

"What's wrong?" Alec Chambers asks. He has been waiting by the front door. "Is there anything I can do?"

"It's a friend, Dad. He needs my help."

After a brief explanation, his father picks up the phone and orders a taxi.

"Don't tell your mother, Sidney."

"What about?"

"Me, calling a cab. She considers it a very great extravagance. She'll never forgive me."

When Sidney walks into the flat he finds Freddie has already arrived, duelling pistol in hand. Frank is lying dead in front of the fireplace. Henry is on the sofa with his tie loosened, his head bowed, and his hands large and heavy against his thighs. He has removed his paisley-patterned pocket square to wipe the sweat off his forehead. It no longer matters that he took care in choosing it that morning.

"Henry's been accusing me of the most dreadful things," says Freddie, "and so I've brought protection. I won't have him maligning me."

"I told you to give the pistol back."

"But I didn't. It's just as well, isn't it? They say that hell hath no fury like a woman scorned, but what about a man?"

"You're making this whole thing worse, Freddie."

"Am I now? The situation was bad enough when I came in."

Sidney stoops down to look at the body. He checks Frank's pulse. The man's been shot in the side of the head. From what he's seen of dead bodies in the past, it must have happened several hours ago. Dark blood has spilled on to a burgundy carpet that disguises the colour but not the stain. There is no sign of a weapon. The living room, with its deep green walls, its blue-and-white lamps in Chinese porcelain and rococo architectural engravings, remains irrelevantly stylish.

"Did you do this, Freddie?" Sidney asks.

"Don't you start. Of course I didn't."

"Hand me the pistol."

"I'm not doing that."

"I just want to check if it's been fired recently."

"I'm not giving you anything."

"Don't be absurd, Freddie. Do what I say."

Freddie waves the duelling pistol in the air. "'Do what I say.' The war's over now. You're not in charge of the troops any more."

Sidney thinks of taking a step forward but doesn't want to provoke his friend. "Give me the pistol."

Freddie's head twitches. "You know the cardinal rule of drama? You can't have a gun in a play and not fire it. I've never killed a man in a drawing room. You'd better watch out, Henry."

"Give me the gun," says Sidney.

Freddie aims the duelling pistol at Henry's heart. "One shot. I can hardly miss from here."

Henry leans back, stretches his arms out, and closes his eyes. "Oh, go ahead, Freddie, why don't you? What difference does it make?"

"I didn't know how much jealousy could make a man change the way he thinks," says Freddie. "It can even make a man mad. People think I'm ridiculous. Well, so be it. I am ridiculous."

The doorbell rings. Freddie walks towards Sidney but holds on to the pistol. "I'll answer. I don't want you taking charge of any of this, Captain Chambers."

"What does he mean by that?" Henry asks.

Freddie goes out to the door. Sidney and Henry wait until they hear it open and listen to sounds from the summer night.

"Freddie! Are you all right? You mustn't frighten us so."

"Amanda, I'm in hell. We're all in absolute hell."

"What have you done? Tell me."

While the two friends are out in the hall, Sidney sits beside Henry. The sofa has more give than he had been expecting. The comfort feels wrong for the situation they're in. "You've been brave to stand up to him. He could have killed you."

"And what if he had? Life's little more than a game of Russian roulette. The pistol's an old single-shot flintlock. They miss most of the time. Not that I fire them that often."

"You ended the relationship with Frank."

"How do you know?"

"Isn't it obvious?"

"I gave him the afternoon to pack and go. And I left him to it. That's why I went out."

"Had you argued before you gave him the ultimatum?"

"He threatened to blackmail me, but I'm used to paying men off"

Sidney sits up, as formally as the sofa allows. "When you were out this afternoon, where did you go? And did anyone see you? Witnesses?"

"A whole theatreful. Why do you ask? You don't think I've done anything untoward, do you?"

"People might think —"

"Why would I have telephoned you if I'd done something compromising?"

They hear Amanda in the hall asking, "Is Sidney here, then?"

She walks into the room, passes Henry and stoops down beside the dead Frank.

"How ghastly. When did this happen?"

"Hours ago," says Henry.

"And no one's called the police? Why ever not?"

"Why do you think?"

"What else were you planning on doing? You can hardly cover it up."

"We'd better get our story straight," says Sidney.

"I thought I'd just make one up," Freddie replies as he returns to the room. He throws the gun on the sofa. "You can have this after all. I feel calmer now that Amanda's here. Besides, I need a drink. At least I know where to find one."

"Help yourself, why don't you?"

"What happened, Henry?" Amanda asks.

"I don't know. I came home and there he was."

Sidney picks up the gun and tries to think it through. If Freddie is guilty then this pistol will have been fired recently and there should be traces of gunpowder on it — but there aren't. If it's been a burglary with murder, then the police will ask why nothing has been taken. And if Frank's death was suicide, why is there no weapon lying by his side?"

"How many guns do you keep?" he asks Henry. "Is this the only one?"

"I have two," he replies. "They're a pair. I've been restoring them. When I have a moment."

"And where is the other?" Sidney asks.

"In my dressing room."

"Can you fetch it?"

When he brings it back, Sidney sees the second pistol is, indeed, similar to the one he is holding: French, late eighteenth or early nineteenth century, with carved walnut handles, fixed sights, and the words *Acier Fondu* engraved on the barrel. Sidney compares the two and sniffs them both.

"When did you move it?" he asks Henry.

"What?"

"From the scene of the crime. The gun that you've just fetched is the one that's been fired."

"I don't know what you mean."

"Oh, Henry, I think you do."

Sidney weighs the two weapons and holds up the one in his right hand. "This is the pistol that was used. Freddie's is still loaded. He didn't kill Frank. The timing doesn't work either. Did you do it, Henry?"

"No, of course I didn't. I've told you. I was elsewhere, at the theatre. There are witnesses. And in any case, why would I have telephoned you if I was guilty?"

"There are plenty of reasons. Panic, the double bluff, the need to buy time . . ."

"None of which are true."

"No, I don't think they are. But nor is the possibility of an intruder, a man, or woman, who took nothing — not the monogrammed cufflinks there on the side table, the little Canaletto painting, the silver candlesticks — even the duelling pistol itself."

"One's not worth very much without the other."

"Like us, Henry," Freddie says quietly.

The window is open and they can just about hear a drunk man singing in the street outside: "I'LL be loving you . . . I'll BE loving you . . . I'll be LOVING you . . . I'll be loving YOU . . ."

Sidney continues. "You decided to cover yourself, Henry — and make it look like burglary or murder — anyone or anything but your being responsible for someone else's despair. Rather cowardly of you, I'm afraid."

"I don't know what you're talking about."

"It was suicide, wasn't it?"

"I don't know about that."

"You do. Face facts."

Henry sits forward but looks at the floor, avoiding eye contact. "I never believed Frank would do such a thing. I suppose I've been trying to protect him."

"By accusing me!" Freddie shouts.

"I didn't accuse anyone."

"You bloody well did."

"Where is the note?" Sidney asks.

"What note?"

"There must have been one."

"I can't remember."

"What were you wearing when you came in? Was it raining?"

"I'll fetch his coat," says Amanda. "I saw it on the stand."

"You bastard, Henry."

"Oh, shut up, Freddie. I don't need your condemnation. You've done enough for one day."

"You do. Face facts."

"I haven't done anything, more's the pity."

Amanda brings the raincoat in from the hall and pulls a piece of paper from out of the pocket. She reads aloud. *Now you'll never forget me*.

She shows it to Freddie. "Not your handwriting, is it?"

"It's Frank's," says Henry. "He took the paper from my desk and wrote it with my fountain pen. Just to rub it in, I suppose."

"So, we call the police," she continues. "Frank committed suicide. You panicked."

"He did a bit more than that," says Freddie.

"They'll have to deal with this now . . ."

Sidney takes a step towards her. "And we should pray for God's mercy on Frank's soul. You've made such a mess of this, Henry."

"Oh God, don't I know it?"

"It's a bit too late to ask for his help," says Freddie.

"No, it's never too late for that." Sidney kneels beside the body and the other three stand in silence: "I am the resurrection and the life, saith the Lord: he that believeth in me, though he were dead, yet shall he live: and whosoever liveth and believeth in me, shall never die . . ."

The police keep them until past three in the morning. Sidney does most of the explaining. Frank's body is removed, and Freddie is allowed to go home. Henry says he can't bear to stay on and will try to sleep at his club (provided he can wake the porter). It's not far to the Garrick.

Amanda and Sidney wait for a taxi in Piccadilly. It has rained again and the night streets are slicked black, and gleam under the street lights. They are going in different directions and he lets her take the first cab. He opens the door for her and, before she steps into the back seat, he thanks her for all she has done.

"The trouble love gets you into, eh, Chambers?" she says.

"Desperation will make people do all manner of things."

"You were so calm. Did you know what had happened all along?"

"As soon as I saw the body, I was pretty sure it was suicide."

"I should start calling you Sherlock."

She leans forward and kisses him on the cheek. He can smell her perfume, Guerlain's L'Heure Bleue. He asked her once what it was, after she had changed it from Joy, and she was amazed he had noticed. Now he can't think how she can have applied it in the midst of all the chaos. She touches his cheek. Her hand is cold and it wakes him.

"You're a good, impossible man."

"I am what I am."

"What on earth are we going to do with you? Goodnight, Chambers."

CHAPTER TWENTY-SIX

The next time they see each other it is just before Sidney's ordination. Jennifer Chambers is singing in the BBC Choral Society and has reserved them seats for a performance of the *Messiah* in the Albert Hall. The venue is filled with members of the armed forces, Boy Scouts and Girl Guides, with the great and the good in the stalls and the music students higher up in the balconies. The conversation is animated by the expectation of Christmas; whom people have seen recently, what their plans are, if they'll be in London, where they're all going to spend the New Year.

Amanda looks at the concert sheet and notices that the bass soloist is a Mr Murray Dickie. She thinks he sounds like a friend of Freddie's. "Have you met Mr Dickie, duckie?"

Enough time has passed for the jokes to resume but an undercurrent of melancholy is never far away. In another life, Sidney realises, Robert might have come with them, but he knows he has to stop thinking like this.

Amanda is keen to hear the latest news. "Has Freddie calmed down, do you think? I felt so sorry for him. And that poor dead boy. What a waste of a life."

"His parents never even knew . . ."

"That Frank was a homosexual? What did the police tell them, do you think?"

"Oh, some kind of story, I imagine."

"It must be terrible to know so little about your son. The secrets people have to keep. I never quite realised before now. In our family, we always used to think pansies were a bit of a joke . . ."

"When they're not at all."

"Some of them must be utterly miserable. To have to hide your feelings all the time — we have no idea. Does Freddie ever talk to you about it?"

"Sometimes."

They are interrupted by a burst of applause as the conductor, Frederick Jackson, takes his bow from the stage. There's a full orchestra with extra brass and trumpets and an enormous choir, so that when the music is at its fullest, in a hall filled with Londoners dressed in their finest clothes, it feels not so much a celebration of Christ's birth and triumph over death as a reminder of the Allies' victory over fascism. At this moment, and on this day, God is most definitely British.

Sidney finds the beauty of the music impossibly moving. Every word (*blessing, honour, glory* and *power*) takes him away from the memory of its opposite in wartime (*curses, shame, disgrace* and *weakness*). The strings support and dance around the singers with all the buoyancy of faith. It is a defiant proclamation of Christianity, and when the soprano sings "If God be for us, who can be against us?" Sidney is so struck by the fact that the higher notes in the aria are reserved for the words "God" and "Christ" that his tears come unbidden.

He is not sure if he has ever heard anything more beautiful. *Who shall lay anything to the charge of God's elect*? Here is the joy that his life has lacked.

It is God that justifieth . . . it is God that justifieth . . . Here is consolation. *Who is he that condemneth*?

He cannot quite cope with the surge of music and emotion and, finally, it proves too much. He bows his head forward into his lap and covers his face. He tries to pretend he is doing something other than crying — praying perhaps — but he cannot stop himself.

Amanda hands over her handkerchief without looking at him and he knows that he will be teased afterwards and it will be impossible to explain himself.

Still, he can do nothing other than weep.

"Who would have thought that you were such a softie, Chambers?"

He tries to smile, to make light of it all. It's hopeless to think that anyone else can understand his need for faith. "I'm sorry. I wasn't expecting to cry."

"If all your church services were like that then more people would come. You could even charge them admission. Twelve and six, those tickets."

They fetch their coats and emerge into the smog, dark and damp of a South Kensington winter that no amount of privilege can alter. "I think if people had to pay to come to church, we'd struggle," Sidney replies.

"It's so much easier to believe in God when you hear music like that. I can feel it all coming back to me."

"It never quite goes away, you know."

"That's what you hope."

"I think you have to have faith when it's hard, Amanda, when life has no music and your belief is tested to the limit."

"Well, I think I've been tested quite enough, thank you very much."

"Then it's strange," Sidney answers, "because I feel that my trials are only just beginning."

"You mean it's going to get worse?" Amanda asks. "I'm not sure if I can bear seeing you go through it all."

"You don't mean that, do you?"

"Oh, Sidney, sometimes I don't know what I mean. I just want to have a nice time."

It takes a while for Jennifer to join them, and they smoke a cigarette on the steps as the crowds depart in search of Tube trains, taxis and buses to take them out to dinner or back to their homes with the Christmas trees up, presents still to wrap and the cards over the fireplace. Ordinary life continues regardless of anything else, Sidney thinks, even his impending ordination.

"Only a few days to go," Amanda continues. "Not too late to back out and join the Foreign Legion."

"Please don't tease me any more."

"If I wasn't able to do that, Chambers, then there wouldn't be much of our friendship left."

"But I do hope you take me seriously."

"Not as much as you take yourself these days. You're nervous about it all, I can tell. It's looming over you like a cloud."

"You are still coming to the service, aren't you?"

"You don't think I'd miss it? I'm chumming Freddie. Or he's chumming me. I'm not sure which way round it is. We're both your oldest friend. He says he'll fight me for the title."

"It shouldn't be a contest."

She hands him her cigarette to put out. "We do love you, you know. And I'm sorry if, sometimes, you feel we're not properly on your side. I suppose it's just that we can't all have your faith."

"I don't expect you to."

"Sometimes you give the impression that you do."

"I don't mean to, Amanda. But it will be my job to preach the gospel . . ."

"But it can be quite irritating outside church, Sidney. What if we don't have enough faith, or we *can't* believe, or don't want to believe, or don't want our lives changed?"

"Then I have to be patient."

"And that's precisely what I find annoying about some vicars: the assumption that we'll get there in the end."

"I'm not 'some vicar'."

"You're about to become one, Sidney. There's a vicar in Wiltshire where the Mannings live. He looks at you with this mixture of sorrow and pity, but also with a kind of smugness. He's like the cat that's got the cream. 'If only you know the joy I know.' It's infuriating."

"I'm not responsible for the facial expressions of my colleagues."

"And I don't want faith to be a condition of our friendship."

"It isn't. But you must believe something, Amanda? I know you have doubts, but surely you must acknowledge that we cannot be alone? This earthly life cannot be all there is."

"I'm not sure what I believe, Sidney. I'm perfectly happy to sing along and take part in the rituals, but I can't really believe that God is looking out for every single one of us, as you know full well. But I don't want to cause offence. We can't all be like you . . ."

"I'm not asking you to be like me."

"But sometimes I think that's exactly what you're expecting."

Jennifer arrives, all of a fluster, carrying the music score, bags of shopping and her concert dress. "I'm so sorry. I got held up. Some dreadful man was insisting I accompany him to a cheese and wine party. I told him I was otherwise engaged. I hope I'm right about that? We're still having dinner together, aren't we? I'm starving. Did you both enjoy the concert?"

"So much so that we appear to be having some kind of argument," Amanda replies.

"Oh dear, I hope my brother's not being too judgemental?"

"When am I that?"

"Oh, please. You're worse than Daddy . . ."

"Dad's not judgemental either."

"You should hear him when you're not at home, or after Matt's asked him for money."

"I don't believe it."

"Sometimes, Sidney, you are in a world of your own. You've no idea . . ."

"Now you're for it, Chambers," Amanda laughs. "Two against one. There'll be no end to the teasing."

"It's really not fair."

"It gets worse," adds Jennifer. "You're paying for dinner."

The two women link arms and forge ahead. Sidney waits for a moment and watches them recede into the fog and street lamps. Perhaps they will never understand the need to set his trust in God so badly; and maybe his faith will always remain necessarily personal; a private mystery?

Jennifer turns and shouts back through the London gloom, "Don't sulk. I was only joking. We'll go Dutch."

"We both know that priests can never afford a decent meal, Chambers."

The women wait and then, when he joins them on the outside of the pavement, Amanda adds, "So, you'll just have to pay up in other ways."

"What do you mean?"

"By being excellent company. You can do that, can't you, Chambers? You're still allowed to have fun, I hope? We don't want to lose you for ever."

CHAPTER TWENTY-SEVEN

Despite his desire to be taken "seriously", there is much amusement when Sidney tells them that he, a man with so many witty and chatty friends, is being "sent to Coventry". He is to begin his ministry at Holy Trinity Church in Priory Row and the ordination service will take place in the open air and at dusk, amidst the ruins of the city's bombed cathedral.

It is a crisp, cold Christmas Eve, dry and clear with so many stars, all very different from the choking smog of London. There are braziers with flames leading the way to the altar of rubble, and a charred Cross that symbolises determination, survival and, above all, the possibility of Resurrection.

The Provost of Coventry gives each ordinand a small crucifix bound with wire and made from nails found in the ruins.

"Hold fast, Sidney," he says.

The congregation stands to sing the processional hymn, accompanied by a Salvation Army band.

All of the Chambers family, apart from Matt, attend. (He is having problems with his girlfriend in Manchester and some kind of property "deal" that is "too complicated" to explain, especially to "the women of the family".) Rev Nev assists at the service, along with several members of the Westcott House staff. As promised, Amanda has come with Freddie Hawthorne. She is dressed in a dark green loden coat and veiled pillar-box hat and sits with her gloved hands in her lap, as if waiting to be entertained at a night of amateur theatricals. Freddie has put on a bow tie, has a white silk scarf, and beams throughout.

When Sidney hears the Bishop of Coventry's words, carried on the wind as his breath turns into frosted clouds in the cold, he cannot help but remember what has led him to this.

"Good people, these are they whom we purpose, God willing, to receive this day unto the holy Office of Priesthood . . . but yet if there be any of you, who knoweth any Impediment, or notable Crime, in any of them, for the which he ought not to be received into this holy Ministry, let him come forth in the name of God, and shew what the Crime or Impediment is."

Sidney thinks of Robert, the war, his friends and his failings. All he can do is ask once more for mercy and the grace of God in the midst of a ceremony that feels unstoppable.

The sermon is preached by Michael Ramsey, the newly appointed Regius Professor of Divinity at Cambridge, a man who states that the priest should be, in St Paul's words to the Corinthians, "sorrowful, yet always rejoicing".

Sorrow and joy are two sides of the same coin, he argues. "It is with this ahead of you that you become a deacon or a priest. It is for this that you are committing yourself to the Lord Jesus. 'Lord, take my heart and break it: break it not in the manner I would like, but in the way you know to be best. And, because it is you who break it, I will not be afraid, for in your hands all is safe and I am safe. Lord, take my heart and give to it in your joy, not in the ways I like, but in the ways you know are best, that your joy may be fulfilled in me. So, dear Lord, I am ready to be your deacon, ready to be your priest.' "

Sidney kneels down for the laying on of hands. He is stunned by the import of what he is doing. It isn't the joy that everyone has told him about at theological college, the wash of grace, but the sharp pain of responsibility, the fear that he has done something irreversible.

He takes his first communion service in the crypt, remembering all he has been taught about giving a firm lead through the prayers and sacrament. He is the shepherd; the people are his flock. He has to help them feel secure in the love of God.

He is relieved and thankful when it is over. Afterwards, Freddie gives him a hug and tells him that he's been so moved, far more than he ever is at the theatre. Amanda kisses him on the cheek.

"The adventure begins," she says. "Congratulations, Chambers. You're a new man."

"I'm not so sure about that."

"You're committed. From now on, there'll never be a time when you're not a clergyman. There's no escape."

Freddie puts an arm on his shoulder. "God bless you, dear old Sidney."

"Aren't I supposed to say that to you?"

"Oh, please, I can't bear it. Don't be kind to me. You've been generous enough in the past."

"And I will continue to do so, I promise."

"I'll cry if you are too nice."

"Nothing wrong with tears, Freddie."

"I've been so moved today. I've blubbed twice. Just watching you kneel down set me off. Then there was the laying on of hands. So humbling. So brave. I'm going to cry every time I remember it. You did it, Sidney. You've got your feet on the first rung of the ladder towards infallibility. You make us all better."

"I don't know . . ."

"To think of you as a priest: it's beyond anything I ever thought possible. You will promise to look after us all, won't you?"

"It is my bounden duty."

"Then, God bless you again. I'm so proud of you, so grateful, I'm crying all over again."

"Don't, Freddie. What would Robert say?"

"He'd laugh," says Amanda. "Then he'd shake your hand very hard and try not to be embarrassed."

"Yes, I imagine he would."

Freddie is accosted by an old army friend whom he hasn't seen for years, and Alec Chambers announces that the family is heading on to the reception that the Provost is hosting so, for a moment, Sidney is alone with Amanda.

"Are you at peace now?" she asks quietly. "Is this really the right thing for you?"

"I hope so. Sometimes I think I'll never be at peace."

"Don't you think that, after so much suffering, you deserve it?"

"I don't deserve anything."

She smiles, opens her handbag and picks out a rectangular object wrapped in red-and-green paper for Christmas. There's even a sprig of holly. "I brought you a present."

"There's no need for you to do that, Amanda."

"There is. I am sorry I was horrible after the *Messiah*."

"You weren't horrible. You were just being yourself."

"There was rather too much teasing. I hope you'll forgive me."

"There's nothing to forgive. Shall I open it now or wait until morning?"

"Open it now. I'd like to see your face. It'll be quite amusing to see you pretend to like it if you don't."

"There's a challenge."

He finds two plain wooden chairs near the door of the crypt and they sit side by side as he unwraps his gift.

"Happy Christmas, Chambers. Happy new life."

It is a watch. The Roman numerals are picked out in gold against a white face. "It's so you'll never be late for church."

"That's so kind of you. It's beautiful. I'll think of you every time I put it on."

"Don't go overboard. Once in a while will do."

He kisses her on the cheek and there's a moment when their eyes meet before she turns away. They can hear carol singers in the distance, other people saying their goodbyes or offering quick trips to the pub. They know it's time to join everyone else at the Deanery, but just before they go back, the two of them stop to look at a nativity scene made by local children. Still no baby Jesus. He will arrive in the morning.

"Can you imagine having a child?" Amanda asks.

"Not yet," says Sidney.

He does not dare ask her the same question.

PART FOUR

LOVE

CHAPTER TWENTY-EIGHT

Sidney's lodgings are in Peggy Carter's Boarding House in Spon Street. It's a detached mock-Tudor family home that has been converted into separate living arrangements with linoleum flooring, shared bathrooms, lockable doors and an air supply that combines everyday oxygen with the odour of cooking fat, mothballs, disinfectant and a last whiff of lavender from the laundry bags.

The bedroom is appropriately spartan; a single bed, a desk, a chair and a wardrobe. It could almost be monastic if it wasn't for the famous Pears soap print of *Bubbles* on the wall. Sidney is allowed to hang his crucifix of nails above his bed because his landlady approves. She's pleased that the new priest won't be causing the kind of trouble she has had with actors in the past, bringing home men and women at all times of night, thinking they are quiet enough on the stairs when they never are, using the inside toilet when they should have gone outside, missing breakfast because they are too hung-over. At least with Sidney there won't be any "carrying on" with some of the local girls who, she has heard, offer all manner of "services".

"I can assure you, Mrs Carter, that all my services will be religious."

"That's very witty of you, Mr Chambers. Very quick. I like a man with a sense of humour. My Alf had that."

She is a small woman of indeterminate age (mid fifties, early sixties?) with short arms and sharp elbows that give her room to move through the tightest of spaces. Her grey hair is curled once a week and tinted with alternate washes of colour that frustrate her as never being quite right. She has a sensible, economical wardrobe of navy, cream and grey; wool for the winter and cotton in summer, never linen (too time-consuming to iron) or satin or silk (they lose their shape so quickly). This winter, she has made sure that she dresses in plenty of layers to keep out the cold. Gas is so expensive these days and the best way of staying warm is to move about as much as you can, although she will allow herself a sit-down, a cigarette and a Tia Maria on Saturday nights in front of the wireless.

"Have you been a widow long?" Sidney asks.

"My Alf got pneumonia in the middle of that terrible winter. Christmas 1946, it was. He'd just given me a new ironing board. I asked him, 'What kind of present is that after thirty-two years of marriage?' Honestly, I could have murdered him. Then, in the New Year, we had snowdrifts up to ten feet deep. You couldn't move. All the traffic stopped. We thought he'd get better but he kept on sinking and there was nothing the doctor could do to stop it. He just melted away like when it goes funny in the films. What do they call that?"

"The fade to black."

"That's right, Mr Chambers; and now my whole life's a bit like that."

"I think you're being hard on yourself, Mrs Carter."

"At least I've had a bit of love in my life. Someone to watch over me, as the song goes. I know Alf's looking after me now."

"I am sure he is, Mrs Carter."

She tells him about the other four residents: a married couple who used to run a hotel but have fallen on hard times ("He thought he was a chef and she liked to be a hostess, but they got it the wrong way round, if you ask me"); an engineer at the Singer Factory who "like you, Mr Chambers, should have found a wife by now"; and a French dressmaker who copies the latest fashions in cheaper fabrics and makes adjustments "at very reasonable rates and I just hope that's all she's offering".

Mrs Carter explains the dinner menu. It's at half-past six. On Monday, there's rissoles and salad or veg; Tuesday, Welsh rarebit; Wednesday, sliced tinned sausages; Thursday, cauliflower au gratin; Friday, stuffed haddock — "fish on a Friday, you'll approve of that, I'm sure"; and on Saturdays they have a bit of gammon if the butcher's feeling friendly enough to give a discount.

"You'll have to fend for yourself on a Sunday, because that's when I go to my sister's in Birmingham, but you'll soon find people to give you your tea. In any case, that's the day you're busy, isn't it?"

"I do work in the week, Mrs Carter."

"I'm sure you do, Mr Chambers, but it's not really proper 'work' when you think about it, is it? Not like the others do . . ."

Holy Trinity Church, Coventry, is a predominantly fourteenth-century building that has survived the bombing of the city in November 1940 through the actions of its vicar, Canon Graham Clitheroe. He had prepared for the attack, bought in a supply of hydrants and ladders, and kept a nightly watch from the North Porch. The previous curate had organised a small team with a couple of vergers and a few parishioners to stay alert for incendiaries, put out fires and even, at one point, to push bombs off the roof. As a result, the church remained standing when the cathedral did not. The sign erected afterwards still remains: *It all depends on me and I depend on God*.

Canon Clitheroe is something of a chameleon; a scholar in round-rimmed glasses when seated at his desk and yet athletic when in motion, always up and doing, ready to make the most of each day. His favourite parable is of the wise and foolish virgins, and he is keen to discuss matters of faith straight away.

"What do you think is 'good' about the 'good news' of the Gospels, Sidney?" he asks. "How are you planning to develop your spiritual awareness and well-being?"

"Through prayer and reading, I hope. These are complicated questions, Canon Clitheroe."

"I do not expect immediate answers. Please call me Graham. How do you sustain yourself theologically?"

"I start by searching for quietness and grace."

"Well, let's hope you finish with them. Although our work, it seems, is never-ending. I always think that our ministry is a bit like gardening. Everything comes round, year after year, but you never quite know what's going to pop up next."

"I suppose we can't plan for everything."

"Not at all. And what would life be like without surprise? Unpredictability is what makes it so wondrous."

Wondrous. Sidney realises he has never used the word.

He has been allocated the Canley Estate in the southwest of the city as part of his pastoral ministry. It is a new development where families from slums and bombed-out areas have been relocated but have yet to recreate the closeness they knew before.

"People have had these new places designed for them," Clitheroe explains, "with central heating and running water and proper sanitation, but what they seem to want more than anything else is a feeling of belonging. We are in danger of losing our community spirit. This is where the Church comes in. The ministry of the Good Shepherd is not simply about keeping the flock safe, Sidney. It's about guiding them to new pasture. They may have moved *geographically* but have they moved *spiritually*? That's what I want you to work out. There's a mass of souls out there in very great need of God's mercy and grace. We have to show them that they have not been forgotten; that they are still loved."

This is true, but hard to achieve, and Sidney finds his pastoral ministry far from straightforward. He is given respect (most of his parishioners have been brought up well), but the people he talks to have more urgent priorities than listening to a Church of England priest rejuvenate the good news of the Gospels. They are more concerned with money, health, food, children and their employment prospects than Christian direction. They also want Sidney to prove his credentials before they let him into their homes.

Did you fight in the war then, Reverend?

People assume he has not, so he has to disabuse them without ever quite explaining everything he's been through: the mud and the fire, the fear and the cold; the dead that still infect his dreams. Sometimes he can hear Robert answering for him: *Of course I bloody did. Do you think I went there on holiday*?

But his presence is only a step away from having the police or the doctor round; the professions who only turn up when something is wrong. They'd rather he didn't bother. They'd rather be coping.

There are, however, more rewarding times, when the purpose of his ministry becomes clearer. He visits an elderly couple who are ailing — arthritis, poor sight and bronchitis. They have no children or close relations. It is Sidney's duty to tell them that their well-being is not just a matter between them and their doctor. The whole family of God is affected when people are ill.

Edith and Jackie Charles live in a Victorian terraced house that has been spared the bombing. Neighbours have moved their bed into the living room because the husband can no longer manage the stairs and they don't want to be in separate rooms at night. The house smells of gas and stale tobacco. They have taped up the windows to keep warm. Their wedding photograph is on the mantelpiece. The service was fifty-two years ago, when Queen Victoria was still on the throne.

"They hadn't even started the Boer War then," says Jackie.

It is eleven in the morning and they have just finished eating porridge. The odour of boiled milk hangs in the air.

"You've had porridge for your breakfast?" Sidney asks.

"We have it late so we don't need lunch. It saves money and it fills us up. In the evening, we have it again. Sometimes we add a teaspoon of honey. Or even marmalade. That's a nice treat."

Sidney notices the kitchen at the back of the house. "Can I make you a cup of tea?"

"We're all right, thank you."

His wife fumbles for her spectacles. She can't find them even though they are in her lap. "What about you though, Reverend?"

"Don't mind me. I've just come to see how you are."

"That's good of you."

"Everyone's kind," her husband adds. "The nurse comes every week and dresses my ulcers."

Edith continues. "The doctor visits once a fortnight to see how my breathing is."

"We have a home help for the shopping."

"The milkman's always friendly."

"Then there's the chiropodist. She does our feet." Jackie Charles gives a little laugh that turns into a cough. "Although we can't reach our toes so well any more, can we, chuck?"

"And now you've come, Reverend. Seeing you reminds us of our blessings, and where they all come from."

"We've had a good life."

"And we've had each other," says Edith. "That's the best thing we've ever done. Get married. Now we just have to see each other out of this life and into the next."

"It would be nice to go at the same time, but I don't think that's likely."

"Don't you worry, pet. I won't be far behind."

"You think I'll be first off, then? I should watch what you're putting in the porridge."

"I'm joking. Plenty of life left in us yet."

"Would you like us to pray together?" Sidney asks.

"That would be nice, wouldn't it, Edith?"

"It's so very kind of you, Reverend."

"O Lord, look down from heaven, behold, visit and relieve these thy servants, Edith and Jackie. Look upon them with the eyes of thy mercy, give them comfort and sure confidence in thee, defend them from the danger of the enemy, and keep them in perpetual peace and safety, through Jesus Christ our Lord. Amen."

After Sidney has said his goodbyes ("You're so very kind, Mr Chambers . . . you've cheered up our day"), he starts his journey back to the bus stop but realises that he's not quite ready to go home.

He's pleased with how the morning has gone and he wants to take a moment to recognise all that has happened. There are kids playing football, a couple of teenagers tinkering with a motorbike and a young mother seeing some children safely across the road ahead.

"This is what I'm here for," he says to himself. "This is what matters. I was bloody well right to do this."

CHAPTER TWENTY-NINE

It takes him a year to become accustomed to the rhythm of his daily tasks. Whether it is taking the minutes for the meetings of the Parochial Church Council, sorting out the syllabus and the staffing of Sunday School, supervising the organisation of the flower rota, advising on the purchase of hymn books or a new mower for the churchyard, Sidney comes to realise the truth of the advertising adage of local handymen: "No job too small".

He is a long way from Cambridge feasts and philosophical speculation, the glamour of London theatre and the front line of war. It is a quieter, gentler life, and although it has its moments of birth and death, trauma, reaction and, indeed, overreaction (he can't understand how a parishioner can care so much about the smell of petrol from the garage next door, but then he doesn't have to live there), Sidney is reassured by the fact that he's not too bad at his job after all. People come to rely on him, trust him, and most of the time they are glad to see him. They wave at him in the street, they smile when they see him coming. He could almost be happy.

He wonders if Graham Clitheroe is right and that it really is a bit like becoming a gardener, waiting for things to develop and grow, letting everything take its own time. He doesn't want to preach on the subject of his parishioners as plants and seedlings (or some of the more matronly members of the congregation being blowsy old roses), but he considers the natural rhythms of the year, of moving at a slower pace; of listening rather than talking. He thinks of the Gardens of Eden and Gethsemane, the Parable of the Mustard Seed, and of Christ appearing in a garden after his Resurrection: Jesus, the Gardener. It is his way of remembering the roses in Subiaco and the thoughts that brought him to this state of being.

He lets his former life drift away from him. His old friends have their daily concerns and now Sidney has his. All those old preoccupations of careers and dinner parties, gossip and dance, courtship and betrayal, seem far away. He enjoys the novelty of separation and the time apart from his past until Freddie Hawthorne telephones to say that he is coming to Coventry on an emergency visit since "you've clearly gone off us all. No one has a clue what you're up to."

"It's not that, Freddie. It's just that I am very busy. I do have my work."

"People use the word 'busy' to cover all manner of selfishness."

Sidney is shocked by Freddie's honesty. "That's quite an accusation."

"I thought I'd start off on the front foot, my old mucker. Being a priest does not make you immune from criticism, I'll have you know, and you've been absent from civilisation for far too long."

"Coventry is actually quite civilised, Freddie. We even have a theatre. But I'm sorry if you feel neglected."

"I bet you don't feel guilty at all. You must be having a wonderful time. Have you got a secret lover?"

"No, of course not."

"You disappoint me."

"I'm sorry to hear that."

"You're not at all sorry, I can tell. So, I'm coming to check up on you whether you like it or not. Please book us a table somewhere extraordinarily nice, if you have such a thing in the Midlands. I'll pay."

"You don't have to do that."

"Oh, I do, Sidney, believe me, I do. I'm going to need something more than spam and eggs when I see you."

They have lunch in one of Coventry's newer restaurants, with special offers for businessmen and tablecloths of laminated calico. Freddie inspects the clientele around them, examines the cleanliness of the water glasses, is amused by the accent of the waitress ("positively Shakespearean") and declares that his crab cocktail starter is "almost bearable". He's dressed in a grey flannel suit with a lemon-yellow tie that feels a bit too summery for January and he can't help but complain about the building works around them. "I almost expected that we'd have to eat our meal in the middle of a roundabout. This town is *enslaved* to the motor car."

"There's far more to the city than that," Sidney replies. "The people here are lovely. Young families are popping up all over the place. It's modern Britain, Freddie. This is the future and I'm right in the middle. Exciting times."

"I'm not so sure about that. Stand still for too long round here and you'll find yourself *encased* in a mound of concrete. It's the Midlands answer to Pompeii. You could save Henry Moore the bother of making one of his dreadful civic sculptures."

"There's more to life than London, Freddie."

"But not much more, alas. Talent does tend to *coagulate* in the metropolis."

"One of the things I have learned from being away from the capital is how ignorant most Londoners are about the rest of the country."

"But if you've ever had to stay in digs on a theatrical tour you find out pretty sharpish that you should never have left the West End."

"I'm in digs now, actually, and they're not as bad as you make out."

"A diet of endless rissoles, I should imagine. You've forgotten how to live, Sidney."

"On the contrary, I've learned that many people can't afford extravagance, even if it's a treat. All the world is *not* a stage."

"Then those of us who are in the theatre should 'spread a little happiness'. Isn't that how the song goes? Did you ever see *Mr Cinders*?"

"No . . ."

"I don't suppose you have much time for musical entertainment these days. But how are you going to pull in the crowds for worship? What are you doing to add to the gaiety of our great nation?"

"I'm trying to build a faithful, healing, morally responsible community."

"Is that what it says on the tickets? You're going to have to make it sound more exciting than that."

"The Church is not a circus, Freddie."

"It jolly well might be. What is the Mass if not a piece of theatre? There's not much difference between a priest and a ringmaster."

"There's a very great difference, as well you know."

They eat breast of chicken with a hunter's sauce, and the waitress is surprised when Freddie requests a second and then a third bottle of beer. Sidney sticks to water because he has a busy round of pastoral visits that afternoon and it won't do to smell of drink.

Freddie asks if his friend has ever heard of toothpaste and then, out of nowhere, he changes the subject to Amanda Kendall. Has Sidney seen anything of their mutual friend recently? Has she paid a visit?

"Not yet."

"But you've been here over a year. Why haven't you asked her?"

"I don't know," he replies.

"You can't just abandon her. What would Robert say?"

"Perhaps she's abandoned me?"

"Nonsense. You can't think like that. You have to be loyal to your friends."

"I am."

"And you shouldn't have to be a priest to know that."

"I do know that."

"Then you need to prove it, Sidney. Not everyone can make random trips to the provinces. Do you think they might furnish us with a dessert? They seem to be offering a 'plum cobbler'. There must be a joke in there somewhere. A handsome shoemaker . . ."

"I suppose I could have a crème caramel. I'm sorry if you think I've let you all down, Freddie."

"You haven't. Just ring her up. That's all I'm asking. How difficult can it be?"

CHAPTER THIRTY

Sidney makes sure he reads *The Times* on each anniversary of Robert's death. The announcement has been in the paper on 26 January for the previous five years.

BIRTHS

Heatley, Holden, Ingledew, Lasko.

MARRIAGES

Fooks, Lygo, Maling.

DEATHS

Jones, Kirkness, Lee, Lovell.

IN MEMORIAM

Harmsworth, Jessell, Kendall, May.

The following week he goes down to London to see the Kendalls. He takes a bowl of hyacinths because he knows that snowdrops are Lady Kendall's unique tribute to her son's memory and he doesn't want to provide the same flowers.

Amanda greets him in the doorway. "It's kind of you to come, Chambers. I don't know if this will ever get any easier."

"We may become accustomed to the routine, but the loss will always be as keen."

They climb the stairs and visit Robert's bedroom as usual, standing in silence, listening to the distant sounds of London, wondering how long it is decent to stay there. Lady Kendall tells them that, no matter how much she thinks about it all, she still can't understand how or why her son has never returned from the war.

"It doesn't seem fair. I always thought we were a lucky family . . ."

She's sorry to go on, but there are moments when she doesn't know quite where she is any more; she loses all sense of time and place. Sometimes she feels she is still carrying Robert inside her; that she could go back to that time, start life all over again and do things differently.

"Men can never know what it's like to bear a child, Sidney; how it stays with you for ever. I remember him as a little baby. He was always so alert. Demanding, too. You always knew when he was in the room . . ."

"I can vouch for that."

"I sometimes think that if he had been born a day later, or a day earlier, and not in a leap year, then Robert's whole life might have been different. He could have survived because the events leading up to that day would have been changed. I know it is foolish to think like this but I can't stop myself. I cannot help but feel that everything has been my fault. I didn't love my son enough to protect him."

"You can't think like that, Lady Kendall."

"Are you not plagued by the same fears? We could all have done more."

"Sometimes."

"Why not all the time?"

Amanda interrupts. "That's not fair, Mummy."

"We have to live our lives," says Sidney. "But it doesn't mean that we don't remember him."

"Yes, I suppose we do. But my own life is past. I have given up on any hope for a future."

"One has to hope . . ."

"That is very Christian of you, Sidney — the belief that all may yet be well. But I find it very difficult to forgive God if he knew that this would happen all along . . ."

"I'm not sure he did . . ."

"I thought he was supposed to be all-seeing and all-knowing?"

"Robert's death was fate, Lady Kendall. There's nothing any of us could have done."

"Are you sure about that, Sidney?"

"In the heat of battle, no one has control of their destiny."

"Then why has God made us all so helpless?"

"None of this will bring him back, Mummy . . ."

Lady Kendall sinks on to the bed. Amanda puts her arm round her mother. Sidney sits alongside. They wait until they can't stand it any more.

He takes Amanda to a performance of *Madam Butterfly* at Covent Garden. Elisabeth Schwarzkopf is in the title role and they sit high up in the amphitheatre because these are the only seats Sidney can afford. Amanda tells him not to worry as "these are where the true music-lovers sit. I can see my friends in the stalls any time."

Sidney has not realised that the story is about a clash of cultures — love, religion, betrayal and finally suicide — and he is embarrassed when Amanda knows so much more about Puccini's opera than he does.

"Cio-Cio-San is fifteen at the start. That's how old I was when we met, do you remember?"

She knows so many people in the foyer that it's impossible to talk without interruption and so they agree to go to a pub off Drury Lane afterwards. There's time for one drink before closing but it's so crowded they have to stand.

Amanda asks for a double brandy. "It's good to see you again, Chambers."

Sidney has a pint of bitter. It will be Lent soon. Time to withdraw and economise: no booze, no trips to London, no opera.

"Freddie's been worried about you," he says.

It's so hard to hear each other that they have to keep the exchange brief and to the point.

"And you haven't been? I'm sorry if it needed Freddie to tell you."

"What's wrong?"

"I don't know, Chambers. I think, like Hamlet, that I have of late lost all my mirth. But seeing you brings it back. You cheer me up."

"But you have so many friends. The opera house was full of them."

"I have a gay old time really. It's only when I get home and close the door that things aren't so good. But I mustn't complain. There are plenty of others in the same boat. I've got so many friends who lost their sweethearts as well as their brothers. We just have to keep going. Are you enjoying your work?"

Sidney does not know quite how to answer. He's not sure if "enjoy" is quite the right word.

"I think it's the right thing to be doing."

"Still?"

"Yes." He thinks of all his parishioners back in Coventry; his new family. "I can't imagine anything I'd rather do. What about you?"

Amanda has begun work in the conservation rooms of the National Gallery. They have a scheme where she is attached to different departments for the next year so that she can get an understanding of how the organisation works. As long as she can surround herself with beauty and routine for some of the day ("I suppose it's not unlike your life, after all, Sidney. Art is my religion"), then she can spend the rest of her time with friends, enjoying weekends in the country and holidays on the Isle of Skye.

"I have plenty of things to fill my time, to stop me thinking too much about what's past. And lots of friends. People are very kind to me. I can't complain."

"Anyone special?"

"Cheeky."

"Sorry."

"No, Chambers, don't worry. You'll be relieved to hear that there's still nobody like you."

CHAPTER THIRTY-ONE

Everyone in Sidney's youth group is exhaustingly young. As they are teenagers, he's learned to expect them to behave up to five years either side of their biological age on any given day. A girl of thirteen can act like an eight-year-old having a strop one night and then, on the next, like a young woman on the cusp of marriage. Sidney never knows which version of the child he is going to get.

They are devising a pageant play about the history of Coventry for Easter Monday. Sidney has discussed his rehearsal plans with Freddie Hawthorne and called in a music teacher from a local school to write some songs. He splits the children into groups to work on scenes featuring Saxon settlers clearing the land, monks founding the monastery, and masons building the three spires of St Michael's, Holy Trinity and Christ Church. He devises the show himself, describing how the city became the capital of England in the Wars of the Roses, and develops scenes involving the first weavers and the beginnings of industry, with animated dance and mime routines as the children become watches, clocks, sewing machines, bicycles and motor cars. The idea is to show that Coventry is continually evolving, at the forefront of technology, alive with ideas.

Unfortunately, the older members of the youth group are more concerned about who is going to play Coventry's most famous citizen, Lady Godiva. Is anyone going to ride naked through the streets? Who has hair long enough to hide 'their bits', who is going to play the horse and how is she going to ride it?

Most people suggest Julie Jordan, but she is nowhere to be found. It turns out she is having a fumble in the broom cupboard with Johnny Fisher.

When the group guess what is going on, they start up a series of animal noises, which Sidney finds hard to stop. He loses concentration and discipline. He still has a lot to learn.

As the season of Lent continues he reconsiders the idea of retreat and contemplation. This is the time to be alone and to listen in prayer and meditation. It is more important than being out and about in the world and continually expressing his opinion. He thinks of the teaching of St Benedict: "A wise man is known by the fewness of his words."

He remembers his retreat in the monastery, just before he decided to become a priest, and tries to make everything he does an act of prayer. When he climbs a staircase, he thinks of the person who made it, the wood it has come from and the planting of the original tree. Each step connects his life with what has gone before: the carpenter, the soil and the oak. He concentrates on acts of tranquillity and thankfulness, offering short, frequent prayers, aware of the silences and the sounds around him, stepping back from the world just as one might step back to look at a painting, to see it more clearly, as a whole.

He preaches on a text from the Gospel of Mark. *At once the Spirit sent him out into the wilderness* . . .

"The war was, for all of us, a time of wilderness," he begins, "a place where the familiar could be recognised no longer, a land of terror and unfamiliarity and darkness, where we were separated from our friends and all that we knew and could trust. We have had to find our way back home to God and to each other. But, perhaps, in coming back, we have learned to appreciate what we left behind in the first place? Perhaps we need wilderness moments to appreciate the importance of the love and kindness that we, so often, take for granted. We might crave solitude, time away to address our fears, but then, in the middle of that exile from our lives, we discover that most of us cannot live alone and apart. Few of us survive for long in the wilderness. We either need to tame its wildness or return to those who have loved and nourished us in the past and whom we know we must care for in the future. For we have learned that we are nothing without each other. No man, or woman, is an island apart from the main."

To Sidney's enormous surprise, Caitlín Delaney is waiting after the service with her husband to say "hello". They have come to Coventry, she says, for her cousin's wedding. They are making a weekend of it while her mother looks after the children back in Listowel. They have twin boys now — Conor and Sean

— and another baby is on the way. They are hoping it will be a girl.

"Say what you like about Darragh, he knows how to look after me."

"Don't make a holy show of yourself, Caitlín."

"How do you know that's what I meant?"

"He may be a clergyman but he's no eejit."

Sidney is about to tell them it is all right when the husband continues. "I'm sure you think it's a fair shame you missed out on her, Father. Just as well I snapped her up. You must have been out in the wilderness at the time!"

"Ah yes," says Sidney, unable to comprehend how the man in front of him could possibly interpret the hard-thought theological musings of his sermon as a lament for Caitlín Delaney.

What would it have been like had he ended up sharing his life with her? He feels guilty about being snobbish — yes, she was probably right — but he can't help but be relieved at their mutual escape. She is far happier than she would have been had she married him. That is one thing that's for the best, he thinks, even if he could have handled it better.

"It's very nice to see you again, Caitlín. I hope you're keeping well."

"And I assume you're behaving yourself too, especially now that you've joined the Church."

"I don't think I have any choice these days."

"I never thought of you turning out as a clergyman. We were just passing and I saw your name on the noticeboard. I couldn't believe it! I said to Darragh,

'How many people called Sidney Chambers can there be in the world?' We wouldn't normally come to a service that's not Catholic, but I wanted to get a square look at you. You're not married, then?"

"Not yet, no."

"That's a shame. But I suppose you must be a different person, these days . . ."

"I try to be the same old Sidney."

"It doesn't look like that to me. But you were always a funny one, weren't you, keeping your cards close to the old chest? I expected you to be Prime Minister."

"I don't think there's much chance of that now."

"Funny how life turns out."

"Yes, Caitlín, it is."

"Who'd have thought *any* of us would be like this? We were so green in those days, weren't we?"

"Yes. Indeed. Who'd have thought it?"

They part with promises to keep in touch — "when you're back in Coventry" . . . "if you're ever in Ireland" — but they both know that they will never see each other again.

CHAPTER THIRTY-TWO

The West Indian cricket team is touring England and their opening game is against Worcestershire. Sidney's father is keen to combine a visit to see his son with an opportunity to watch the great West Indian middle-order batsmen of Walcott, Worrell and Weekes. They are the great "Three Ws", the cricketing counterblast to a seminar Sidney had recently attended on "Worship, Witness and Work".

It is an overcast day and, despite the threat of rain, some 7,000 spectators are packed into the County Ground. The West Indians win the toss and decide to bat, scoring at a fast rate despite the absence of sightscreens, indifferent light and a slow outfield.

"This is how the game should be played," says Alec Chambers, "with flair and pace. Your mother has provided cucumber sandwiches — goodness knows where she got the cucumber so early in the year, but they're not exactly filling. Fortunately, she's made a sponge cake as well. I hope that's all right?"

"I should have brought something myself."

"Perhaps we can get a pie for lunch and have this as our tea? We don't want to be greedy."

"Odd, though . . ."

"That she went for the cucumber sandwiches? I know. But she's preoccupied at the moment. I didn't like to say anything. She would only have told me to make them myself."

"What is she preoccupied by?"

"The romantic prospects of your brother and sister. I think she's rather given up on you, by the way."

"That's a relief."

"I'm not sure who Jennifer and Matt are seeing. None of you tell me very much."

"We do if you ask."

"But none of you ever tell us the whole truth."

"Probably because we're not sure you want to hear it."

"That's the odd thing about a family though, Sidney, isn't it? No matter how close you are, you can never be sure who knows what. It's impossible to guess the secrets siblings share with each other without telling their parents."

"I suppose that's why they're called 'secrets'."

"It's nonsense, really. Everything comes out in the wash."

"Are you saying all this to try and find out if I'm seeing anyone myself? You just told me that Mother's given up on me."

"That is only to get you going. It's the first thing she'll ask when I get home."

"And will you tell her?"

"It depends what you say, Sidney. She still hasn't quite recovered from my revealing that you wanted to become a priest. She thinks she should have known first."

"I was going to talk to her about it all . . ."

"But you took too long to get round to it. Never mind. She still loves you. You know that. Only it's probably time you found a wife, don't you think? I hear Amanda Kendall's seeing Guy Hopkins. I'm sure she can do better than that."

"Is she? She never told me."

"I don't suppose she has to ask your permission."

"I saw her only the other day."

"Perhaps she didn't want to give anything away."

There is an edge of the bat, an appeal to the bowler, shouts from the crowd and then applause for the departing batsman. "Aha . . . look, Sidney, they've got Rae. I didn't see it properly. That's what happens when you take your eye off the ball. You get caught out."

CHAPTER THIRTY-THREE

The next time Sidney sees Amanda it is at a house party in Wiltshire. Hattie and Timothy Manning have invited three or four friends down to their house in the village of Lake, just along the road from Stonehenge, in the heart of the Woodford Valley. Also attending are Hattie's no-nonsense school-friend Fliss and, to Sidney's surprise, Guy Hopkins who, it turns out, is confident, rich, broad-shouldered and the possessor of the fiercest handshake known to man.

"Amanda's told me so much about you," he begins. "I knew Robert, of course."

His cheeks are ruddy, he's wearing tweed even in late spring, and his voice has a natural boom to it, all hail-fellow-well-met.

"Everyone knew Robert," Amanda replies, with a softer, kindlier and less nervous voice than is usual when talking about her dead brother. Sidney notices that she is almost on the man's arm.

"Such a loss."

"I gather he was your best friend, Mr Chambers?"

"He was."

"You must miss him then?"

"We all miss him," Amanda says quickly before Sidney can elaborate.

Their hostess interrupts. "Now then, everyone. No gloom. I'm determined that we must all have a very jolly time."

The Manning residence is a former vicarage with tasteful floral displays in fluted vases, supported by felted coasters on mahogany furniture, set beside deep chintz sofas. A couple of Labradors, one black, the other golden, mooch around for mainly decorative purposes.

"Just think, Sidney," Timothy Manning announces as they are shown round and told of the improvements made and those still yet to come, "if you'd been born a hundred years ago, you could have had somewhere like this for free."

"He still might," says Amanda, realising, perhaps, that she has been rather abrupt with her old friend. "There are plenty of lovely vicarages left."

"I'm not sure I have a choice," Sidney says.

"You've surely earned one after the concrete of Coventry?"

"I don't think it works like that."

"Whatever happens, you'd better get on with it before they sell any more of them off. You don't want to miss out," says Timothy, as if this is a comment on the whole of his guest's life and not just a matter of finding the bricks and mortar where he might one day settle.

Is this going to be his role now? Sidney worries, to act as a spiritual court jester to his friends, or will he have to discard them altogether and live a completely different existence? Perhaps he should go the whole hog and become a monk after all?

"How shall we address you in future?" Timothy asks. "Vicar? Reverend? Father?"

"Sidney is still perfectly acceptable."

"I know you think it's rather infra dig when people refer to you as 'Sid'."

"That's why I call him 'Chambers'," says Amanda.

"I don't think any other woman does that," Hattie replies.

"Perhaps it's a special thing between the two of you?" Guy asks.

"Oh, I don't mind what anyone calls me," Sidney smiles, "as long as it's not rude."

Timothy Manning offers champagne to kick off the evening and pushes the wire cage off the cork. "Isn't there a special name for it?" he asks.

"Yes," Sidney remembers, "a *muselet*."

Their host balances it on the end of his nose and everyone laughs. "Are you *amused* by my *muselet*?"

The drinks are accompanied by quails' eggs with a celery salt and aioli dip. This is followed by poached salmon, roast pheasant, and bread-and-butter pudding, washed down with a crisp young Chablis, a blackcurrant-tinged claret, and what Timothy describes as "a rather pushy little Sauternes".

Sidney wonders how on earth they've managed to achieve such decadence with rationing still in force, and what his parishioners might have to say about it. He can certainly imagine what his frugal mother would think; she who never eats in restaurants, seldom uses the telephone or takes a taxi, and wastes nothing, reusing or composting scraps, boiling up stock, drying out soap, sharing bathwater, darning socks, diluting shampoo and always squeezing out the last of the toothpaste.

The guests chat about how they all know each other and whom they have seen recently. In the midst of her teacher training, Fliss has been to the most dreadful dinner party with a man who never dries his hands properly after visiting the bathroom and is "certainly not safe in a taxi". Hattie has plans for the flower beds surrounding the upper lawn, but the gardener who did for the previous owner "has a gammy leg and no sense of smell or colour" and no one in the village has much taste. Some of the women, she says, hardly bother with make-up at all.

"Pond's Cold Cream is about as good as it gets."

"I suppose they don't worry so much about appearances if no one sees them," Amanda replies.

"Or notices. Once their husbands take them for granted, they've only got the dogs left. And if it's good enough for the dog . . ."

"I do think women should make an effort, though, whatever the circumstances," Amanda continues. "We have to do our bit to add to the gaiety of the nation."

Timothy says he's thinking of building a lake at the bottom of the garden. "It makes sense, don't you think? Then we can pretend the village is named after our house."

"Seems rather extravagant," Amanda replies, "but I suppose it's cheaper than a swimming pool."

"I've said I'd prefer a tennis court," says Hattie.

"Perhaps Sidney could take a few baptisms; give the vicar a run for his money?"

"I don't think that would go down well."

"You never know . . ."

The conversation continues with an extended rally of exchanged information on home improvements, the inadequacies of local shopping and the difficulty of finding a reliable cleaner. The last one the Mannings had was, apparently, a bit of a kleptomaniac, although the house is filled with so many possessions it must have taken them a while to notice.

After dinner, they sit on sofas and play the "in the manner of" adverbs game taken from Noël Coward's *Hay Fever*, acting out scenes "seductively", "jealously", "candidly" and "foolhardily". Sidney is expected to draw the curtains "lustily", which causes enough merriment to make him question why on earth he has come.

"Cheer up, Chambers," Amanda calls out. "You're amongst friends. No one in Coventry can see you now."

Early the next morning there is a group outing to Stonehenge. "We don't have to get up at dawn and do the full summer-solstice thing," says Hattie Manning. "We're hardly druids. But it's nice to have the circle to ourselves."

They set off in the Morris Six and the Land Rover so they have plenty of space. Timothy read Archaeology and Anthropology at Cambridge and considers himself an expert. Consequently, he talks about the stones with proprietorial entitlement. He explains the geographical location, ley lines, Neolithic funeral rites, the movement of the sun and the nature of sacrifice. Guy and Amanda drift off as he points out the differences between sarsens and bluestones, and walks Fliss and Hattie round the inner horseshoe, but they bump into Sidney almost straight away. He has already detached himself from the group, trying to find a moment of solitude and contemplation, even prayer.

"I don't suppose you approve of pagan rituals," says Guy.

"I don't disapprove."

"Do you think Christianity was ever considered in the same way?"

"It must have been when it started," Amanda argues. "A blow to all those Roman gods everyone is supposed to have worshipped."

"I think some people will believe in anything," says Guy. "And it's perfectly possible Christianity will go the same way as Mithraism or the sacrifice of virgins."

"I didn't realise you knew so much about it," Sidney answers, his tone edged so slightly with sarcasm that Guy doesn't know whether to take him up or ignore it.

"How can you believe in a loving God after all that war?" he asks.

"I've quizzed him about that too," says Amanda, "and I've yet to receive a satisfactory reply."

Hattie Manning returns to join them and can already detect a scene in the offing. "Don't gang up on him, you two. It's his day off. Everyone needs a break from religion from time to time, even priests. Otherwise life gets so terribly dreary."

"It's all right," Sidney answers. "It's a fair enough question. There are things beyond human comprehension. God can't be responsible for every human action."

"He can if he created us," says Guy.

"And will you be responsible for all the actions of your children when you have them?"

"That's different. I'm not God, despite what my friends think."

Hattie and Amanda laugh and Sidney knows that it is useless to continue. He says he plans on going to church. Would anyone like to join him?

No, they wouldn't. They are too hungry. They would rather have a leisurely breakfast with the papers and a walk round the garden. Amanda wants to "make the most of the company". She can go to church another time.

Once they are all back at the house, Sidney walks a mile down the road to St Andrew's in Great Durnford. It's a medieval English flinty, higgledy-piggledy building that dates back to the twelfth century, with a stopped clock, leaning gravestones and a warped wooden porch that bears testament to its powers of survival. Sidney is reassured by its unpretentious solidity, the squat ashlar tower, the wide whitewashed nave and fifteenth-century carved-oak pews.

There's a goodly congregation, a wobbly organist and a stooping elderly vicar with thin grey hair and thick eyebrows, who preaches on the subject of spiritual renewal. "Britain may be rebuilding its cities but is it rebuilding its souls?" he asks. How can we create a lasting peace? It is impossible, he argues, without the peace of God, which passes all understanding.

Sidney would like to suggest that if it does, indeed, "pass understanding" then the congregation are liable to find it hard to go along with what the man is saying. The priest would do better to concentrate on Christ as the living embodiment of our salvation from the noise and violence of the world, but he is not going to get drawn into a debate on his weekend off duty.

Although Sidney has come incognito he can't avoid the priestly welcome on the way out. He's asked if he's new to the village.

"No, I'm staying with the Mannings."

"We don't see very much of them these days, I'm afraid. Christmas and Easter only. They used to come when her father was alive but standards are slipping. My predecessor had a Jack Russell with a lovely little party trick that always went down well with the family. He would throw himself on to the ground with his legs in the air whenever he heard the pop of a champagne cork or the word 'Amen'. I'm afraid I can't compete with that. Do you go to church much yourself?"

"I do . . ."

"I thought so. I can always spot a fellow pilgrim."

"I'm not sure about that."

"We're never sure. That's why what we do is always a matter of faith."

Sidney admires the man's uncomplicated generosity Other people are waiting to be greeted. "God bless you," the vicar says, shaking Sidney's hand. The priest has a large, warm, old hand, not damp like Fliss's suitor's, or powerfully controlling like Guy's, but the kind of handshake that a carpenter or a gardener might give.

There's a full Sunday lunch back at the house with sherry and gin beforehand and plenty of laughter. Guy is now having a bit of a flirt with Fliss.

"What are you having?" she asks him.

"Gin and Cin."

"Gosh."

He drops his voice. "Amusing, isn't it," he says, "to think of sin with an 's' rather than the 'c' of Cinzano?"

"I don't think I've ever had it."

"The gin or the sin? Perhaps it's time you started?"

A different seating arrangement is in play from the previous evening and Sidney finds himself at the far end of the table from Amanda. He can hear her laugh but not what she is saying as the conversation breaks up into twos and threes over lamb and redcurrant jelly, new potatoes and the first mint from the garden. Fliss asks Sidney what his daily life is like as a priest and he goes through his weekly routine, trying to make his stories as entertaining as possible, describing his exploits with the youth group, the elderly couple who only eat porridge and the unrelenting predictability of his landlady's weekly menus. Fliss wonders if he's been to see any Shakespeare plays at Stratford and what his plans are for the next few weeks. Does he ever get any time off? How often does he come to London? Perhaps they can go to a concert together? It's only then that he realises she has been set up as a potential vicar's wife.

She's going to be a primary schoolteacher. What could be better?

There's a brief walk after lunch to exercise the dogs and get some horticultural ideas from a neighbour who has offered them some cuttings, but Sidney is keen to leave before tea. The train connections are complicated and he has a parish meeting the following morning that he doesn't want to miss. It will be a relief, he thinks, to get back to Coventry. It occurs to him that he belongs there far more than he does here.

CHAPTER THIRTY-FOUR

Back on the Canley estate, he is asked to take the wedding of Julie Jordan, the butcher's daughter. She is still only seventeen. With her pale skin, roundly trusting face and long dark hair she was one of the most obvious candidates to play Lady Godiva in the pageant play, but Sidney had thought her too young at the time and had offered the part to her confident friend Georgie instead. It's been a while since he's seen Julie and he's worried that she's still too young and that it's a bit early for marriage. It's also the first time he has ever given premarital advice.

The prospective groom, Ray Shearer, is the son of a local farmer and, while they are discussing plans for a reception in the parish hall, it becomes clear that there is an arrangement of black-market proportions between the two families. It is easy to see how a farmer might have close business dealings with a butcher, but it also involves the local brewer, "Yeasty" Yates, and a Welsh baker, known locally as "Bread of Evans".

"We can pay your fee in crates of beer if you like?" Julie's father asks. It is clear that Sidney's ability to turn a blind eye is being tested but his discretion is challenged further when Julie asks if she can see him on his own.

There's a brief discussion about why she needs to do this and where the rest of the family should go. Her dad's the only man allowed in her bedroom but they suppose a priest might be all right. Or can everyone go out?

Mrs Jordan says she still has the tea to get on, so the men say they'll have a swift pint in the pub and ask if Sidney wants to join them when he's finished. It won't take long, will it? As long as he doesn't put her off the whole idea of getting married . . .

Julie says she'd just like to ask the curate a few special things and everyone shuts up when they assume it's about sex. Her mother asks if she should be present, but Julie says no, she just wants Sidney.

They go up to her bedroom, and he sits on the chair by the table where Julie used to do her homework. Gone are the mathematics and the geography and the history textbooks. In their place are a diary, fashion magazines, a hairbrush, combs, scissors, ribbons, pins and rollers. She is training to be a hairdresser.

Julie sits on the edge of the bed so her pale-blue skirt won't run up too high. Her legs are bare. It's been a hot day, and she wears a simple white blouse with no jewellery. Sidney says it's a nice room and to begin with they talk about her old dolls' house, her china poodle and the teddy bear with the wonky eye called Charlie. It used to be her mother's, Julie says, and the conversation runs on into a discussion about her childhood, her hopes and plans, all the preparations for the great day, who is going to wear what, how many bridesmaids there are going to be and how the salon is going to do all the hair for free, when she suddenly stops the politeness and says: "We need to do it soon."

Oh, thinks Sidney. *That*. "I see."

"Do you, Mr Chambers?"

There is a silence and he tries to remember what he was taught during his training. How much do you need to help people say what they want to say, and how much should you wait?

Don't be afraid of silence. Embrace it.

A strange noise comes from the girl's mouth, somewhere between a sucking sound, a sigh and an intake of breath. No words are forthcoming. She is afraid of words.

"Are you pregnant Julie?"

"I am."

Sidney swings into pastoral mode. He can do this. He picks up the pace of the conversation. "Well, that need not necessarily be a bad thing. There's plenty —"

"Yes, I know, but . . ."

". . . I mean, we can have the wedding as early as possible. I can say something about the availability of the church. So many weddings, we have a full house for the autumn, but there is a little space in the diary if you'd like to have it. A nice Saturday afternoon. Besides, plenty of babies are born prematurely."

"The thing is, Mr Chambers, Ray's not the father."

Good heavens, Sidney thinks, and remembers his tutor always asking when trainee priests requested confidential meetings: *What fresh hell is this?*

"Are you sure?"
"Yes, I am."
"And he doesn't know?"
"Only the doctor knows. And Mum."
"What does she say?"
"That I shouldn't tell anyone at all. But I feel bad. I don't think it's good to have secrets."

Sidney is aware that, as an alternative parent, he has to be slow to judgement and quick to praise, but he also has to be wise. He's not sure if he's ready, if he can be enough for this young girl, but he recognises that he is probably all she has outside her own family. "Who is the father?" he asks.

"Johnny Fisher."

"I remember him from our youth group. Lively chap." (That is one way of putting it. Sidney had been on the verge of kicking him out when he left of his own accord.) "He doesn't know about you being . . ."

"No, I haven't told a soul. Johnny won't want anything to do with it anyway. He's gone to London. But do you think I should tell Ray, or just pretend? I feel bad about not saying anything but if I confess then he'll cancel the wedding and I'll be on my own, no one will want me and Dad'll go mad."

"Forgive me, Julie, but it's important to know all the facts before we make a decision. Have you had sexual relations with your future husband?"

"That's the problem. He thinks we should wait. We've done some mucking about but not the full you-know-what, so he can't be the father."

"How pregnant are you?"

"Two and a half months. That's why I have to get on with it. It's got to be in the next few weeks, but Ray says there's plenty of time. He says we can wait until the harvest's done but it'll be too late by then. I'll be showing."

"You don't want Ray finding out after you're married, Julie."

"I just don't think I can tell him now, though. I could try and make him sleep with me. That would be something. But he'd guess. Sometimes it's like he knows what I'm thinking. It's spooky, Mr Chambers."

Sidney thinks he might say that having a partner who is sensitive to your thoughts can be considered a good thing. It is his duty to be optimistic as well as practical, but just as he is about to continue, Mrs Jordan knocks on the door to say that tea will be ready soon. They are having ham and eggs with sliced fried potatoes and baked beans. Would he like to stay? It's no trouble.

As Sidney declines, politely, he wonders if Julie's mother has been listening outside the door and he waits until he is sure she has retreated down the stairs before returning to the subject.

"It seems to me that you have three choices, Julie: tell no one and have the wedding as soon as possible; tell Ray now; or cancel the wedding altogether, talk to Johnny Fisher, and hope he does the decent thing."

None of these suggestions seem right. The only other option is to disappear, have the baby and give it up for adoption. He wonders if he should warn Julie about the dangers of an illegal abortion. Surely that's not his responsibility? Or maybe it is?

Julie picks up her teddy bear and starts directing the conversation towards it rather than Sidney. "I'm an idiot, I know. Johnny's such a creep. I don't know why I did it. He dumped me and went on to my friend Georgie. Bastard." She throws the teddy bear on to the pillow.

"You may have to confess everything to Ray then, Julie. I don't think you can marry him under false pretences."

"But I do love Ray and if I tell him he'll dump me!"

Sidney holds firm. He remembers the Cross he was given at his ordination. *Hold fast*. "You don't know that."

"It's such a risk."

"Perhaps loving someone means risking everything," Sidney replies, saying out loud what he didn't think he knew.

CHAPTER THIRTY-FIVE

It is his mother's birthday and Sidney comes down to London for the celebration; a trip that he combines with the Thursday matinee of *Seagulls Over Sorrento*, a "naval comedy" at the Apollo, which he goes to with Freddie Hawthorne. He thinks it might amuse them both.

It doesn't.

Freddie is full of opinion ("the whole of the first act could go") and insists they leave for a cocktail to console themselves. It will help put Sidney in the right frame of mind for his family dinner.

It's so dark after the light outside that they have to check their steps on the stairwell and then again on a green interior carpet that's covered with spilled drink, ash and fag burns. The hostess is wearing a sleeveless purple cocktail dress that shows the sharpness of her collarbone. She doesn't smile but gets off her stool to take their orders. Someone is playing the piano very badly, a bit of ragtime, but it keeps stopping and then starting up again, elite syncopations that are neither syncopated nor elite. Two men in identical lime-green blazers are drinking vermouth and playing backgammon in the corner; a woman in a white blouse and beret smokes at the bar and crosses her legs when Sidney catches her eye. She is wearing red fishnets that don't match anything else.

The hostess brings over the gin rickeys. "We had your friend Henrietta in last week," she says to Freddie. "She's let herself go a little, I must say. Be a Grimms' fairy soon enough if she doesn't watch out. Lacks your attention to detail, Winnie."

"You know me. I'm all detail. Don't miss a trick."

"Plenty of tricks in here, I can assure you."

"I'll have to be careful," says Sidney. "I don't have long and I don't want to turn up four sheets to the wind at my mother's birthday. Are you going to stay here all night?"

"I might see what comes up. You never know what the tide might bring in at six o'clock. I would have quite liked seeing Henry again."

"Oh, Freddie. Have you seen him at all?"

"I have, but I'm too old for him these days. He's still a chicken hawk."

"Poor man. He's too old to be playing that game . . ."

"We should be friends, I suppose, but I can't quite manage it. Sometimes you just have to give up on people. What do you think?"

"I think it's important to support the people you love."

"Even when they reject you?"

"That is the lesson of Christ. I'm sorry to bring him into the conversation, but that is my life. He was 'the most despised and rejected of men'. Yet he loved."

"But he was the Son of God, Sidney. I'm the offspring of a gas engineer in Bromley. I don't think it's quite the same thing."

"No, Freddie, you've got me there. But this is what we have to aspire to. Somehow we have to love people unconditionally."

"And you can do that, can you, Sidney?"

"Not all the time, no. But I have to keep trying."

Someone laughs at the other end of the room and says, "Come off it." The piano player stops and calls out, "Time for another?" There's a chink of glasses, a struck match, the sound of a window being opened and checkers being moved on a backgammon board.

"Friendship," Sidney continues, "can be as important as love. We know that."

"And we've lost that too. Robert. All those other chums in Italy. I'm amazed you were able to go back and see the graves."

"It did help."

"I hate the past, Sidney. And most of the time, I dread the future. What's to become of us?"

"We just have to keep on fighting."

The hostess brushes past, leans down and kisses Freddie on the back of the neck without appearing to stop. It's one fluent movement. Sidney wonders if she has heard the conversation or if she just thinks they need cheering up. How often does she hear stuff like this and is she always so disinterested?

Freddie sings out loud and out of nowhere. He doesn't care who hears. His eyes are defiant rather than drunken. "Fight the good fight with all thy might. Christ is thy strength and Christ thy light."

One of the blazered men calls out, "Give over, Winnie."

Sidney puts his hand on Freddie's to console and stop him at the same time. "I didn't know you knew that hymn."

"I know about much more than you think I do, Sidney. And I will support you, I promise you that. If everything goes wrong one day."

"Do you think it will?"

"I don't know."

"I do have the strength of my faith."

"But do you always believe it when you sing those glorious rhyming couplets?"

"I hope so, Freddie. I really do. Sometimes you have to sing yourself back into belief."

"It's strange, to believe so wholeheartedly, to risk all we have on something we can't ever know."

Freddie signals for another drink already. The woman with the fishnet stockings has gone, replaced by a large man in a double-breasted pinstriped suit and a golden tie. He is smoking a cigar and looks as if he's telling the world he's either done a massive deal or had sex with a prostitute.

Sidney wonders how all this late-afternoon laziness can go on, unaware of his life or his news. It's a deliberate absence, a smoke-filled, drink-fuelled vacating of any responsibility, a dream of denial.

The hostess serves up another couple of gin rickeys. "I've put it on your tab, Winnie. There's a lovely young boy who has just started behind the bar."

Freddie raises his glass. "I'm too old, angel, we're all too old." He turns back to Sidney. "Sometimes I wonder what's to become of us all. What do you think of this Guy Hopkins chappie? Amanda seems quite taken with him."

"Really? He's pleasant enough, I suppose."

"He's from the cream of society, you know. Rich and thick."

"Why are you asking?"

"It might be worth having one of your chats."

"About Guy?"

"I think so."

"Is there something you're not telling me?"

"Have a word, Sidney. We don't want her making a mistake."

"You mean . . ."

"Always best to keep your eyes open. That's all I'm saying."

Sidney books a table at Mon Plaisir. The dining room is full of couples enjoying a romantic dinner or catching up with friends, secure in their temporary haven from the outside world, reassured by the comfort and the cleanliness of the linen and glass and all the attention given to contrasting pink detail. There is enough noise, chatter, and even laughter, to cover up for the fact that Amanda is trying not to cry.

"Do you think there are certain things, Chambers, from which it's impossible to recover?"

"I do now, yes."

"So do I."

"Robert."

"I don't know if it will ever get better. Time's not the healer everyone says it is."

"I wonder what he would think of our lives now."

"I've no idea. I try not to think of him too much, but then it all comes back . . ."

"He's always with us."

"Or even between us. People expect me not to be gloomy, but there's the future to think about. The older generation keep asking me about marriage and I wish I could talk to my brother about everything. Everyone says ridiculous things or asks the most impertinent questions."

"And what do you say to them?"

"Most of the time I laugh mysteriously. I've got it down to a fine art, now. It's my old friend, the mysterious laugh."

Sidney looks at the menu, pretending to consider the options, but he doesn't feel like eating anything at all. What difference will any of his choices make? Croquettes de volaille or French onion soup? Noisette of lamb or coq au vin? None of it matters.

"What about Guy Hopkins?" he asks. Someone has to be the first to say the man's name.

"What do you think, Chambers?"

"I'd like to know your views first."

"I think I'd want your approval."

"If —"

"You know why."

"In place of Robert?"

"No, because . . . oh . . . if I have to explain it . . ." She looks in her handbag for a handkerchief.

"Perhaps some things are best left unsaid."

"Are they really?" Amanda dabs at her left eye. "You don't like him, do you?"

"It's not that."

"Is it intellectual snobbery? You don't think he's clever enough?"

The waitress arrives to take their order. Amanda wants something light: melon, trout and tarte tatin, and a nice wine to go with it all, Chablis perhaps. Sidney says he will have the same. He can't think. It's easier. Yes, the 1948. No, it doesn't matter if it's still a bit young.

"I thought you didn't like trout, Chambers?"

"I do. It's fine."

"Why don't you have the duck?"

"No, Amanda, I promise you." He turns to the waitress. "The trout will be lovely, thank you. Could you just check that the wine is properly chilled?"

The waitress asks if the two of them are celebrating anything special and is told that they are not. Amanda smiles, briefly and unconvincingly. She puts away her handkerchief. There is a brief silence that Sidney can only puncture with a direct question.

"Do you love him?"

"Not yet. But I might grow to love him. I'm not sure I want to talk to you about all this."

"But we can't pretend that nothing is going on."

"Technically, Chambers, nothing is happening at all. Guy takes me out to dinner. We go to the opera. He's very spoiling."

"And he's rich?"

"It's pretty obvious. I have been to stay at the family home. It's probably an improvement on Coventry."

"Now you're the one that's being snobbish."

"I don't know how you stand it up there. Freddie tells me the town's just one giant roundabout. Everything could have been so different for you."

"We have to work with the hand God deals us."

"But you can't abandon yourself entirely to him. You have to make your own luck, don't you? Isn't there something about that in the Parable of the Talents?"

"There is, Amanda."

"I'm not as theologically ignorant as you think I am."

"I don't think that at all. Looking at all those paintings must give you an advantage. How is your work, by the way?" Sidney asks, deciding to move on to safer ground.

Amanda tells him about a restoration project she has been following at the National Gallery. X-ray detection has discovered a forgery in a Van Dyck portrait of Cornelis van der Geest. The original, small-panel painting of the head alone was reset and expanded in the eighteenth century in order to improve its value and fetch the higher price that's normal for a larger work. So, what should the gallery do now? Break the picture back down to its original size or continue to display it and explain which parts are real and which fake?

"Should one look at the original or what the picture has become since it was first made? That's surely an interesting philosophical dilemma, Chambers, don't you think?"

"If the later additions are a forgery then they surely don't count."

"But that is what people are familiar with: both the forgery and the original hidden inside it."

"Amanda, are you trying to tell me something?"

"No, I am being amusing in case you haven't noticed. But I won't go on because I know you'll be tempted to make a sermon out of our conversation."

"I think you are the one doing the preaching . . ."

"Heaven forfend . . ."

"There are sermons in stones, Amanda. I've been a priest for long enough already to recognise that a man can preach about anything at all if he sets his mind to it."

"And a woman has to listen. Anyway, I am sorry if you're upset about Guy."

"I'm not."

"I don't *have* to marry him. He's just a companion. Not as good a one as you, of course — or at least you when you were the old Chambers, *the original*, before God came into the equation and added in extra edges. I hadn't accounted for you changing as much as you have."

"I'm sorry if I've disappointed you. I haven't meant to. But I don't think that any part of me is a forgery, Amanda, and I don't want you to be unhappy."

"I'm not unhappy. I'm just not happy, that's all. I can't make life the way I want it to be."

"Then perhaps —"

"Don't preach, Sidney, please. At least, not to me."

"I wasn't going to . . ."

"I know what you're going to say, anyway."

"Has Guy proposed to you?"

Amanda leans back, putting her hands on the arms of her chair. She corrects hair that doesn't need correcting. She is about to answer when the melon arrives with an unexpected glazed-cherry decoration. Sidney wonders how much of the meal they are going to manage. She scoops up a teaspoonful and mutters something. He thinks it is the word "sharp".

"Have you said yes already and you're not telling me?" he asks.

"No. I would never lie to you, Chambers. And I hope the same is true of you with me."

"But Guy assumes" (he hates saying the man's name) "that you are going to accept?"

"I told him I needed time to think about it. But my parents are certainly on his side."

"You've told them."

"I've warned my father that he can expect a visit, but Guy won't come unless he knows the answer is yes."

"How long do you need to make up your mind?"

"I didn't say."

CHAPTER THIRTY-SIX

Julie Jordan's wedding to Ray Shearer takes place in Holy Trinity with a knees-up in the Scout hut afterwards; pork pies and sausage rolls, cheese and fish-paste sandwiches, an iced wedding cake with proper marzipan and crates of beer.

If people know Julie is pregnant it is easy enough to see the signs; if they don't, then it is still possible to assume she has just put on a bit of weight. Her knee-length dress is in ivory lace and tulle, accommodatingly sashed, and her hair is pinned in a low, oversized chignon that sits at the nape of her neck. The salon has pulled out all the stops.

The bride's father makes a speech in which he says how proud he is of the little girl he could never have imagined as a grown-up. Now that she is a beautiful woman, he loves her even more; and, if she experirnces even half the love he has shared with his wife, then she will be a happy woman. Then he bursts into tears and everyone sings "For He's a Jolly Good Fellow", cracks on with the beer and gets swiftly drunk.

Sidney sees out the first and second dances and is just deciding that this really would be a good time to leave when Julie notices him stand up and insists that he sits back down with her, just for a moment, at a corner of one of the trestle tables. She wants to tell him something. There is so much noise that no one can hear them and she leans in to his left ear and thanks him for all he has done for her. Ray knows everything now.

"And what did he say?"

"It was very hard. But we agreed we would go on and never mention it or speak about it to anyone else. We know, but from now on, it's our secret, it doesn't matter, we're going to ignore it for ever and ever."

"That's very generous."

"Of Ray, you mean?"

"Of both of you." He puts his hand on hers. "I wish you every happiness. God bless you, Julie."

It takes a long time to say his goodbyes, the joviality is extreme, but eventually people start to drift away, the older generation who have known two wars and the young who have escaped battle by only a few years. There is hardly anybody in the room in their late twenties, Sidney's age, and he is momentarily disorientated. They may be his parishioners, but he feels separate from them, as a priest, a Londoner, and as a surviving soldier. He wishes Freddie could be with him, just to keep him company, or Robert of course, or even Amanda.

"Tell me it will all turn out all right, Mr Chambers?" says Julie.

She wants to be the last person to say goodbye to him. What a nice girl, he thinks, realising that he has probably drunk too much. Why aren't more people like her?

"If you start with the kind of honesty and generosity you've shown each other, then that's a very good place to begin," he tells her. "Always remember what you've found with each other."

"But you're not married are you, Mr Chambers? How do you know?"

"I don't. I hope I know. That's a bit different."

"Have you got a special friend? We never see you with one."

"I think so."

"Why doesn't she come out with you then?"

"It's a little bit difficult at the moment, Julie."

"Do you love her?"

It's a straight forward request but, as he looks back at Julie, he is unable to quite take in what this young, lovely, pregnant bride is asking. He admires her patience and her hopefulness and her directness, and he realises that she deserves a straight answer.

"I think I do," he says. "But I can't be sure if it's the best thing for either of us."

"Does she know that?"

"I'm not sure she does."

"Then why don't you talk to her about it? Honestly. Like you talk to me."

CHAPTER THIRTY-SEVEN

Sidney chooses his text for Christmas Day from St Paul's Epistle to Titus: "The grace of God has dawned upon the world with healing for all mankind."

He asks the congregation to imagine a world before electricity or to remember the blackouts in the war, and think how dawn comes quietly and almost imperceptibly. This was how Jesus first arrived on earth, he says, in an obscure place, as a small light in the darkness. He took time to make himself known just as, after his Resurrection, he appeared quietly in a garden, at the seashore and on the road to Emmaus. The grace of God does not come with a roll of thunder. It is a small, growing and steady light. It arrives as the dawn comes, slowly and truly, each day a new birth.

After lunch with Graham Clitheroe and an exchange of presents (what do bachelor clergymen give each other apart from a bottle of wine, a good detective novel or a tin of Quality Street?), he drives down to London to see his parents. There's little traffic on the road and it is dark sooner than he has anticipated, but they welcome him with more food, music, presents and an evening round the fire. His mother sings a song at the piano, Jennifer insists on charades and their father takes off his shoes and asks, as he does every year, "I don't suppose anyone has furnished me with the luxury of a new pair of socks?" They all pretend to have forgotten and then bring out the last gifts of the day. Alec Chambers feigns surprise and astonishment at the calf-length argyles and everyone is happy. Sidney knows that, despite the jollity, his parents can tell there's something on his mind, but they are tactful and ask him few questions.

Sidney is grateful but tired after the morning service and the drive down and he is fearful about Amanda, although he's convinced there is still time to talk to her about her future. He tells himself that she can't be that serious about Guy because she has taken so long to make up her mind. Hesitation is a sign of insecurity.

He hasn't decided exactly what he will say apart from asking her about her true feelings and discussing the nature of their friendship. Why can't they carry on as they have always done? Love takes so long to find itself, he thinks.

The Kendalls are away on a Boxing Day shoot in Hertfordshire but have said that he will be welcome to come for tea in Chester Row on 27 December. It's still light when Sidney arrives, but they have lit the candles and there's a small Christmas tree in the hall. It is tasteful without being extravagant, polite rather than showy. He brings presents: wine and chocolate and an inlaid jewellery box for Amanda that he found in a Warwick antique shop. He even has a brooch for Alice, the maid. It's one that his landlady helped him choose.

He's shown upstairs for tea and Christmas cake. He might be asked to stay on for drinks, but he's sure the family will have a dinner of some kind and so his visit must be contained to an hour and a half unless he can find an excuse to speak to Amanda on her own. The mood is curiously formal. There is the usual exchange of news and conversation, but the Kendalls are less interested in what he has to say than they have been in the past and are guarded about their future plans. Sidney wonders if they are embarrassed by his presence and he feels excluded as they talk of the parties they have attended, the friends he has never heard about (doesn't he know the Pembertons up in Norfolk?) and "a most enjoyable weekend" they all spent "with the Ambassador in Paris and his charming wife Francine". They even met Coco Chanel.

In exchange, Sidney can only talk about the rebuilding of Coventry, the daily liturgy, pastoral care and youth initiatives on the Canley Estate. He tries to make his conversation entertaining, but the Kendall family response only falls slightly short of them wondering why on earth he has come when he must surely have so much else to do at this time of year. They look at each other with folded arms and crossed legs until Amanda finally blurts out that she has some news. She has agreed to marry Guy after all.

"It's all very exciting," says Lady Kendall. "We've waited so long for this."

Sir Cecil has spoken to a very good vicar at Holy Trinity, Sloane Square, who has agreed to do the honours. The ceremony will take place in July.

"Then I am delighted too," says Sidney. "When did you accept, Amanda?"

"On Christmas Eve."

Sir Cecil describes how Mr Hopkins came round for cocktails and his wife tells Sidney how excited they all were because everyone knew why he was there. Alice followed the two men into the study and she was tempted to listen at the door while Amanda waited with her mother in the drawing room. Lady Kendall says she was so nervous that she was even quite weepy. It was especially romantic with it starting to snow outside — you could almost imagine sleigh bells — and then they went on to hear carols in the Abbey as a new family all together.

"Guy planned the whole thing impeccably."

"I'm sure he did. He's a decent chap."

Sidney is not going to be allowed to speak to Amanda on her own either this evening or in the next few days or, perhaps, ever again. She will be spending New Year's Eve with the Hopkins family in Wiltshire, she says. Hattie and Timothy Manning are coming, and even Fliss will be there. It's such a pity Sidney has not been able to see more of her. She's engaged too. Geoffrey Wilkinson. A geography teacher with prospects. He's at Rugby School. Once they're married they're sure he'll be made a housemaster and he's not yet thirty.

Sidney tries to keep up the conversation but knows he must leave as soon as he can. Sir Cecil takes a telephone call and Amanda excuses herself. There is something she says she has to do to get ready for the evening and, momentarily, he is left alone with Lady Kendall.

She tries to make the situation better. "I'm so sorry if all this comes as a bit of a shock."

"Not at all."

"But it's such *a blessing*. After Robert . . ."

"Yes . . ."

"Life can be so unpredictable. Amanda is getting married. You've become a priest. That took us by surprise, I must say."

"It was something I realised that I had to do."

"Yes . . ." Lady Kendall's voice breaks off again but she adds, "I suppose it was . . . I mean . . . I imagine there might have been other possibilities."

"It was the only one I could manage at the time."

"Yes, it did seem that way."

"I'm sorry if I've disappointed you, Lady Kendall."

"Not at all, Sidney. I'm glad you've found your way. And Amanda's very happy, don't you think? You can see that, can't you?"

"Yes, I'm sure she is."

Sir Cecil Kendall comes back into the room, having finished yet another diplomatic discussion. His work never stops, he says. Foreigners make no concessions for Christmas.

"It's kind of you to drop round, Sidney. We do appreciate it. I know we can count on your support."

"Of course."

"I think Amanda's already gone out for the evening. She asked me to say goodbye. Lavinia will want to show you Robert's room before you leave, won't you, darling?"

As they climb the stairs up to the top of the house, Sidney notices that Lady Kendall is walking more slowly. She takes his arm. They exchange the briefest of looks, both knowing that there might yet be more to say but neither of them wanting to take the risk of using the wrong words or describing feelings about which they still can't be sure, even after all these years.

There is the sound of a car passing outside, a rook in the garden, a child riding her new Christmas bicycle along the pavement, trying out its bell, even though it's long since dark.

CHAPTER THIRTY-EIGHT

Sidney is grateful for Lent, a time of retreat and reflection, but knows that he must not concentrate too much upon himself. This is a time to think about people and focus on what he can do for them as both minister and friend.

On Easter Monday, Graham Clitheroe asks for "a serious conversation". Sidney worries what this might be about. Has a parishioner made a complaint? He does not think he has been neglecting his duties. On the contrary, he has been working all the time. Perhaps the vicar thinks he has been too lenient with Julie Jordan? Or maybe someone has died? Or Clitheroe has decided to retire?

They sit in deep old sofas, inherited and in need of reupholstery, drinking sweet dark sherry that Sidney does not like but won't say. There's a loud clock too, and he wonders why people need to be so constantly reminded of time.

"Do you fancy a trip back to Cambridge?" Clitheroe asks. The tone is kindly, almost amused.

"Why there?"

"I've had a letter from the Bishop of Ely. I don't think you know him, but he's been asking after you.

They need a new man in Grantchester and he wants to know if you might be ready for the task. It's quite a job."

"I do know the village."

"It's in the gift of Corpus, as you are probably aware. You were a student there, weren't you?"

"I was."

"Simon Opie thinks you have the necessary mixture of youthful energy, intelligence and gravitas. Quite a recommendation."

"I'm not sure I've got any of those qualities."

"You are too modest, Sidney. Why don't you go and have a look round and meet them all? It can't do any harm. If you're interested there'll be an interview and all sorts of other things."

"Don't you think it's a bit soon, Graham?"

"I was hoping to hold on to you for a little longer, I must admit, but perhaps you need a change of scene, and if it's God's will . . ."

"I don't know that it is."

"Then you'll have to have a good pray about it. Only it's probably best not to dither too much."

"And do you think I dither, Graham?"

"It depends on the subject. You're good personally and theologically, of course, and pastorally I would say you get top marks. I'm only sorry that we didn't find you a decent wife while you were here. You really should get on with it, you know."

"It's not something I want to rush."

"Perhaps there'll be a nice young lady in Grantchester?"

"That's not a reason for going."

"It might be, Sidney. You could look on it as an added benefit."

"I'm quite at home here."

"Ah well, then perhaps you should be moving on after all. You need a new challenge. We can't have you getting complacent."

"I don't think there's much chance of that."

"We should all do the things that quicken the pulse; tasks that make us fearful."

"I had enough of that in the war, Graham."

"Well, now, perhaps you should see what it's like in peacetime."

The college of Corpus Christi was founded in the fourteenth century and has been Patron of the Living of Grantchester since 1380. Close on fifty priests, both Catholic and Protestant, have served the parish of St Andrew and St Mary over the centuries and the job of vicar is considered to be one of the most coveted in the Diocese of Ely.

Sidney's only obvious disadvantage is that he is still young and that the opportunity has come too early. It's only eight years since he was a student. The porter still remembers him ("Once a member of the college, sir, always a member") and greets his former undergraduate with a respectful yet knowing smile that seems to say: "I thought I had seen everything. Who would have thought that you, Mr Chambers, would become a clergyman?"

Some of the more outrageous exploits of youth may be tolerated but they are seldom forgotten. Sidney walks round New Court in a clockwise direction, even though it's a longer route, so he can pass his old rooms on the way to the Master's Lodge. In his last year, he had lived on the same staircase as Robert, and he remembers a midnight somersault race across the grass after far too many pints of beer in the Eagle. Sidney won, and his friend had insisted on a rematch and then on to a "best of three" before they were stopped by the Proctor. It's quite hard, he recalls, to somersault while drunk and holding a pint of beer.

Sidney pulls on the bell to the Lodge and the Master's secretary opens the door. She, too, is pleased to see him again. Would he like a cup of tea and some shortbread while he waits? They won't be long. Perhaps he'd like a copy of *The Times*, or even the Grantchester parish magazine? He could do a bit of last-minute swotting up. She doesn't want to give him any unfair advantage but it's good to see him looking so well. He and Robert Kendall were always amongst her favourites.

Three men conduct the interview: the Master, Sir Giles Tremlett, a former diplomat who fought in the Great War with the Grenadier Guards; the Archdeacon of Ely, an evangelical Christian who once played cricket for England; and the local squire, who owns a stable at Newmarket and is chairman of the parish council. Sidney knows the Master is a friend of Humphrey Waldock and the Archdeacon is one of Rev Nev's old muckers, so it's the local man he'll need to convince that he's up to the job, probably by concentrating on his pastoral gifts rather than his academic ability.

The conversation begins lightly, with talk about the journey down from Coventry, the restoration of the cathedral and the modernisation of the city centre. They ask when Sidney was last in college and what he thinks of Grantchester. Is he ready to be a vicar? He hasn't been a curate for long.

Sidney replies that he first visited the village as a student and he knows it's a far more interesting and varied community than any tourist can imagine. It's a mixture of tradesmen and Nobel prizewinners, agricultural labourers and the landed gentry, whatever their walk of life, all in need of God's mercy and truth.

"It's hard to think of a place where the British class system is so fiercely concentrated," the Archdeacon pronounces. "How do you think you'll fit in?"

"I think a clergyman has to be able to go anywhere," Sidney answers. "He is of all places and yet no place. Like a doctor, he must speak to everyone, calmly and with the authority of his profession. But he mustn't be pompous or entitled. This may seem a rather bold, or even an unwise thing to say, but, in many ways, I think he has to be a bit like the fool in a Shakespeare play."

"A fool, you say?"

"Someone who tells the truth — and makes it understandable. I think that's what the best of Shakespeare's characters achieve. Even the gravedigger in *Hamlet* is a clown. These people are the bridging points between the other actors. That's what a priest has to be."

"A bridging point?"

"It's also important that, although a priest obviously wants to be taken seriously by his parishioners, he doesn't take *himself* too seriously. You have to have a sense of compassion and humour, whether you are dealing with broken windows or broken engagements."

(This is a line Sidney has stolen from Rev Nev. The Archdeacon smiles. Has he heard it before?)

The Master breaks off the flight of fancy. "But faith is a serious business, Mr Chambers."

"I am aware of that. My job is to listen, first to God and then to other people. Then I have to guide and steer. I cannot always tell people what to do, but I'd like to think I can help them make better decisions about the course of their lives."

"What do you mean by 'better'?"

"More thoughtful. Morally aware."

"You seem a good man," the squire interrupts. He is wearing a green tweed three-piece suit in need of letting out. Sidney also notices that the top button of the man's shirt is loose underneath the tie to give his neck a bit of air. "And you make your calling sound noble. That's as it should be. What do you think is your greatest weakness?"

At first, Sidney cannot answer. He had not been expecting such directness. The room feels hotter and more enclosed. He thinks about asking if they can open a window or if he can have a glass of water.

"I wouldn't know. I have many faults."

"What's the worst?"

"I think that may be a matter for me and my Maker."

"It's of great matter for us if we need to decide whether to employ you or not."

"I'm not sure," Sidney replies, surprised that there is a man in the room who may not like him. "Perhaps there are times when I wait too long to reveal what I think."

"And why is that?"

"Because I'm not always clear that I'm right."

"You have doubts?" The squire pulls a red handkerchief from his pocket and dabs the sweat from his forehead. Soon it'll be time for a whisky. "Isn't it a clergyman's job to provide strong leadership?"

"There can be strength in thought as much as action, I would hope?"

"As long as people know what you are thinking, Mr Chambers."

"But I hope it's also surely permissible, sometimes, to dwell in mystery. There are times when we can only see through a glass darkly . . ."

"Then you must bring us face to face."

"That is my hope and prayer."

Sidney goes on to explain how there might yet be delight in the cloud of unknowing. Certainties may be simpler, he argues, but he is determined to bring his own thoughtfulness to this new opportunity if he can; to have the courage to be slow to judge or condemn except in matters where lives are in danger or evil is made manifest. He will learn and love and care and dwell in mystery, recognising that the greatest happiness often comes from outside ourselves, that life needs to be spiritual as well as physical, and that the transcendent, in whatever form it is embraced, can redeem the everyday.

"It's good of you to come," the Master concludes, after it is clear there will be no further questions.

The Archdeacon extends a hand. "God bless you, Sidney."

The squire smiles. "I suppose you'll do."

CHAPTER THIRTY-NINE

Sidney is offered the job and decides to tell Amanda about it in person. He's not quite sure why; perhaps it's just because it's something he is used to doing, letting her know what he's up to, wanting her approval, even if the news hasn't always gone down well. It's a matter of clarity, he thinks.

He telephones and suggests that they meet at the Festival of Britain. He fancies a bit of optimism, fantasy and colour, he says, especially after the recent tension between the two of them. She asks what he means by "tension" and if it is urgent. She has a lot of things on her mind: her job, preparations for the wedding, a new house.

Sidney says that it is quite important, actually, but if it's too difficult . . .

"No, no, I'll do anything for you, Chambers. At least, anything before I am married. It might be a little difficult afterwards . . ."

"Guy could come too."

"I don't think he'll want that."

She and her fiancé have already attended the opening concert in the Festival Hall but Amanda doesn't mind going again now that the weather is better. She can even show him round. They can "skip the duds" which, she explains, are the working model of a power station, a full-size gas turbine and a display that shows the interior of a sewage-disposal plant. Instead they concentrate on the Dome of Discovery and the Lion and the Unicorn Pavilion with its "Alice Through the Looking Glass" exhibition and "Eccentrics' Corner".

"We'll have to hurry through that bit, Chambers. If you stand still they'll think you're an exhibit."

They eat in the Regatta Restaurant. It is crowded and understaffed and they queue for a table as people order rump steak and chips, morue aux tomates and chips, Coquilles Saint-Jacques au vin blanc and chips, spaghetti and chips.

Once they've been shown to a quieter corner table, Amanda gives him all her news about the wedding plans. Then he tells her his ecclesiastical news.

"So, it's a promotion?"

"Quite a big one."

"And you've accepted?"

"The induction is on the Feast of Corpus Christi."

"Which is when?"

"About ten days' time."

"That soon? Why didn't you tell me before?"

"I've been leaving you alone. I believe it's considered polite."

"What if I don't want to be left alone? You could have written or rung me up. I never intended for us to be on 'no speaks'."

"I know that."

Sidney is aware that Amanda is the best-dressed woman in the room, and is proud to be lunching with her, but it only increases his feelings of inadequacy.

"So why do you need to see me now all of a sudden?"

"Because I'd like you to come to the service."

"In Grantchester? You've left the invitation a bit late, haven't you?"

"I thought you might not want to come. I suppose I was worried you'd say no."

"I came to Coventry, didn't I?"

"But you weren't engaged then."

"What difference does that make?"

"Quite a lot, I would have thought."

The waitress interrupts and asks if she can take their order. They'll both have the cod, if there's any left. No, they don't do wine by the bottle, only by the glass. There's beer if the gentleman would like it. No, there are only two types of wine, red or white. They'll have the white. If it can come before the food? No, it'll come when it's ready.

"Will this mean," Amanda asks, "that we might see more of you since you're closer to London, or will you be too busy being a vicar?"

"I will always have time for you."

"Then I'm glad. I'm sorry if you think I've been a bit icy, Chambers, but I've needed time to adjust. It's why I ran away when you came at Christmas."

"I wasn't going to mention that . . ."

"Don't. I couldn't face your bemusement any more. I don't know why you were so surprised. I gave you enough notice, didn't I?"

"Yes, I suppose you did."

"All I want to say is that, whatever happens in the future, I would still like us to stay friends . . ."

"Good."

". . . as I have always promised and despite your many failings."

"I rather hoped I'd reduced the number of my faults."

"Not at all. They might even have increased over the past year or two. I don't know why I have to keep reminding you of them. Although we probably won't be able to see each other as often as we have in the past. I don't suppose that matters too much, does it? You'll have plenty of demands now you've got your own parish. Not as many as when you become a bishop, though. How long do you think it takes?"

"Really, Amanda, that's a long way off."

"I can just picture you in a palace."

"I'll be happy with a vicarage."

"Will you have a woman 'who comes in and does'? You could always ask our Alice, I suppose?"

"I think she's a bit old."

"Giving her that brooch nearly finished her off. You are ridiculously charming when you want to be."

"It's manners, Amanda. Nothing more."

The wine is served without the opportunity to taste it. It's white and warm. Sidney wonders what he can do to bring the conversation round to what he wants to talk about.

"Do you think you'll be happy in Grantchester?" Amanda asks.

"I don't know. I hope so. I intend to be."

"Good."

"And what about you, Amanda?"

"Oh, you know me, always cheerful." She looks off to the left, puts her hand to her right eye, brushes something away that might not ever have been there.

The cod with the tomato sauce arrives. It's just about hot enough. The chips are on the soggy side. Sidney wonders how soon Amanda will complain and the amount of fuss she will generate. He doesn't suppose it will make much difference.

"So why are we here?" she asks. "It can't just be the news. You could have told me in a letter. You're good at them."

"There's something I need to talk to you about."

"Something I don't know?"

"That's right."

"Why now?"

"Because it's time. Only I'm not sure if this is the right place."

"Perhaps you should have thought of that before we came. We've never been very good in restaurants, have we? Is it so very terrible?"

"Yes, Amanda, I think it is."

"Oh, God."

She picks up her glass of wine and downs almost half of it. "Now you're frightening me. In the past, I've always had to keep guessing about everything you've not been saying. And sometimes I've thought the less of you as a result. But I suppose it can't be worse than anything I've already imagined."

"It's about Robert."

She puts down her glass. "Oh, Sidney, do we have to go over all this again?"

"Yes. We do."

"What is it?"

And so, Sidney talks about the war. He tells her about the darkness of an afternoon in January seven years ago; of the tension, panic and uncertainty. He remembers shouting, "Down," and how, as he did so, firing his Bren gun from left to right, a figure came into his peripheral vision.

Sidney says that he told himself to stop, that he worried immediately that this soldier might have been one of his own men, but there was a delay between the thoughts in his brain and the action of his hands. The rhythm of his firing was too advanced. He couldn't stop.

The man dropped.

He didn't have a moment to question his instincts or his timing. The battle was on. He had to keep his fire going, tracing the line back across from right to left, the 120 degrees ahead of him. But he felt a deep terror, and it's one that has never left him. He knew, at the time, that he could not dwell on what had happened. He could not think it through. Thinking is no good in battle. He has been told this so often. It's all instinct. You have to fight. You have to survive.

And Sidney did.

But Robert did not.

And he was the man down.

Amanda has her hands on the table, either side of a plate of abandoned food. People around them are discussing whether there's time to go on to Battersea Park, what they are going to have for their tea, what's on the wireless that evening, and who is staying with whom when it comes to Christmas. She looks at him steadily, careful to have understood every word. "So, this is what you're saying, Sidney. You think you killed him. You killed my brother."

"They say these things are never black and white, that we can never be entirely sure what happens, but the fear has never left me."

"And who are these 'they'?"

"Freddie. Rev Nev. Those who were there."

"You've discussed it with them?"

"Not directly."

"So how do you know?"

"I don't."

"So, it may not be true. You may be exaggerating."

"That's right. But . . ."

"Why didn't you tell me before?"

"I suppose it's because I didn't want you to be even more upset than you were already. I needed you to know that Robert died a hero. I couldn't face telling you the full truth about his death. There are so many reasons."

"And you think this *is* the truth?"

"I do."

"Friendly fire. Isn't that what they call it? Accidental death. Is that why they gave Robert a medal? To cover it up?"

"It's not quite like that."

"But if it is true, then everything we have been told has been a lie."

"Not a lie as such."

"A distortion."

"Not the full facts."

"Even though the facts aren't entirely clear."

"That's right," Sidney admits. "They are opaque."

"And you a clergyman . . ."

"I wasn't then."

"But you are now."

"I am."

Amanda looks at her unfinished food, thinks about eating it, but can't. In any case, it's cold.

"When you were ordained, Sidney, I remember feeling so confident when they asked if there were any 'crimes or impediments' that might prevent you becoming a priest. Is that why you looked so nervous?"

"It wasn't that. It was everything."

"I can't understand how long it's taken for you to tell me."

"I'm sorry."

"I could have helped you. We could have shared all this. Why didn't you just confess to your fears the first time we spoke about it?"

"Because I thought you shouldn't know. I thought if everyone could remember Robert as a hero, then it would be better for all of us."

"Wouldn't that have been for me to decide? He still fought bravely, didn't he? His death is not the only part of his life."

"You can't unsay things. If I'd told you then you wouldn't have had a choice."

"Everything would have been different. Everything."

"It might still be . . ."

"Perhaps. But you haven't been honest and I can't believe in anything you say if there isn't clarity between us."

"I'm sorry if I've never been what you seem to want me to be."

"I just wanted you to be yourself. But since you've been back from the war you've been such a different person."

"It's hard to recover; and, if that is the case, then now perhaps you understand why."

"Do I know everything?" she asks.

"I think so."

"You think? Is that all?"

"I don't always know what I'm thinking."

"You do. You're just trying not to hurt me."

The waitress interrupts and asks if they've finished and whether they want a dessert or not, otherwise she needs the table back. There's a queue. Amanda tells her to bring anything but the woman, strong forearms, unimpressed by poshness, is not satisfied. She requires a specific order. Amanda loses her temper and shouts, "I said anything," and Sidney says they'd like something chocolate.

"There's no chocolate."

"What is there, then?"

"There might still be some treacle sponge left."

It is the first thing she mentions and they order it straight away. Sidney wonders why the Regatta Restaurant can't offer a summer pudding. They ask for more wine at the same time.

"I was trying to protect you, Amanda."

"No, you weren't. You were trying to protect yourself"

"Isn't it better if your parents think Robert died a hero rather than as the result of an accident?"

"Is that what you've decided it was? A mistake? Why are you telling me this now?"

"Because I couldn't stay silent any longer, Amanda."

"That bloody war. It hasn't ended at all, has it?"

Amanda leans back in her chair, looks away, can't find anything on which to concentrate — a London pigeon, the leaves on a plane tree, the river, other diners, there's nothing that can take her away from this — and then she speaks.

"You were right to tell me. At least I know the truth at last — or another version of it. It's like that play we saw. *Dangerous Corner*. You remember? 'Telling the truth is about as dangerous as lighting a match in a gunpowder factory.' I always thought, in the back of my mind, that there must be something you've been keeping from me. But you have sacrificed your happiness, Sidney. And you've also sacrificed me. Perhaps it was unconsciously deliberate. You needed an excuse to avoid me."

"I couldn't live a lie."

"But if you'd told me . . ."

"I didn't, though, did I?"

Amanda pushes back her chair. "I must go."

"I'll get the bill. I'll come with you."

"No, Sidney, not now. I need to be alone. I'll be all right. Don't you worry about me. I might have guessed it would be something like this. You've been so strange. There had to be some kind of explanation."

"Well, now I've given it. Are you sure you don't want me to take you home?"

"Please let's not talk any more, Sidney. Just let me go away and think for a bit on my own. I can't stay here any longer. I'm not even sure I can breathe properly."

"I'd like you to come to the service."

"Are you really saying that you can't go through with it all without my forgiveness? Because if you are, then that's quite a burden to put on me. You should have said all this before you became a priest in the first place."

"I'm not saying anything, Amanda."

"I do think your timing is extraordinarily bad."

"I'm sorry."

"Yes, you keep saying that. I'm sorry too."

Sidney remains at their table. So, this is where the truth gets you, he thinks.

"I'm not even sure I want you to come to my wedding. Although it'll be hard to explain."

"I'll do whatever you want me to do, Amanda."

"I have to go."

Two treacle sponges arrive, covered in custard, together with the glasses of wine. Sidney doesn't touch any of it but asks for the bill. It reminds him of the time Amanda walked out of the Mayfair Hotel when he saw her at the end of the war. Was this how the friendship was going to be from now on, provided it survived at all: a mixture of secrecy and disclosure, scenes in restaurants, affection undefined, an indissoluble ambiguity?

How long can one remain silent — or do some truths need to be kept secret for ever? He tries to imagine what might have been if he had told her sooner; if he had not thought what might be best for her and for himself; if he had been honest.

He thinks then, and perhaps at last, that it isn't right to make assumptions about what is best for people or to take decisions away from them; that it is perhaps better to give them the choice; that no matter how well a secret is kept, you cannot control the moment of its revelation; that you do not always know what will be remembered, what forgotten or what forgiven; that memory is supple, fragile, fickle; that friendship survives beyond the grave; and that love depends upon the time we give it.

CHAPTER FORTY

The Archdeacon of Ely insists on following the medieval ceremony of induction at Grantchester. He places Sidney's hand on the latch of the church door with the churchwarden as a witness. He then walks him round the interior and asks him to toll the church bell to signify *habemus vicarium*: we have a vicar.

Sidney loves the village already; not only the church but also the high street with its thatched cottages, pubs, garage, shop and school. It is a small community by the River Cam, two miles south-west of Cambridge, but it has history and fellowship and is close enough to a town and railway station not to feel insular. It also has the most beautiful elm trees, standing tall as if they are in a Dutch landscape painting, lining the meadows and cricket ground. He loves the height of summer but, at the same time, he looks forward to autumn, winter and spring. He can see that this is his chance of healing, of becoming the man he has to be.

Before the service, the Master of Music plays Henry Purcell's "Trumpet Tune and Air". He has been imported from Ely Cathedral — much to the chagrin of the local organist Mrs Phipps, a retired piano teacher with an unsteady left hand and a sense of rhythm that never extends beyond the funereal.

The choir leads off a procession of lay ministers, ecumenical partners, visiting clergy, parish clergy, Crucifer, Acolytes, Sidney, the Presenting Officer, the Area Dean, the Bishop of Ely, and the Bishop's Chaplain. It is the Church of England putting on its best, timeless show.

"This has been going for centuries," the service is saying to both priest and parishioners. "*Don't mess it up.*"

Sidney is supported by friends old and new: his parents and siblings (even Matt this time), Rev Nev, Freddie Hawthorne and Simon Opie from Westcott House, together with all the regular villagers, including Mrs Maguire, a fierce-looking woman who has been earmarked as his housekeeper, the Mayor of Cambridge, and Inspector Geordie Keating from the local police.

Sidney looks out into the congregation and spies Amanda at the back of the church. She must have arrived late and on her own. The people in the row have budged up to let her in. She is in all her finery; a naval-looking summer dress with white piping and a large hat that makes it look as if she's just stopped off on her way to Ascot. She smiles, he thinks rather sadly, but he knows then and there that she is telling him: *You wouldn't expect me to miss all this, would you?*

The Bishop of Ely preaches on the subject of saintliness, how holy men such as Peter and Paul weren't perfect human beings. They had their flaws and their anger and didn't always behave in "saintly" ways.

St Peter denied Christ and ran away from death. St Paul lost his temper with his flock and indulged in orgies of self-concern. They were touchy men, the Bishop continues, quarrelsome and wanting approval. They are the examples that show how there is no such thing as all-round perfection in a human being.

"So, don't expect too much of Sidney," he says to the congregation. "Your vicar will not be a saint."

They laugh. Sidney catches Amanda's eye and she points at him discreetly as if to say *I don't need anyone else to tell me that*.

The Bishop hopes that, as a priest, Sidney will reveal something of the love of Christ, the goodness and mercy of God, and His generous love. It might not all come out at once, he warns, and it will never be perfect, just as human beings can never, ever, be perfect. We can only assimilate God's love slowly and by degrees. The journey of faith is one of unfolding discovery.

Beloved, now are we the sons of God, and it doth not yet appear what we shall be.

There is a buffet lunch in the village hall: tea, orange squash and sandwiches together with a selection of home-baked cakes and biscuits. There are so many people for Sidney to meet and be polite to that he finds it far more tiring than he thought he would. The geniality is relentless.

He tries to make the most of his pastoral training and his experiences in Coventry, but this is a different crowd. They ask him about everything from the Oxford Movement to hedge trimming and grave maintenance; from the use of incense and anointing oil to the flower rota; from the limitations of religious education in the village school to the potential installation of a new lavatory.

Sidney asks Amanda if she can stay on afterwards. Perhaps they can go for a walk by the river?

"Oh, I don't know," she replies. "Won't there be gossip? I don't want to put off any local admirers."

"You could show them the standards they'll have to reach."

"Flatterer."

"Come on, Amanda, it's such a beautiful afternoon. I'd like you to feel at home here."

"Really?"

"I want you to feel you can visit at any time. Both of you."

"You don't mean that."

"I do."

They walk down to the Meadows and along a river edged by comfrey and lady's-smock. The blossom on the hawthorn is at its height. The days will soon stretch out into a lazy heat and the fields will be filled with summer picnickers, impromptu games of cricket, mothers with prams, parasols and babies, young lovers enjoying larks and laughter after their exams.

"Did you come here when you were a student?" she asks.

"Often."

He remembers Robert swinging naked from a rope over Byron's Pool, high above the water, laughing and carefree, before dropping down to swim confidently away downriver: another time, another life.

"And what do you think of it now?" she says.

"I'm not sure. Perhaps it's as if God is calling me to come back here and start my life again. Maybe I have to do things over and over until I get them right?"

"Like practising a piece of music. You keep going back to the start. Remember when we danced the quickstep? I was just a girl but I still had to remind you of the steps."

"'*Bei Mir Bist Du Schoen*'. Everything would have been different without the war."

"You told me that only God could help you recover. I haven't had that."

"You still could. He's still there."

"It's just as well. I'm good at making people wait."

"It was kind of you to come, Amanda. I wasn't sure you would."

"No, I wasn't sure I would either. But then I realised that being here is all part of the story. Our story. And who knows how it's going to end?"

"I suppose that, if we knew, then it wouldn't be such an adventure."

They walk on up to the weir and beyond, the grasses thicker, the path less certain. Brimstone and meadow brown butterflies flutter out of the hedgerows; swifts and house martins dart overhead.

"There is something though, Chambers, isn't there? You've got that ominous look in your eye that I know of old. It's why you wanted me to stay on after the event and it's why we're on this walk."

"I don't have an ominous look, do I?"

"If I'd known we were going to do all this as well I'd have brought a second pair of shoes. But it doesn't matter. Tell me. As long as it's not another bombshell you've been keeping from me. Don't be shy."

He stops, looks at his feet, then back down the river; anything to avoid her eye. "I don't know. Everything has taken such a long time, Amanda . . ."

"And yet so many things seem long ago."

"They do."

"So, what do you want to ask? Perhaps I can guess."

He faces her at last. "Will you always blame me?"

The silence is filled with the sound of water and bird-song. "For which one of your crimes? I'm sure there's more than one."

They walk on, through a gap in the hedgerow and into a field where they find themselves entirely alone. A large fallen elm tree has been left to rot. The cattle trough is empty of water.

"That means you haven't," he says.

"No, it doesn't. It means I'm still trying. It's ironic, isn't it? You've become a priest but I'm the one who's got to come up with the forgiveness."

"I'm sorry."

"My parents would counsel that it's character-building. They still don't know exactly what happened, by the way, and I'm not going to tell them. I've decided it won't help and it won't bring Robert back. In any case, perhaps you don't need my forgiveness to get on with your life?"

"I think I do, Amanda."

"But it may be a matter for you and God alone. That is the only relationship in your life that matters."

"Not the *only* one . . ."

They come to the end of the field and, because there's a slight breeze and they have been out for long enough, they turn back, instinctively and without consulting each other. Young jackdaws skirl in the sky and swallows hawk midges over the slow-moving water. They climb the rise in the Meadows towards the church as its bell strikes the half-hour and they can hear a mother calling her children in for tea.

Amanda takes Sidney's arm as they head on to the vicarage. "Will you promise me something?" she asks.

"Is it something I can keep?"

"It's not to waste your life; to use your talent. Because God has provided you with the gift of survival so that you can be useful to others. That's what you believe, is it not?"

"That is my hope and prayer."

"Then we must have no regrets; either of us."

"I think most of my life is regret, Amanda. Now I have to do something about it."

"And this is where you can do it. In this village. At this time."

Sidney stops again. They are late returning but he wants this to finish so that they do not have to talk about it ever again. There should be no more scenes, difficulties or confrontation, at least for the time being. There's been enough confusion.

"I'd like you to answer another question," he begins.

"Questions, questions, Sidney. Whatever next?"

"Will you look after me, Amanda?"

"That sounds like a proposal of marriage. You know I'm engaged to someone else?"

"I think it's more than that."

"More than marriage?"

"Yes, probably, given our history, given all that we know about each other, given my hopelessly uncertain and impoverished future . . ."

"And you expect me to answer that?"

"I do."

"There you go again. Is that the only time you are going to use those two words in my company?"

"Probably."

"Then I will answer you."

"And what is your answer, Amanda?"

"Always, Chambers. Always. You don't get away from me that easily."

She smiles. Soon she will have to leave on a train back to London in muddy shoes that will, in turn, irritate and amuse her throughout the journey. She will think of the day they have shared. She will wonder when they will see each other again, what they might say, the people they might become and even, perhaps, how long they still have yet to live. They have survived so much uncertainty, but the days last longer now, lengthening and lightening. The sky's expanse seems wider and it lifts their hearts with possibility. It is the return of hope.

Acknowledgements

I would like to thank Diana Balfour for giving me access to her husband's letters home from the Second World War; Marilyn Imrie, Jo Willett and Stuart Rock for coming with me to Trieste; friends David Kynaston, Allan Little, Joanna MacGregor, Juliette Mead, Siobhàn Redmond and Susannah Stevenson for advice, as well as Pip Torrens for a stringent but kindly reading; also, my editor Alexandra Pringle, copyeditor Sarah-Jane Forder, publicist Philippa Cotton, and agent David Godwin for their fierce but loving professionalism.

The following books have been particularly helpful:

WAR

Trieste, Roberto Bazlen, Paris, 2015
The Law of Nations, J. L. Brierly, revised C. H. M. Waldock, Oxford, 1963
A Pilgrim of Remembrance, Michael Curtis, Salisbury, 2004
Trieste, Daša Drndić, London, 2012
Cassino: The Hollow Victory, John Ellis, London, 1984

The Scots Guards 1919–1955, David Erskine, London, 1956
Battle Diary: Tunisia, Italy & Palestine, George Forbes, Ampleforth, 2013
Cassino: Marking the Gustav Line, John Ford, Oxford, 2004
The Face of War, Martha Gellhorn, London, 1959
Italy's Sorrow, James Holland, London, 2008
Trieste, Neil Kent, London, 2011
Salerno 1943, Angus Konstam, Oxford, 2013
Naples '44, Norman Lewis, London, 1978
Savage Continent, Keith Lowe, London, 2012
Eastern Approaches, Fitzroy Maclean, London, 1949
Trieste and the Meaning of Nowhere, Jan Morris, London, 2001
Monte Cassino, Matthew Parker, London, 2003

PEACE

The Love-charm of Bombs, Lara Feigel, London, 2013
The Blitz, Juliet Gardiner, London, 2010
Austerity Britain, David Kynaston, London, 2007
Family Britain, David Kynaston, London, 2010

FAITH

Evil and the God of Love, John Hick, London, 1966
The Office and Work of a Priest, Robert Martineau, Oxford, 1972
The Problem of Pain, J. E. McFadyen, London, 1910

The Life and Work of a Priest, John Pritchard, London, 2007
The Christian Priest Today, Michael Ramsey, London, 1972
What Are We Doing Here?, Marilynne Robinson, London, 2018
Windows Onto God, Robert Runcie, London, 1983
After War, Is Faith Possible?, G. A. Studdert Kennedy, ed. Kerry Walters, Oregon, 2008
The Hardest Part, G. A. Studdert Kennedy, Worcester, 1918
Love's Endeavour, Love's Expense, W. H. Vanstone, London, 1977
Fare Well in Christ, W. H. Vanstone, London, 1997
The Stature of Waiting, W. H. Vanstone, London, 2004
True Wilderness, H. A. Williams, London, 1965

LOVE

A Tonic to the Nation: The Festival of Britain 1951, Mary Banham and Bevis Hillier (eds), London, 1976
Ruined and Rebuilt: The Story of Coventry Cathedral, R. T. Howard, Coventry, 1962
Beacon for Change, Barry Turner, London, 2011

Other titles published by Ulverscroft:

SIDNEY CHAMBERS AND THE PERSISTENCE OF LOVE

James Runcie

It is May 1971, and the Cambridgeshire countryside is bursting into summer. Archdeacon Sidney Chambers is walking in a bluebell wood with his daughter Anna and their ageing Labrador Byron when they stumble upon a body. Plunged into another murder investigation, Sidney discovers a world of hippies and psychedelic plants, where permissive behaviour seems to hide something darker. This is the first of many disturbing secrets that Sidney unearths beneath the tranquil surface of the diocese: a celebrated photographer is accused of rape; a priceless religious text vanishes from a Cambridge college; the authentication of a lost masterpiece proves a slippery business; and Sidney's own nephew goes missing . . .

SIDNEY CHAMBERS AND THE DANGERS OF TEMPTATION

James Runcie

Archdeacon Sidney Chambers is beginning to think that the life of a full-time priest (and part-time detective) is not easy. So when a bewitching divorcee in a mink coat interrupts Sidney's family lunch, asking him to help locate her missing son, he hopes it will be an open and shut case. The last thing he expects is to be dragged into the mysterious workings of a sinister cult, or to find himself tangled up in another murder investigation. But, as always, the village of Grantchester is not as peaceful as it seems. From the theft of an heirloom to an ominous case of blackmail, Sidney is once again rushed off his feet!

SIDNEY CHAMBERS AND THE FORGIVENESS OF SINS

James Runcie

Six new stories about the full-time priest and part-time detective, set in 1960s Cambridge. On a snowy Thursday morning in Lent 1964, a stranger seeks sanctuary in Grantchester's church, convinced he has murdered his wife . . . Sidney attends a shooting weekend in the country with his wife Hildegard, where they find their hostess has a sinister burn on her neck . . . A firm of removal men "accidentally" drops a Steinway piano on a musician's head outside a Cambridge college . . . Sidney's friend Amanda receives threatening pen letters when at last she appears to be approaching matrimony . . . During a cricket match, a group of schoolboys blow up their school's science block . . . And on a family holiday in Florence, Sidney is accused of the theft of a priceless painting.

SIDNEY CHAMBERS AND THE PROBLEM OF EVIL

James Runcie

It is the 1960s and Canon Sidney Chambers is enjoying his first year of married life with his German bride Hildegard. But life in Grantchester rarely stays quiet for long. Our favourite clerical detective soon attempts to stop a serial killer who has a grievance against the clergy; investigates the disappearance of a famous painting; uncovers the fact that an "accidental" drowning on a film shoot may not have been so accidental after all; and discovers the reasons behind the theft of a baby from a hospital. In the meantime, Sidney wrestles with the problem of evil, attempts to fulfill the demands of Dickens, his faithful Labrador, and contemplates, as always, the nature of love.